JOSEPH
vanPEARCE

and the Prophecy of
the Dragon's Head Medallion

Brampton Publishers Ltd,
The Gate, Keppoch Street,
Cardiff CF24 3JW

Text copyright © by C. C. Brampton 2016
Cover illustrations by Julie Dillon copyright © 2016
Design by Mecob © Brampton Publishers Ltd 2016

This book is copyright under the Berne Convention.
No reproduction without permission.
All rights reserved.

This edition published March 2017

The right of C. C. Brampton to be identified as the author of this work
has been asserted by him in accordance with the Copyright, Designs and
Patents Act, 1988. This book is a work of fiction. Names, characters,
places and incidents are either the product of the author's imagination
or are used fictitiously. Any resemblance to actual people living or dead,
events or locales is entirely coincidental.

All rights reserved. This book is sold subject to the condition that it
shall not, by way of trade or otherwise, be lent, hired out or otherwise
circulated in any form of binding or cover other than that in which it is
published. No part of this publication may be reproduced, stored in a
retrieval system, or transmitted in any form or by any means (electronic,
mechanical, photocopying, recording or otherwise) without the prior
written permission of Brampton Publishers Ltd.

www.ccbrampton.com

A CIP catalogue record for this book is available from the British Library

eBook ISBN: 978-0-9935568-0-7
eBook ISBN: 978-0-9935568-3-8
Hardback ISBN: 978-0-9935568-1-4
Paperback ISBN: 978-0-9935568-2-1

Printed and bound in Great Britain by Clays Ltd, St Ives Plc

MIX
Paper from
responsible sources
FSC   FSC® C018072
www.fsc.org

JOSEPH VANPEARCE

and the Prophecy of the Dragon's Head Medallion

C.C. BRAMPTON

Dedication

For Ira-leigh and Ava, who are the most precious gifts in my life, and for Sarah, who has stood by my side through everything and so was the first one to read my book.

Though harsh and painful reality may be, it can never impede your fantasy.

Contents

Chapter 1

BLOOD SPILT

Dawn was breaking and the colossal battle continued to rage across the land. Blood soaked into Ettonina soil from the Clytums and Morgs as they clashed gruesomely. Corpses of dead dragons littered the once beautiful and glorious green land of Ettonina, and the smell of the deceased soldiers polluted the air. It was no ordinary battle; it was a battle that Joseph was willing to give his life for in a bid to save those who lived in Ettonina from the evil and ruthless Dark Lord Sadon Rage.

Lord Sadon loathed the mortals and wanted to kill every last living soul and rule the world. He was filled with such violence that he could cause a dead person's bones to rattle with fear even within the grave. The Dark Lord fought with his powerful and monstrous dragon named Malus and the black-hearted Morgon army to completely destroy his adversaries. Dighted all in black armour, with a helmet as hideously ugly and twisted as he was, he hovered in the sky, straddled upon Malus. His ungodly eyes peered through his helmet at the bloody battle below. 'I will rule this world!' he hailed, and pounded the air with his stave in his hand.

Malus roared.

They spiralled down towards their enemies on the ground at ferocious speed. The evil dragon spat out ferocious fire that shot across the army of Clytums and other alliances. Some of the soldiers who were caught astray screamed as they burnt to death, while others grouped together defensively and hid behind their protective shields.

The King of the Clytums, Daninius, swung his mighty sword with immense power and smashed a Morgon to the ground. He thrust the hilt of his sword high into the air with both hands and drove it down into the Morgon's chest. He gritted his teeth with disgust and tore his sword out from the Morgon and raised his head up towards the sky. The King's eyes flashed from the fire as it ripped through the air from the menacing dragons as they engaged in battle and lit up the skies. Daninius charged forward, quickly picking up speed, striking and killing Morgs along the way with his sword. Suddenly he leapt into the air off the back of a Morgon that fell to the ground. A dragon roared as it swooped down and jetted out a burst of flames that scattered Morgs. It scooped up the King, who landed safely in the saddle on its back. Arrows shot from Morgons' crossbows narrowly missed the King by just inches, whizzing past his head as he soared high into the dangerous skies.

As hundreds more Morgs stampeded forward on the

ground, Joseph helped to drive them back, along with the Clytum soldiers. Light and nimble on his feet like a dancer, yet lean and slightly muscular, he twisted and turned as he wielded his sword and sliced a Morgon clean in half, then turned and clashed swords with another, and then pivoted and drove his sword backwards through the Morgon's abdomen. Black blood spewed from the Morgon's crooked mouth, and before it fell to the ground Joseph grimaced as he withdrew his blade. Expecting to clash swords with another as he turned around, he looked on with shock when the Ungar ogre, standing tall as a house, charged at him.

'Uh-oh,' Joseph murmured to himself, and before he had chance to move, the Ungar ogre swung its club and struck him high into the air. He soared across all of the soldiers and ploughed into the ground hard and slid across the dirt.

Hurt from the blow and with the wind knocked out of him, he shook his head and rolled onto his back and gasped. All of a sudden the ground started to tremble around him and when he raised his head he saw soldiers being struck up into the air like skittles by the Ungar ogre. Joseph closed his grip, thinking he still had his sword in hand, and clutched nothing but air, and turned his head with disbelief to see his sword a few yards away from him.

Out of breath, he slowly began to crawl along, scuffing his shiny red and gold armour against the filthy ground, when he glanced back again and saw the Ungar ogre only a few feet away. He froze and his eyes flashed wide open with fear, when unexpectedly the Ungar ogre collapsed and crashed down and shook the ground. The ogre slid all the way up to him and came to a halt just yards away. Joseph stared worryingly at its huge ugly head, and slowly shifted his eyes upwards to see Eglan the Elgarian Elf, standing on top of the ogre proudly with multiple arrows harpooned into the back of the Ungar ogre.

'You should be more careful, young Joseph,' said Eglan, raising his one eyebrow with a smug grin. 'Now we are even,' and he leapt down and ran off to continue the battle.

'Huh,' said Joseph, and a smile lifted the corner of his mouth at his wry comment. He tilted his head upwards to the burning sky and stared with eyes that looked like dark, swirling liquid gold. All of a sudden his pupils narrowed and became long and thin and out of nowhere a flash-forward occurred and he saw the King's fate and gasped with shock.

Back in the sky, the King of the Clytums began to chase the Dark Lord on his dragon. As he swept through the mountains, his dragon dangerously skimmed the very edges with its wings. The King's dragon fire-balled Malus from behind and just barely missed the monstrous creature, as they edged closer and closer to the evil pair. Both dragon-riders flew through the spine of the canyon at breath-taking speed and bore to the right, when suddenly it began to bottle-neck and unknowing-ly up ahead an enormous crag made it a dead end.

Undeterred, Lord Sadon continued towards it. With the crag almost upon them he blasted out a beam of light from his stave, which struck the crag and created a small jagged oval opening that was just large enough to fit the pair through.

At the last second and simultaneously, the Dark Lord leant forward on Malus and turned the dragon to a sideways flying position. Malus quickly shut its wings and they both shot through the hole like an arrow and just scraped out to the other side.

Not far behind, the King looked on with shock at the death-defying move and, unconvinced that they would make it through, he sharply halted the reins on his dragon. The dragon roared thunderously and pivoted its wings to a vertical position, and up the face of the crag they skimmed. The King clenched his teeth and held on for dear life at the speed they soared. As they ascended high above the canyon, a Morgon dragon-rider headed directly towards them, blazing fire. The King's dragon quickly tumble-rolled to avoid the flames just in the nick of time. But as soon as they came out of the courageous manoeuvre, unexpectedly they were both side-swiped by another Morgon dragon-rider which struck them with its razor-sharp claws. The King was instantly thrown from his dragon and began to plummet to the ground. His face was frozen with shock as he stared with vulnerable eyes at the sky above. The last precious seconds of life seemed like an eternity to him as he freefell and closed his eyes and saw images of his wife and children flash before him. Suddenly he crashed into a huge tree and bounced helplessly off the branches and landed into a small brook. Not a stir came from his lifeless body as he lay face down, with blood slowly trickling out of his mouth and into the water.

Chapter 2

DREAMING IN REALITY

Present Day

Cough, cough. 'Mr Van Pearce!' said the man beside him in a calm and stern voice, his hands on his hips. The man tightened his lips and waited for a response from the teen whose head was happily plonked on the desk and clearly not in reality. 'MR VAN PEARCE!' the man boomed.

Joseph awoke with a screwed-up face. 'The KING . . .' he slurred, lifting his heavy head up, while dribble ran down the side of his cheek and landed on his book. Disorientated by his surroundings, he nonchalantly wiped his wet cheek with the back of his hand and glanced up to see the class full of students. Suddenly he realized where he was again and felt a deep sense of vulnerability slowly seep inside of him. He moved like a sloth and slowly began to lean back warily into his chair and felt the presence of someone standing beside him. He nervously glanced up to see the teacher with his arms firmly crossed, an ireful look on his face.

The teacher tilted his head backwards to glare through the bottom of his glasses, unimpressed at his pupil's apathetic behaviour. 'Why, how nice it is of you to join us, Mr Van Pearce. Please, no need to call me the King. Whilst I might behave like that, conducting lessons for your benefit and others, I am more than happy to be called Mr Dowinlade, but most of all SIR!' he said, as some of the students chuckled unkindly around the room. 'Please could you tell me, Mr Van Pearce, what I have orated to the class over the last fifteen minutes?' He shifted his head downwards to beady-eye him.

Joseph heard all the students start to shuffle in theirs chairs and screech them against the floor as they turned around to stare at him. He sat uncomfortably in his seat and gazed around to see them stare with the look of impatience in their eyes, and he felt as though he was about to address the nation with a big speech.

'Err, Jerusalem,' he spouted, and nervously looked back to Mr Dowinlade.

The whole class burst out laughing unsympathetically while some of the girls whispered to one another and rudely pointed their fingers to mock him.

Mr Dowinlade smirked through clenched lips and blinked behind his glasses as he pressed them to his nose. 'Mr Van Pearce,' he said in a condescending tone, 'it brings me such pleasure to see that you have been paying such close attention to my wonderful history lesson, and for that you get a bonus prize of writing me a two-thousand-word essay on Jerusalem

Christianity. Have it on my desk by Friday morning – understood?'

Joseph lowered his head and nodded. He watched Mr Dowinlade walk off to the front of the class. Sheepishly he shifted his eyes back and forth to see if any of the students were still looking at him. Out of the corner of his eye he caught sight of Philippa Dors at a desk over to his left, staring at him through her huge circular-shaped glasses that looked like giant saucers clinging to her freckled face.

Philippa acted coy and swirled her finger around one of the two long, vanilla-blonde pigtails that stuck out of the top of her head, and gave him a smile through her slightly misaligned teeth.

Joseph scowled at her unkindly, lumped his glum face upon his knuckles, rested his elbow on the desk and turned away to stare at the wall miserably.

Out of the blue, the school bell abruptly sounded to end class. All the students immediately started to shuffle their books and pens frantically into their bags and desperately shoved past one another in a bid to get out of the classroom as quickly as possible.

Mr Dowinlade stood by the side of his desk, repositioned his neat round glasses on his face, and bellowed out to the class as they scarpered past in front of him: 'Please can you all hand in your assignments to me by next lesson, thank you very much – oh, and Joseph, I would like a word with you before you go as well.' He dumped himself down into his chair and sighed with relief as the classroom emptied. He rubbed his forehead gently. Casually he took off his glasses and exhaled his coffee breath onto the lenses and used the bottom of his grey cardigan to clean them, before holding them up to check for smears.

Joseph felt anxious as he cautiously approached Mr Dowinlade's desk and began to wonder whether he was likely to get another ear-bashing for falling asleep. He watched Mr Dowinlade slip his glasses back on and stare directly at him, which caused him to feel uneasy. He swallowed nervously.

'So, Joseph, how are things with you?' said Mr Dowinlade in a calm tone while he adjusted his glasses.

Joseph gave a slight shrug of his shoulders. 'Fine,' he replied.

'Well, the reason why I ask you, Joseph, is because it's not just my lessons you have fallen asleep in – it's other lessons too. Other teachers have said the same thing so it's not going unnoticed,' said Mr Dowinlade as he half cocked his head and narrowed his eyes.

Joseph remained quiet. An awkward silence fell between them. He stared blankly at Mr Dowinlade's desk to prevent eye contact; he didn't want to engage in any sort of conversation and hoped to get out of the classroom quickly.

'How are things at home with you, Joseph?' said Mr Dowinlade, trying a different angle with him.

'Everything's fine. Can I go now?' Joseph snapped back in an abrupt tone, feeling sensitive to the question.

Mr Dowinlade leant forward in his chair and removed his glasses. He propped his elbows on his desk and clasped his hands together with a serious look upon his face. He breathed heavily through flared nostrils and stared at him. 'Here's the thing, you have the potential to be a straight "A" student, Joseph, which can open the doorway to great opportunities such as university. I wouldn't like to see you throw that away simply because you can't stay awake in class. You're a good kid, but you need to start applying yourself more. And if there is anything you feel you need to talk about – the school is here for you, I want you to know that,' he said.

Joseph bowed his head, dispirited by Mr Dowinlade's speech, and stared at the floor vacantly. He felt enormous pressure by the teachers to live up to his late father's unprecedented record at the same school, and he was growing tired of it. 'Can I go now?' he muttered.

Mr Dowinlade paused for a second. 'Yes, you can go, but I want that essay on Jerusalem Christianity on my desk on Friday morning – understood?' he said in an authoritative tone, pointing the finger at him.

'Yes, sir,' replied Joseph woefully.

'Off you go,' said Mr Dowinlade, and fluttered his hand for him to leave. He placed his glasses back on.

Joseph slung his rucksack over his shoulder in a huff and headed towards the classroom door.

All the students shoved and rushed past each another in the corridor like a stampede of elephants, and screeched their shoes against the tiled floor like the sound of basketball players running up and down a court. Some of the misfit girls huddling together could be heard cackling to one another uncontrollably, while others were talking gibberish to each other about their day.

Joseph walked down the corridor as though he bore the weight of the world on his shoulders, with his head bowed and his eyes firmly fixed on the tiled flooring. He bounced off other students like a pinball machine as they trampled past him until he reached his locker in the corridor and inserted his key. He clenched his teeth and yanked hard on the door and clanked the metal locker open, pausing to stare at the picture sellotaped to the inside of the door of his late father pushing him along in a wooden toy car when he was small. He sighed. Then he removed his rucksack from his shoulder and began to swap files to and from the locker ready for his last lesson.

'Late night again, mate?' a voice said behind Joseph's locker door.

Joseph grinned to himself as he instantly recognized the chirpy voice a mile off, and moved the door inwards to see Jamerson Hoggle standing there, grinning from ear to ear like a Cheshire cat. Joseph and Jamerson had grown up in the same street together – Lon Green – and had been best friends from a very young age. It also helped a great deal that they had a lot in common too. They both had the same birthday month, April, both wrote left-handed and both wore the same size shoe size 9. But what really brought their friendship together was that their fathers had also been best friends and attended the very school which they attended called Saint Habir School of Excellence, and went on to both serve in the same Fire Brigade. But needless to say, they had their differences as well: Joseph was taller and slender with short dark brown hair brushed to the side and brown eyes, and Jamerson was shorter and slightly podgy, with blue eyes and mousey-coloured curly hair that he was forever touching.

'No, why?' replied Joseph with a screwed-up face.

'Mate, your head hit the desk as soon as you were in class; I don't think Mr Dowinlade was impressed,' chuckled Jamerson.

'Screw him, Hoggle. Anyway, I got a lot on my mind lately,' replied Joseph with pursed lips.

'Is your mum okay?' replied Jamerson, concerned.

'FINE,' said Joseph bluntly, feeling as though everyone kept asking him the same thing.

'Okay, okay,' said Jamerson, holding his hands up and raising his eyebrows as though he didn't mean to offend him. 'I was just checking.'

'Sorry, mate, didn't mean to snap at you. Just feel a little down at the mo, and I keep getting these stupid dreams lately which are so vivid and—' But Joseph was cut off from finishing his sentence.

'Look, don't worry about it, mate, forget about it,' said Jamerson, and gave him a gentle punch on his arm. 'So what you doing tonight? Want to come over to mine so I can kick your ass again on Thunderblast?'

'Maybe, I'll let you know later or something, mate,' replied Joseph.

'Make sure you do, Joey. What you got for last lesson?' asked Jamerson.

'R.E. with Mr golden balls Twine. Huh, what another

exciting lesson that's going to be, with him preaching to us,' replied Joseph and rolled his eyes, and then slammed the door shut on his locker. 'Look, I'll catch up with you later, mate,' and humped his rucksack onto his shoulders and turned to walk away.

Jamerson began to walk backwards in the opposite direction and raised his one hand to the side of his mouth to throw his voice. 'Hey, Joey!' he yelled, which caused Joseph to stop and turn around. 'Keep ya head . . . off the desk, that is,' he laughed out loud.

Joseph scowled, not amused, and shook his head. He walked off briskly to his next class before he was late.

'C'mon, c'mon, hurry up, hurry up, everyone, and sit down quickly, I haven't got all day,' boomed Mr Twine while he stroked his thick ginger moustache with one hand as though he had a nervous disposition.

Joseph tailed in last behind everyone and sat at the back near to the classroom window. A mobile phone rang unexpectedly and he saw Jenny Broth frantically scramble for her bag to switch the thing off.

'Miss Broth, pass it up here please,' said Mr Twine, not amused.

'But, but I've turned it off,' groaned Jenny.

'I do not care, Miss Broth, you know the rules; it's school policy that no mobile phones are to be switched on whilst in lesson, hence the sticker on the classroom door,' replied Mr Twine in a condescending tone and pointed over to it. 'Now pass it up here.'

Jenny waddled her head from side to side and groaned as she stomped her feet along the floor, walked up to his desk and slammed the phone down. 'Huh!' she said, and continued her stomp all the way back to her desk and plonked herself down on the seat. A sulky look came over her as she crossed her arms whilst her lips clenched together and she waddled her head again.

'Thank you, Miss Broth, you can have it back after the lesson,' said Mr Twine, and he placed the mobile in his drawer and hammered it shut. 'Right, does anyone else have a mobile phone I need to confiscate before we begin?' he said.

Suddenly all of the students began to quickly check their pockets and bags to make sure theirs had been switched off, apart from Joseph who had never owned one. Instead he nonchalantly rested his cheek upon on his knuckles to prop up his head, and began to doodle in the back of his book what he could remember from his dream in the lesson before as it still played on his mind.

'Good, let's make a start, shall we?' said Mr Twine, and got up from his old worn brown leather chair and strangely wheeled a chalkboard to the centre of the classroom.

'What's wrong with the smartboard, sir?' asked one of the students.

'I'm afraid there is a problem with it, so until it can be fixed, I am resorting to using a good old-fashioned chalkboard instead for today's lesson,' said Mr Twine, and he began to grate the white chalk against the blackboard, creating a horrendous scraping noise, and causing some of the students to shudder and flutter their eyes like they were being electrocuted.

Joseph shuddered too, before he casually turned his head to the side to stare out through the dirty classroom window at the thick dark clouds above, and wondered if there was likely to be any more snow. Halfway through the lesson he was still gazing out, when he broke from his reverie to stare at a small black mark in the sky that edged closer and closer in his direction. His eyebrows unknowingly moved inwards, his eyes narrowed and at a snail's pace he slowly lifted his imprinted cheek from his knuckles. He drew a blank at what it could be, until it became large enough in the sky to be recognizable. He realized it was a crow.

His eyes widened and no sooner than he could blink, the crow walloped straight into the window and bounced off. He leapt out of his chair with fright and stepped back. 'What the hell!' he said out loud to himself, on edge. Sheepishly, he turned around with embarrassment to face the other students, expecting all of them to be staring at him by his silly behaviour, but was flabbergasted by what he saw instead. His mouth fell open to see Mr Twine had Sam Durrell pinned over a desk by the collar while his circulation was being cut off from the tight grip he had on him and he screamed in his face.

'You think you can cheek me, boy, do you, do you?' yelled Mr Twine, bright red in the face like a raging bull about to attack the matador.

The other students gasped with horror, with their mouths open as they watched on helplessly as Mr Twine continued to shake and strangle the life out of Sam, when one of the students piped up.

'Sir, sir, let him go, you're hurting him!' said Peter Willstone, pleading with him.

For a second, Mr Twine stopped and cast his devilish eyes sideways to the students before he turned to Sam again. 'Get out of my classroom right now!' he yelled in Sam's face and released him from his grip.

Sam choked for air, shook uncontrollably and held his neck, and without a second to lose, quickly picked up his bag and scarpered across the classroom to the door.

The venomous look of anger in Mr Twine's face slowly drained from red back to white again and he gazed around the class at the other students who were all staring at him like startled rabbits caught in the headlights of a car.

Joseph swallowed nervously and quietly sat back down. He watched Mr Twine place his shaky hand into his trouser pocket and pull out a hanky to wipe the sweat from his moustache, then stroll back to his desk looking clearly unsettled.

A deafening silence fell upon the class as they reeled in shock and looked around at one another, dumbstruck by what had happened. They turned their attention back to Mr Twine who was sitting in his chair in a warped trance of sorts.

'Uh, class dismissed,' muttered Mr Twine.

Knowing there were still twenty minutes left of the lesson, some students shrugged as they looked baffled at each other, but they were not going to argue the toss, and began to quietly pack their books away into their bags. One by one, they gradually got up from their chairs and gingerly headed for the classroom door.

Jenny Broth slowly got up out of her chair, slung the strap from her bag over her shoulder and crossed her arms tightly to stop them from shaking. She took a deep swallow and began to walk towards Mr Twine's desk to ask for her phone back, but at the last second she chickened out and walked straight past Mr Twine and headed for the door with the others and glanced back over her shoulder.

With his eyes firmly fixed on Mr Twine, Joseph accidentally screeched his chair back to stand up and cringed. He quickly slung his rucksack over his shoulders and began to walk sideways to his right like a crab, passing two rows of desks. A hard lump formed in his throat as he warily walked down the end row, and prayed he didn't do anything more irrational until he left the room. The cold air pressed against his face as he entered the silent corridor and gave a quick glance back to Mr Twine slumped in his chair before he ran up the corridor.

He glanced through the other classroom windows filled with students in lessons, finally reached the main doors and thrust them open with relief. Half a dozen students from his class stood near to the steps yapping away whilst they huddled together from the cold and got overly excited by the discussion between them. Not one to engage in conversation or socialize, Joseph placed his grey bobble hat upon his head and rushed down the steps. Just as he was passing them, he overheard one of the girls mention Mr Twine's name and slowed down to listen.

'Yeah, Mr Twine just flipped out and walked up to Sam and

started to throttle him for no reason,' said Kerry Bell excitedly.

'Well, I'm not afraid of golden balls,' said Shawn Bane, acting macho in front of some of the girls, 'and if he done that to me I'd—'

'You'd what?' said Martha Stokes, rudely interrupting, calling his bluff.

'Well, I'd . . . I'd,' replied Shawn, stumbling for words. Caught off guard, he quickly tried to find something to say, when he looked to Joseph. 'Hey, Noddy!' he yelled, turning the attention onto him.

Joseph stopped in his tracks and anxiously clutched his straps over his shoulders with his hands and swallowed. Slowly he turned around and saw them all stood staring at him and felt uncomfortable.

'So did you see anything, Noddy?' said Shawn, mocking him about the other lesson he'd seen him in earlier.

'Who, me?' replied Joseph, hoping he was talking to someone else.

'Yeah you, dozy, did you see why golden balls flipped out on Sam?' said Shawn, continuing to belittle him in front of the others, while some of the girls sniggered.

'No, I, I didn't see anything, honest,' said Joseph, shrugging his shoulders. 'What did Sam do?' he asked.

'Nothing, as far as I could tell,' replied Francesca Borges, as she twirled her hair with her finger, whilst blowing a bubble with her chewing gum at the same time.

'Well, he should be sacked for behaving like that, it's totally unprofessional, and he still has my phone, the nerve of him, huh,' said Jenny Broth, wiggling her head from side to side annoyingly and joining in the conversation.

'Well, it was nice talking to you – got to go,' Joseph said, turned and proceeded to walk off through the wet snow.

'Strange boy, isn't he?' said Martha, tilting her head sideways to stare at him.

'Huh, kid's a weirdo, if you ask me,' replied Shawn, shaking his head.

Joseph overheard the spiteful comments and for a split second stopped and clenched his teeth before he carried on across the school yard.

Chapter 3

BROKEN HOME

Joseph pushed the key into the lock on the front door of his house, sighed and entered. 'Mum, I'm home,' he said in a glum voice, dumping his bag down in the living room and threw a quick glance around to see where she was.

As he whipped back the curtains, the natural light poured through the window. It looked like the living room hadn't seen daylight in weeks; flecks of dust kicked up into the air and glistened like tiny speckles of lights. The shoddy, worn, brown carpet and yellowish wallpaper, faded by numerous of years of sunlight exposure, complemented the rest of the dreary room with its limp yellowish lamp shade that stood in the corner next to a crooked, faded family picture hung upon the wall, opposite a great big old television which sat upon a bowing rickety four-legged table. The tiresome room looked as inviting as going to dinner with a tank full of piranhas.

'Mum, where are you?' he asked, raising his voice with concern.

'In here,' replied a croaky voice, coughing somewhere towards the back of the house.

With shoulders slumped, Joseph trundled diagonally across the living room through an interconnecting archway that led into a shabby dining area. He turned left and stopped at the opening that led into the kitchen. He wasn't surprised to see his mother, Cathleen, sat at the kitchen table looking demoralized, clutching her hand around a glass full of wine, with an empty bottle beside her on the table. Her messy brown hair was uncombed and pinned back behind her ears, displaying her drunken red-rimmed eyes, drowned with misery, the dark circles underneath highlighted against her pale white skin.

'How was school today, Joey?' Cathleen asked in a croaky voice, quickly letting go of the wine glass to pull her hair over her face.

Joseph quickly locked eyes onto the refrigerator and hurried past, pretending he hadn't seen her with the alcohol. 'Yeah, okay, you know, same old,' he replied, as he tugged at the large door and huffed, blowing out his cheeks at the sight of the empty shelves inside.

'Your dad would be so proud of you, Joey, if he was here today,' said Cathleen, slurring her words, and she forced a smile out the corner of her lip. 'Do you want me to fix you something to eat?'

Unable to recall the last time she had cooked him food, Joseph raised his eyebrows with scepticism upon hearing her words and lifted out a nearly empty carton of orange juice from the side door and unscrewed the cap. 'Nah, it's okay, Mum,

I'm not that hungry. Thanks anyway,' he replied, and gulped back the last mouthful of orange juice to quench his thirst. He lazily placed the empty container back into the fridge and slammed the door shut. The moment he turned around, he said, 'I'm gonna head upstairs and get some homework done,' but the words seemed to slow down in his mouth as soon as he locked eyes on her and his heart began to sink. He found it difficult to cope with seeing his grieving mother intoxicated, sat upon the chair wobbling her head and clutching the wine glass like her life depended on it, when from memory she used to be striking with beauty and full of zest for life. It was hard for him to comprehend that this was the same woman who had nurtured him when he was ill; read him exciting bedtime stories every night with her glowing voice, and had a smile so contagious that you couldn't help but feel good about yourself. Nowadays, he felt her soul remained lost somewhere that was not within his reach, and he didn't have it in his heart to tell her he truly missed the way she used to be, as he had spent half of his life now growing up feeling like he was living with a stranger.

Too many times he had shed a barrage of tears about the situation, and he felt she had squandered too many years to drink, which had now become the everyday norm for him. But sometimes he wished he could exchange places with his late father, rather than have to pick up the pieces from a broken home and be left feeling neglected. Still, he couldn't help but feel angry with himself for making feeble excuses to her, knowing full well he had no intention of completing any homework upstairs, but he couldn't bring himself to spend any more time with her than what was necessary, as her inexcusable drunken behaviour was a constant reminder to him of the loss of his father.

'Okay, Joey, just remember I love you,' replied Cathleen, and swigged back on the glass of wine.

Though her words had very little meaning and felt empty to Joseph, somewhere inside of him he yearned to repeat the same words back with his loving heart, but couldn't bring himself to, and instead promptly left the kitchen and strode through into the dining area. He stopped suddenly at the foot of the interconnecting archway to hear his mother cry, and felt a dull ache wrench from his chest and bowed his head with pity. With tightened lips, he ignored the sound and darted across the living room and up the creaky stairs and turned right into his bedroom and slammed the door shut.

He leant against the door and sighed with relief, away from the torturing noise, which he had grown unable to listen to, and he stood for a moment with his eyes closed and head leant against the door. His cold, grim-looking bedroom perfectly matched the rest of the uncared-for house, with its dire blue carpet and distasteful blue striped wallpaper that had peeled in places. Along with the bizarre empty tank that was sat on top of a large wooden chest of broken drawers, and the floor strewn with clothes, it was unwelcoming to say the very least. But his bedroom was his castle, nevertheless, a place where he felt safe and at ease and where he didn't have to deal with the everyday pressures on the other side of the door.

He hurried across and kicked off his trainers and leapt onto his bed. He placed his hands behind his head, took a deep breath and blew out heavily, causing the dream-catcher that his mother had made him to spin around out of control on the ceiling above. The sunlight edging through the dark clouds radiated slight warmth into his bedroom through his dusty wooden blinds and made him feel content. He watched intently as the dream-catcher swirled away freely. A smile formed out at the corners of his mouth as he thought of how beautifully crafted the detailing was, and how chuffed he was the day his mother gave it to him. He gently blew on it again and felt his eyes half close and become heavy. His heart slowed down to a sweet rhythmic sound as he lay still, listening closely to it softly beat away in his eardrums. Finally he gave in and let his heavy eyes succumb and close completely and he slipped off into the darkness.

~

Gradually Joseph opened his eyes and found himself standing on an embankment with the sun shining down blissfully. Everything moved in slow motion as he turned his head and his vision became blurred for a brief moment, then cleared. He spied a man stood in a baseball cap and glasses, casting out across a beautiful glistening lake in front of him. He was unsure of who it was until the man turned around and smiled, when he realized it was his father. Joseph waved to him excitedly but became baffled as to why he did not wave back in his direction.

Curiously he turned around and saw a delightful log cabin up on a hill, with smoke lightly puffing away from the chimney stack, with a woman sat upon the porch in a rocking chair. Intrigued to know her identity, he narrowed his eyes, but with her head tilted slightly down and wearing a large flowery hat that covered her face, it was difficult for him to know. He drew closer and noticed she was sewing something on her lap and he became curious. The woman stopped and looked up with a glowing smile. Overwhelming happiness filled him when he realized it was his mother, and he watched her proudly hold aloft a dream-catcher in her hand. His eyes lit up and began to run as fast as he could towards her, but everything around him still moved in slow motion.

As he got nearer she stood up and dropped the dream-catcher out of her hand and walked to the edge of the porch. Concerned by her behaviour, he stopped and stared and wondered why she held her hands to her face with a look of fright. Out of nowhere a distinctive smell wafted up his nostrils, which caused his nose to twitch. He wondered where it came from and slowly turned around and saw everything was on fire in front of him. His eyes flashed wide open, aghast. Panic-stricken, he called out to his father amongst the bellowing smoke but he was nowhere to be seen. He swung back around to make a quick break for it towards his mother, but a tree on fire had fallen and was blocking his path. In the distance he saw the log cabin had gone up in smoke as well and tears begun to run down his face. Repeatedly he cried out to his mother but she'd vanished into thin air. He began to choke heavily on the smoke and covered his face with his arm.

Everywhere he turned, everything was ablaze around him, then out of nowhere he heard an unexplainable swooping noise pass above his head. He looked up and saw a black shadow sweep in and out amongst the smoke. One by one, trees caught fire and began to fall, causing the ground to shake like an earthquake as they hit the floor. Frightened, he weaved in and out of them, but with every step that he took another tree would fall and block his path. Eventually he found himself cornered and trapped. He stood in a small circle, engulfed by the flames. He whirled around and around, desperately searching for a way out as the heat became unbearable. Suddenly a black shadowy creature's head emerged from the flames with eyes that burnt as bright as the scorching flames and with fire dripping from its nostrils. It drew closer. Terrified, Joseph took a step back but could go no further. He looked back to the creature when suddenly it hurled out a ball of flames towards him.

He closed his eyes and held his arms up to protect himself, then suddenly he leapt up from his bed and gasped for air as though he was still choking on the flames. A cold sweat came over him as his eyes darted all around with panic, when it dawned on him that he was safe and well in his bedroom. He was hugely relieved it was just a dream, but it left him shaken, with his neck hairs standing on end. It had felt so real. Confused as to why his bedroom was pitch-black, he threw a glance over to his bedside drawer. The little red lights displayed on his clock said nine o'clock. Astonished, as he thought he hadn't been asleep that long, he leant over and flicked on the side lamp and squinted from the bright light. Out of the blue, he heard a loud banging echo through the quiet house. Concerned and worried for his mother, he leapt from his bed like a kangaroo and flung open his bedroom door. He sprinted down the darkened staircase like a madman to find her fast asleep on the sofa and wrapped up in a blanket, with the television switched on and lighting the dark room up like a lighthouse to the sea.

'Must have been the TV,' he said under his breath and scratched his head. Calmly he turned back around to head on up the stairs, when the heavy banging sounded again. Startled, he swung his head to look at the internal door that led into the porch, then over to his mother, worried that the sound might have woken her, and quickly rushed through the door and closed it quietly behind him. Warily he opened the front door to see someone standing there in a puffy white coat and red bobble-hat, looking like a huge white cupcake with a cherry on top.

'Jamerson!' he said, and screwed his face up with confusion.

'All right, Joey, how's it going?' replied Jamerson through his chattering teeth and rosy-looking face.

Joseph scowled at him. 'Jamerson, it's like nine o'clock,' he said, unimpressed by his timing.

'Sorry, mate, but you didn't answer the door when I knocked for you earlier. What you been doing anyway? It's freezing out here,' said Jamerson as he bounced back and forth on his toes and rubbed his hands together to keep warm.

Joseph took that as a hint, and not usually one to invite people in, he inconspicuously closed the door a little but allowed just enough room to peer his head around to see him. 'Oh, I must have fallen asleep, mate,' he replied in a low tone.

'So did you hear about Mr Twine today, mate?' said Jamerson excitedly, like it was hot gossip.

'Yeah, I was there,' replied Joseph and nodded calmly.

Jamerson's eyes lit up by his response. 'So did you see what happened, then?' he replied.

'No, I was . . .' Joseph paused and suddenly saw a flashback of the crow hitting the window in the classroom.

Jamerson waited for him to finish his sentence before prompting him. 'Joey?' he said.

Joseph shook his head, trying to get the vision out of his mind. 'What? Oh – oh yeah, umm, how do you know about Mr Twine, anyway?' he said, skirting over the question by answering with a question.

'I saw Martha earlier and she filled me in,' said Jamerson, and grinned with delight. 'But everyone in school knows as it's blowing up all over FB! Dude's gonna be in big trouble now. What do you think made him flip out like that anyway, did Sam cause it?' he asked.

'Not sure,' replied Joseph and shrugged.

'Well, you were there, wasn't you?' said Jamerson, staring at him.

'Yeah, but . . . look, I gotta go, I think Mum's calling me, I'll speak to you tomorrow, mate,' said Joseph in a hurry and slowly began to shut the door.

Jamerson quickly leant forward through the gap. 'I'll knock for you tomorrow,' he blurted out as the door slammed shut in his face. He threw down his shoulders in a huff and scowled at the door before turning away and starting to walk up the small driveway in a sulk.

Joseph trundled back into the living room and gently closed the internal door behind him and threw a quick glance towards his mother. All of a sudden he was struck by an enormous growl of hunger from his stomach and soothingly began to rub it as though it might help ease the discomfort he was feeling. With famished thoughts, he quietly scurried across the living room and headed for the kitchen. He flipped the light switch on and hurried to the refrigerator and tugged at the door, when out of nowhere an unexpected loud clang came from behind him and made him jump with fright. He flung around and cast his eyes suspiciously around the kitchen, but felt them drawn to the internal door that led into his father's integral garage. His unease grew as he edged towards the door and churned over thoughts of what the queer sound could be. That suddenly turned his ravenous stomach into a swarm of nervous butterflies. He reached the door and leant in and heard a peculiar sound of scraping metal and swallowed nervously.

As he reached for the handle with his clammy hand he suddenly froze like a statue to the sound of *clink, clunk*. His heart pounded wildly like a drum while crazy thoughts ran through his mind as he stared at the handle. He proceeded to grab the cold handle and pushed down firmly and swung the door open swiftly to be confronted by freezing cold air that whipped past him and into the house, sending a shiver through his entire body.

'Hello,' he said in a nervous voice. 'Is anybody there?'

His hand trembled, holding the door handle as he stared into the darkness, while his other frantically searched up and down on the inside of the stone cold wall for the light switch. He felt the metal box and flipped the switch the other way. *BOOM*, the strip light powered up every inch of garage, forcing him to squint and blink a couple of times until his eyes readjusted to the bright light.

'Hello?' he muttered again through chattering teeth. Too scared to step inside, he cowardly leant forward and poked his head around to look, but saw nothing out of the ordinary. Eagerly he switched the light off and pulled the door shut, and quickly began to turn the key below the handle to lock the door. Backing away from the door he walked straight into the kitchen cupboards and accidentally caused the crockery to fall over. Spooked by the noise, he dashed out of the kitchen towards the living room and scarpered up the stairs to his bedroom to sleep off his strange day.

Chapter 4

THE TRAGIC LOSS OF A HERO

The morning light wrestled to break free from the dark clouds that kept it at bay, but finally the rays burst through and pierced through the hairline cracks of Joseph's bedroom blinds. An abrupt sound crackled in his ear as he awoke to his alarm clock beeping like a car horn. He reached out and wildly swung his arm to turn it off, but half asleep he accidentally struck the clock off the bedside table and it landed onto the floor.

The sound irked him as it resonated against the thin carpet. 'Would you bloody shut up!' he groaned and pulled the warm duvet over his head to try and block out the noise. After several minutes, the noise finally stopped, to the sweet relief of his ears, and he happily let his tired eyes succumb and he slowly drifted off again. Out of the blue, a bird began to caw loudly outside and unkindly interrupted his slumber. Peeved, he kicked back the duvet and threw his legs wildly over the side of his bed and leapt to his feet and foolishly stood on his alarm clock, setting off the beeper again. 'OWWW!' he cried out, as he fell back onto his bed in a heap, crying in pain. 'ARGHH, that bloody clock, ARGHH!' he yelled, rocking back and forth while he held his foot.

Throbbing with pain, he began to rub his foot while the noisy bird kept up its annoying squawk. Feeling the bird was mocking him, his face turned red with anger and he furiously began to clamber out of his bed. With gritted teeth, he leant down and scooped the clock up and bashed it several times with the side of his fist to shut it off. Finally it stopped and he grudgingly threw it onto his bed. He rose to his feet in a flash and hobbled across his bedroom floor over to his window, yanked hard on the pull cord and thrust the dusty blinds high into the air.

'Shoo, go on, shoo!' he yelled through the window, flapping his arm aggressively at the crow. Startled, the crow leapt from the external ledge and flew off aimlessly into the sky. Joseph watched and scowled angrily, wishing he had something that he could have thrown at it, and said to himself, 'Huh, stupid bird!' Agitated, he carelessly let go of the pull cord and sent the wooden blinds crashing down onto the window ledge with an almighty bang. He turned away and cowered pathetically with his hands over his head at the sound it made.

Gingerly he straightened up and gave a sideways glance to see his blind was all crooked and a couple of the slats had broken. He sighed. 'Great, that's all I need, well done, Joey,' he said, annoyed at himself. With a sullen look upon his face, he vigorously rubbed the sleep from his sticky eyes and let out a big yawn. He scratched his head and looked around his bedroom floor amongst the scattered clothes to find his worn grey slippers and quickly slipped them on. Hobbling over to his bedroom door, he winced from his throbbing foot and shuffled out onto the landing and clutched his hungry stomach.

The open-plan carpeted staircase creaked as he quietly traipsed down it, but halfway down he stopped and peered into the grim living room with a nonplussed look. He let out a heavy sigh and shook his head with clenched teeth at the sight of his mother half hanging off the sofa fast asleep, with a wine bottle fallen on its side beside the sofa. 'I wish she would just give up,' he muttered under his breath to himself with frustration, while squeezing the handrail aggressively. Reaching the bottom, he shivered from the coldness of the room, which made goose pimples spread on his arms. He quietly strolled over and picked up the fallen blanket from the floor and draped it back over his mother. He gritted his teeth with umbrage and snatched the empty bottle from the floor, and casually walked off towards the kitchen with slumped shoulders.

The morning light unkindly shone into the dreary, deteriorated kitchen, showing where cupboard doors had fallen off and the vinyl floor was torn in places. He strolled in, het up by the morning events already, and took one look at the mess of it and visualized throwing the empty bottle at the wall out of sheer anger. Instead, he rationalized with himself and walked over to the chair and slumped down and thudded the bottle down onto the kitchen table. He shut his eyes and leant his head against the wall with despair.

The quietness of the house was abruptly broken by the sound of a faint and mysterious tapping noise. Joseph frowned and glared at the sink's tap, when he realized it wasn't the cause of the noise. He eased his head from the wall and slowly begun to gaze around, baffled by where it came from, and calmly rose from the chair and walked over to the refrigerator and shook it firmly. He stepped back with a smug look, thinking he'd successfully solved the problem, when surprisingly the noise continued, but this time it sounded marginally further away. He scratched his head with confusion and began to search the kitchen high and low, growing more and more agitated by the second. Just as he stepped past the internal garage door heading for the dining area, he stopped suddenly. His legs felt rooted to the spot as he stared at the door, remembering last night's commotion, but he wanted to get to the bottom of the annoying sound and crept slowly towards it.

Gently he leant his ear up against the cold wood, heard a *tap, tap, tap, tap*, and said to himself, 'It's coming from in there.' He moved his head away and began to bite his bottom lip nervously and anxiously rub his thumb across his fingers. Unnerved by the sound, he edged back, when the tapping suddenly stopped for a brief moment, but then resumed. He felt his heart thump against his chest and his throat become tight. He stood and stared long and hard at the door, trying to pluck up some courage, and in a flash he daringly lunged for the handle, pushed down hard and fast, and shoved his shoulder into the door. But foolishly he forgot that he'd locked it the night before. 'OWWW!' he yelped out, as his shoulder crunched against it.

The cranking of the door handle caused the mysterious noise to suddenly stop and not resume. He released the handle and briefly rubbed his shoulder. His sudden burst of courage had all but dissolved and left him jittery. Slowly he moved towards the key and began to turn it. Clunk, the door unlocked. He took in a deep breath and anxiously gripped the cold handle and gradually pressed down. Slowly he opened it to the harsh cold air which rushed past him and quickly fumbled for the switch on the wall. *BOOM*, the light powered up. Nervously he reached out for a large monkey wrench on the right-hand side on the workbench. 'Hello?' he said in a shaky voice. 'Show yourself! I'm armed.'

He heard a *flip flop* noise near to the garage door, but his father's car was in the way and he was unable to see. Warily, he stepped down into the garage onto the stone floor and held the monkey wrench as though he was a batter holding a baseball bat in his hand ready to swing off at the slightest noise. He side-stepped like a crab to his right behind the back of the covered-up car, and leant his head and body over to look down the side of it. 'Show yourself!' he repeated, and quickly straightened back up. His legs trembled as he knelt down onto the floor to glance beneath the car. At the last second, just as he was about to rise up, a large object caught his eye at the right-hand side of the front inner wheel. Hastily he rose up and was slowly creeping down the side of the car when he crunched his foot against something on the ground.

He pivoted his foot out of the way to see that he had stepped on broken glass and looked up to see where it came from, noticing that a pane of glass was broken from the small window high up to the right.

Joseph turned back and stepped over the glass and continued his tiptoeing down the side of the car until he reached the front. Slowly he knelt down and slid his arm underneath the sill of the car. He latched onto a tin and dragged it out across the floor. He climbed to his feet and stared, puzzled, at the rusty thing, when he heard the *flip flop* sound again as though it was right next to him but coming from under the car. Startled, he tripped backwards and fell against all the fishing gear and stacked boxes behind him. He tumbled sideways and landed on the floor with everything falling on top of him. The monkey wrench clunked against the ground as he accidentally let go of it, but with the tin still in his hand he frantically stumbled to his feet and unsteadily ran to the back of the car and around it. He yanked open the internal door and leapt into the kitchen like a frog and slammed it shut behind him. His eyes were wide and his breathing was erratic as he stared nervously at the door, and tried to swallow but his throat was dry. He clanged the tin carelessly down onto the kitchen table.

Sheepishly he backed away and pulled out one of the chairs from under the kitchen table, scraping it against the floor, and plonked his butt down to look at the tin, realizing it was upside down. He quickly flipped it over. A baffled look appeared upon his face as to why it was filled with lots of indentations and scrape marks. He wiped his sweaty hands into his pyjama bottoms and pressed his thumbs against the lid and popped the tin open. The metal lid clanked noisily, and gently he placed it down to the side and immediately noticed a newspaper cutting inside, folded in half. Intrigued, he carefully lifted it out and began to unfold the faded piece of paper, and felt his gut instantly tighten as he read the standout headlines.

~

South Bay Post : *Firefighter Dies in the Line of Duty.*
A family are in mourning after a well-respected Firefighting Officer died yesterday in a blaze at a house. 35-year-old Firefighter Michael Van Pearce, married with one child, was tackling the ferocious blaze and lost his life saving a young child, who was thought to be trapped inside the blazing inferno that quickly ripped through another house.

Chief Dean Huckstable of Greater South Fire and Rescue said,

'Michael Van Pearce was an extremely well-liked and honourable Firefighter who had serviced with us for the past ten years. His dedication and courage will never be matched; he served his community with pride and dignity. My sincerest condolences go out to the family who have suffered the tragic loss of such a great Firefighting hero.'

A full inquest is under way to determine the cause of the horrific fire that took the life of such a brave young man.

~

Choked, a tear broke from Joseph's welling eyes and trickled down his face, hung off the bottom of his chin, then fell off onto the newspaper cutting and soaked through. His stomach churned from the sickening story and he felt an instant heaviness and stabbing pain in his heart as though he had been repeatedly punched in his chest. He closed his eyes, and memories of his father, along with the day he bore witness to his mother breaking down, unhinged by grief, at the front door by fire officers who broke the news to her, soon began to flood his mind like a tidal wave. He had found it hard to believe that his father was never going to return home again when his mother told him, and even harder when he had to attend the funeral and say goodbye to him. Broken-hearted, his bottom lip quivered as he wept uncontrollably from the unbearable pain.

Slowly his teary eyes opened and he placed the newspaper cutting down to one side and wiped his wet nose with the back of his cold hand. Just as he did so, he noticed a large envelope inside the tin with his name and *Private and Confidential* scrolled across it. Taken aback, he picked it up and quickly began to tear it open. He slid his hand inside and to his amazement pulled out a large photograph. He held it up in awe at the sight of his late father and late grandfather Cyril, standing proudly together side by side, smiling, with his father holding a huge fish with both hands, and his grandfather with his one arm over Michael's shoulder, and his other arm holding up something in his hand. He marvelled at the photograph that he had never seen before and felt a sensational rush of warming happiness burn deep within him. His glazed eyes casted all over the photograph detailing, and by chance he flipped it over and looked with utter shock to see a message written to him.

Joseph,
Mad as a hatter, your grandmother called me,
Two dine was devine while we drank afternoon tea,
What I hold in my hand is your destiny,
To get you started I have left you a key.
Love Granddad x
P.S. Are you hungry, Joseph? Look for a fork at Talgar.

Flabbergasted, his mouth fell wide open and he whispered, 'It's a riddle!' Not knowing what to make of it, he repeatedly flipped the photograph back and forth, until his eyes came to rest, staring at what his grandfather held in his hand. He placed the photograph down and quickly picked up the envelope and rummaged inside with his hand, before he turned it upside down, shook it and peered inside. Confused by the uncanny riddle, he searched eagerly through the rest of the tin for a key, but found nothing that remotely resembled one. 'What key? There isn't any key here!' he said out loud to himself, burning with frustration. Out of the blue he heard a faint groaning coming from the direction of the dining room.

'Joseph . . .' Cathleen called out in a groggy voice.

Panic-stricken, Joseph quickly slid the photograph back into the envelope and hurried to place everything back into the tin, and frantically began to look around the kitchen for somewhere to hide it.

'Joseph,' Cathleen called again, coughing. 'Where are you?'

'I'll be there in a minute, Mum,' replied Joseph, praying she wouldn't enter the kitchen. Standing by the sink he spun around and accidentally hit the kickboard with his foot and caused it to fall flat on the floor. 'Perfect!' he exclaimed, and instantly dropped to his knees and slid the tin quickly underneath. Carefully he replaced the kickboard so that it wouldn't fall again and calmly rose to his feet and dusted himself off. 'Coming, Mum!' he called out and nonchalantly strolled towards the living room.

Chapter 5

A TRIP DOWN MEMORY LANE

BANG, BANG, BANG. Joseph stood in his school uniform by the living-room front window and suspiciously eased back the yellowish netting to see who on earth would cause such a noise at eight o'clock in the morning, then huffed. 'Bloody Jamerson, he knocks as though he's the police or something. One day he's gonna break my front door!' he said angrily under his breath whilst he glared through the window at him. He threw a quick glance to his mother who had gone back to sleep on the sofa, and was relieved that the audacious noise caused by Jamerson hadn't woken her.

Abruptly he let go of the netting but continued to stare through and watched him happily scoffing a bag of sweets. Joseph felt slight resentment beginning to brood inside towards his best friend and subconsciously he began to compare his life to Jamerson's. *Huh, he's got it so nice and easy*, he thought. *Look at him stood there, stuffing his face with not a care in the world. How nice it is not to have to worry or be embarrassed about your mother being drunk all the time or be ashamed about your house, because YOUR house is so nice, Jamerson, with your flat-screen TV stuck on your bedroom wall and the new gaming station you're on all of the bloody time . . .* he continued to rant in his mind. With a glum look on his face, he unintentionally switched from his unhappy and resentful thoughts to one of his fondest memories that vividly stood out as clear as a blue sky. He began to cast his mind back to when his father took him on his first ever fishing trip to Cregennan Lakes when he was eight years old, and he drifted off into a daydream.

He had begrudgingly opened his eyes to the booming sound of his father's deep voice that bellowed inside the car from the back, telling him to 'Wake up!' and winced from the pain of his crooked neck where his head had been slumped up against the seat belt on the journey. 'Rise and shine, sleeping beauty, we're here!' he remembered his father saying.

Tired and grouchy, he pushed back his bobble hat that was slightly dipped over his droopy eyes and rolled his dry mouth like a cow chewing on grass. He unclipped his seat belt and with effort reached for the door handle and carelessly flung it wide open and stepped out. Immediately he was greeted by the smell of the fresh morning dew that wafted up his nostrils, the cold and crisp air that wrapped around his face and the marvellous penetrating sun that beamed down on him. His blurred, sleepy eyes narrowed and took a moment to readjust to the sun's brightness whilst he rubbed them. And when they did he would never forget what he saw.

He looked up to see the sky running clear blue overhead without a single cloud to spoil its beauty, before he full circled around in amazement. He held his hand straight against his forehead to create a visor effect, and marvelled at the breath-taking views of the snow-capped mountains in the distance that rose high into the sky, met by a mist that gently wrapped around the tips of them. Below the mountains was a span of bright green grass which complemented the surrounding area beyond an unblemished lake. It stretched as far as his eye could see and was unlike anything he had ever seen before. 'Wow, this place is amazing! Where are we?' he said with excitement in his voice.

'Welcome to Cregennan Lakes, Joey!' replied Michael proudly, standing at the back of the car to unload the fishing gear.

Joseph gazed at the heavenly, picturesque place and grinned like a Cheshire cat from ear to ear. 'So where are we going to, Dad?' he said, strolling round to the back of the car, raring to go.

'Just down that grass verge, son,' said Michael, and spun around and pointed down into the valley. 'We'll have to carry the gear from here but it won't take us long,' and gently he rubbed the top of Joseph's bobble hat.

Joseph stood and watched his father slam the boot shut and keenly began to pick up the fishing gear from the ground. He gazed at Joseph.

'You gonna give me a hand, Joey, or are you gonna stand there and watch me all day?' said Michael, stooping down whilst turning his head sideways on to look at him.

'Yeah, sure, Dad,' replied Joseph with a nonchalant shrug of his shoulders. He heaved up some of the gear that he was able to carry and waddled across the road like a duckling following its parent from behind. The moment he unsteadily descended the uneven grass verge he instantly stepped in a huge dollop of poop. 'Ah, yuck!' he shouted out, and danced around like an imbecile trying to wipe it off his shoe.

Michael began to laugh out loud. 'You might want to watch your step next time!' he said, chuckling to himself. 'There's plenty of that around here, you have the fluffy ones to thank over there,' and pointed to a flock of sheep on the hillside.

Joseph looked across and they all began to bleat in a bewildering way that sounded like they were laughing at him. He huffed and screwed his face up at them and went to turn away but hesitated when an overly large rock caught his attention a little further over to the left from where the sheep grazed. 'Hey, Dad!' he yelled out.

Michael, a few yards ahead, stopped and turned around. 'What's the matter, Joey?' he asked.

'What's that rock thing over there by the sheep?' Joseph replied.

'Oh that, that's a standing stone, there's loads of them things around here,' said Michael with a shrug of his shoulders. 'C'mon, slowcoach, we got some fish to catch,' and he casually turned back around and carried on down the path.

Eager to find out more, Joseph began a half-hearted attempt to run towards his father to catch up. As he stumbled along with his load, he passed a rusty old letter box and wondered why it was there and what it was for. Out of breath, he finally caught up to his father, panting a little. 'So what is a standing stone, Dad?' he said as he trundled along beside him.

'Well, from what I can remember of your grandfather's history lessons that he loved to give me when we would come up here to fish, in the medieval times a standing stone was something people would worship for some strange reason,' said Michael, raising his eyebrows and pouting his lips.

'But I thought people worshipped God?' replied Joseph, looking confused.

'People worship all sorts of weird and wonderful things, Joey. It doesn't necessarily matter sometimes what it is; just as long as you keep believing and stay true to yourself,' said Michael and gave him a smile. 'Anyway, there's a much bigger one than that over the other side, near to the other big lake, with a huge hole in it,' and he nodded his head sideways.

'There's a bigger lake!' Joseph exclaimed, as he looked out across the lake that they were heading towards.

'Oh yeah, I'll have to show you again sometime,' replied Michael, and stopped in his tracks and lowered the fishing gear down on the ground. 'Well, this is it, this is the smaller lake. What do you think?' he asked, and turned to Joseph.

The wondrous sunshine rays bouncing off the undisturbed water blinded Joseph's eyes and caused him to squint, and carelessly he dropped everything to the ground that was in his hand.

'Hey, take it easy, we don't want it all broken before we

start fishing!' said Michael, and scowled, then began to set up.

'Sorry, Dad,' said Joseph, and swiftly made his way over to the water's edge and picked up a flat pebble from the ground. Like a baseball pitcher winding up for a throw, he whipped his arm back and launched the pebble across the water. It bounced once across the gleaming surface and to his great disappointment he watched it sink.

'Unlucky, son, remember what I taught you, always throw it sideways, not so much overarm, that way you'll get a better bounce,' said Michael, and picked up a large pebble from the ground to demonstrate. 'Here, watch.' With his strong arm, he slung it back at waist height and fired it across the lake, causing it to bounce numerous times before it sank. Multiple ripples formed in the water until they faded away and disappeared.

'Huh,' muttered Joseph with envy.

'Practice makes perfect, remember that Joey, in everything you do in life,' said Michael in a stern voice. 'Here, come here,' and he picked Joseph up and tossed him high into the air and spun him around several times, before he dropped him back down.

Giddy and off balance, Joseph fell down onto the wet grass and shook his head, while he heard his father laughing out loud. Unexpectedly he felt his father land beside him and drape his heavy arm around his shoulders. He stared out into the glistening lake with a huge smile and thought that things couldn't get any better than being at the lake with his father, and felt him gently kiss him on top of his bobble hat.

'Shall I tell you something magical about the lake?' said Michael, rubbing Joseph's bobble hat with his hand.

'Like what?' Joseph replied excitedly, turning his head to him.

'Well, many, many years ago before you and I were born, or even your grandfather for that matter, there was a legend that Celtic people would come to this lake and cast all of their wonderful treasures into it,' said Michael, pulling Joseph a little closer.

Joseph's eyebrows drew inwards. 'Why?' he asked.

'Well, they believed that it would bring them good fortune from doing this. And do you want to hear something else real scary, hmm?' said Michael.

'Uh-huh,' replied Joseph nodding his head, intrigued to know more.

'The local folk around here claim there's a ghost that's been seen near these waters,' said Michael, narrowing his eyes at him.

Joseph's eyes began to widen and he felt a shiver run through his body at the very word that passed through his father's lips. 'A ghost?' he replied.

'Uh-huh, and do you know what else they've found?' said Michael.

'What, Dad, what?' asked Joseph, feeling excited and nervous all at the same time whilst looking deep into his father's eyes.

'A sword!' said Michael, lowering his tone and widening his eyes.

'A sword?' said Joseph, scrunching his face up, unimpressed.

'Yep, a sword. Your grandfather reckoned it belonged to the ghost,' said Michael.

'Well, where is it now?' replied Joseph, feeling somewhat sceptical about the story.

'Oh, I can't remember, but your grandfather would definitely know. He loves all of that history stuff and jungle-searching, being an archaeologist an' all. But folks round here claim they have seen the ghost, and it floats along the waters like it's searching for something,' said Michael.

'Do you think it is looking for the sword?' replied Joseph curiously.

'Maybe . . . who knows. Or maybe it likes to eat young – little – BOYS, RRAAAHH!' said Michael, grabbing Joseph with both arms and pretending to bite on his neck.

'Arghhh, Dad, get off me, get off me!' Joseph said, smiling, and pushing his father off him, he readjusted his bobble hat.

Michael giggled and straightened back up and draped his arms over his knees. 'I'm only playing with you, son, but maybe's it's worth asking Grandfather next time you see him. He reckons he saw it,' he said.

Joseph pondered for a moment at what his father said. 'Do you think Granddad did see it, Dad – I mean, the ghost?' he replied, sounding slightly more enthusiastic.

'I very much doubt it, Joey, but who knows, that's what he reckons. I've never seen it in all the years I've fished up here. Your grandfather can be a bit cuckoo at times. He once told people that he'd seen a different world with a lime-green moon and evil birds were chasing him and stuff. I love him to bits, but I think he lets his imagination get the better of him at times. It's no wonder your grandmother calls him the mad hatter, having to put up with all his crazy behaviour,' said Michael, smiling, and he turned to gaze at the lake.

Joseph stared at his father nonplussed before he too turned to stare at the lake and suddenly became lost in its hypnotic beauty.

BANG, BANG, BANG, BANG, the door went again. 'Joey, JOEY!' shouted Cathleen in a groggy voice from the sofa.

The sound of Cathleen's voice broke Joseph from his reverie and he shook his head and repeatedly blinked. 'Uh, what?' he said.

'Get the door, Joey,' yelled Cathleen.

'Sorry, Mum, I'll get it now,' replied Joseph. Swiftly he moved across the living room to fetch his school bag and coat from the bottom of the staircase. He dashed through into the porch and quietly closed the door behind him. Anger boiled inside as he pulled open the front door, but he didn't know that Jamerson still had hold of the knocker in his hand and he fell inwards onto him. 'What's wrong with you, Jamerson? You couldn't knock any bloody louder, could you?' he fumed and shoved him backwards.

'Oh, sorry, Joey, didn't think you heard me,' replied Jamerson, red-faced, whilst he let go of the knocker. He stepped back outside and quickly moved aside and stood in front of the garage door. 'You okay, mate?' he said, puffing up his curly hair.

'Yeah, I'm okay,' replied Joseph begrudgingly, feeling as though he didn't have a choice but to talk to him as he closed the front door behind him.

'Good, good. So what did you do last night? I was smashing some muppets online,' said Jamerson, thumping his clenched fist into the palm of his hand. 'Should have seen me rain down on these fools, *BOOM, BOOM, BOOM*. Mate, I am the King of Thunderblast!' and he bounced around like a lunatic on Joseph's driveway.

Joseph couldn't contain the smirk that formed at the corners of his mouth as he watched him behave foolishly and shook his head. He shivered from the cold before he slipped his rucksack over his shoulders and began to walk in front of the garage door, when suddenly it clanged and shook for a split second. He leapt back with sheer fright and backed away nervously, bumping into Jamerson.

'What the hell was that?' blubbered Jamerson.

Joseph ignored him and stood frozen like a statue. Dread rose inside of him as he stared wide-eyed at the door. His heart raced and his mouth ran dry with grave concern at who or what was in there. He needed to know and slowly edged forward.

'Joey,' said Jamerson in a shaky voice. 'What are you doing?'

Joseph snapped his head around, annoyed, and held one finger to his lips and scrunched his face up at him. 'SSSSHHHHH,' he replied. He stood next to the garage door and cautiously held his ear close to it, but heard nothing more than the sound of his own heavy breathing. His trembling hand reached out for the handle that was partially covered in ice and began to turn it clockwise. Out of the corner of his eye, he saw Jamerson cowardly step back.

Clunk went the handle as the lock released. Joseph held his breath, and gave the garage door an almighty push, sending it sliding up and over into the garage. The moment the door opened, a big black crow walloped him straight in the head and flew away squawking. Shocked, Joseph gasped and tumbled backwards, slipping on the thin layer of snow that covered the driveway, and he landed directly onto his rucksack with a thud.

Jamerson, wide-eyed, gasped, but then rudely began to laugh out loud at Joseph as he rolled around on the floor in the scattering of snow.

'Shut up, you idiot, and give me a hand up, would you!' yelled Joseph at the top of his voice.

Jamerson extended his arm and gripped Joseph's hand and hoisted him up back onto his feet, but continued to laugh hysterically at him.

Joseph glared at him with anger. 'Shut up, would you, it's not that funny,' he said, and gave him a shove.

'Mate, you should have seen yourself, you looked like Tonto with that bird flapping around your head, *SQUAWK, SQUAWK!*' said Jamerson, creating a funny squawking sound with his voice and he flapped his arms, pretending to imitate a bird.

Joseph scowled. 'I don't know what you're laughing at, you were just as scared,' he fired back.

Jamerson instantly refrained from laughing and clowning around. 'No I wasn't,' he replied with a blank look on his face.

'Oh yeah, so why was you stepping back then, huh?' said Joseph, smirking at him.

'I just thought you needed some room, you know, didn't want to CROWD you and all that,' said Jamerson, mocking him, and he held his hands up.

Joseph screwed his face at him. 'Whatever, Jamerson, you were just as scared and you know it,' he said, and walked over to the garage door and slammed it shut. He huffed and quickly pulled out his bobble hat from his coat pocket and shuffled it on. Peeved off, he tightly gripped the straps on his shoulders, stooped his head and walked past Jamerson, leaving him playing with his hair on the driveway. Thoughts of the photograph and the peculiar riddle began to occupy his mind as he walked down the slippery pavement, ignoring Jamerson's whining behind him.

'Hey, wait up!' yelled Jamerson, scurrying to catch up while slipping and sliding along. He draped his arm over Joseph's shoulders and said, 'You know, I wasn't scared, Joey, I really wasn't, just thought I'd let you know that, being my best mate an' all,' and he grinned as they walked off down the street together.

Chapter 6

EVIL EYES

The evening had drawn in and the dim light from above shone down onto Joseph, who sat in the doldrums in his cold, gloomy kitchen. He rested his miserable face in the palm of his hand and leant his thin arm heavily upon the table. He stared with despair at the spoon that he kept lifting out of the bowl of stone-cold Scotch Broth soup, repeatedly pouring it back in, time and time again. He yearned for wholesome food and thought about all the delicious meals he used to eat at his grandmother's house, and how he missed her, and he wondered why he hadn't seen her in such a long time. But the pleasing thoughts did little to relieve his empty stomach or the unhappiness he felt, and he began to dwell on the years that had passed and how hard it had been to deal with his mother.

Carelessly he dropped the spoon into the bowl, causing some of the soup to splatter onto the table. With a disgruntled look he shoved it to one side and sighed heavily. He stared at the blob of soup on the table and felt his nose tingle as his emotions started to get the better of him. He closed his eyes and muttered to himself, 'Wish Dad was here.' All of a sudden a light bulb went off in his head. 'Dad, the photo, THE TIN!' he said out loud as his eyes flashed open.

With great enthusiasm he leapt from his chair and rushed over to the cupboard, quickly crouched down onto his hands and knees and carefully prised back the loose kickboard with his fingers. He shifted it out of the way and lowered his head down. A smile beamed across his face at the sight of it and he promptly reached under in amongst the dirt and cobwebs and slid it out. He stood up with a huge grin, wiped his snivelling nose with the back of his hand and leisurely strolled back to his chair, placing the tin down quietly onto the table.

Gently with both thumbs he pushed the lid open and placed it down to the side. He stared at the envelope on top of all the other bits and bobs, and eagerly pulled it out and shook it upside down until the photograph fell out. He held it up proudly by the tips of his fingers and gazed deeply into the picture. The sight of his beloved father looking happy thrilled him. His heart began to melt and he felt all warm inside. His narrowed eyes curiously stared at what was in his grandfather's hand, and he flipped the photograph over to read the peculiar riddle again. 'I don't get it – what key have you left me? There isn't any key here and I'm always bloody hungry!' he exclaimed to himself in a low tone and screwed up his face with annoyance. Overcome with confusion he rubbed the back of his head and then flipped the photograph over once more. 'What are you holding, Granddad? What are you trying to tell me?'

Question after question began to burden him and he grew more and more agitated by the second at the lack of answers. He felt like a shaken bottle of fizzy pop ready to explode and banged the table with frustration with his hand. Immediately he leapt to his feet and began to bite his fingernails aggressively as he paced back and forth in the kitchen. *I'll ask Mum*, he stopped and thought, but quickly dismissed the idea, knowing it would be pointless to get any sort of straight answer without her getting upset or crying.

For a few more minutes he paced, racking his empty brain further and then said, 'Balls to it, let's go and see if Jamerson can figure it out,' and slipped the photograph back into the envelope, placed the lid back onto the tin and quickly slid it back underneath the cupboard. He picked the envelope up from the table, proceeded towards the living room and quietly crept across to the coat hooks. He kept one eye on his mother fast asleep on the sofa whilst he whipped on his coat and bobble hat, and gently eased open the internal door and closed it quietly behind him.

The harsh, cold wind howling in the dark of the night greeted him soon as he stepped outside and was swirling up the settled snow in all the front gardens of the street. He felt his whole body tremble as he pulled the door to and quickly zipped his coat all the way up to his mouth. He tucked his hands inside his pockets and quick-marched off across the driveway. Suddenly a bellowing squawk came from the trees to the left and caused him to jump out of his skin with fright.

An unsettled feeling came over him and he squinted at the trees, but the winter's darkness mingled with them made it difficult to see. The loud squawking continued. Joseph edged closer and to his surprise saw something glowing red. He tilted his head up and stared hard, when out of the blue a crow revealed itself upon the branch and stared right back at him with burning red eyes, then another and then another. Trepidation grew and he nervously began to back away. They all simultaneously began to squawk aggressively at him and in a flash he turned and ran as fast as he could down the middle of the road and didn't look back once. He reached Jamerson's house and ran straight up onto his driveway and banged the hell out of his front door. He glanced back down the road with worry.

Bella, Jamerson's sister, opened the door with the look of disgust on her face. She glared at Joseph. 'Well, what do we have here? Oh *look*, it's the little *freak*. What do you want, little *freak*?' she said in a nasty tone of voice, while she played with her beautiful blonde hair.

Joseph swallowed hard and bowed his head slightly to avoid eye contact with her, knowing how confrontational she could be towards him. 'Hi, Bella,' he muttered. 'Umm, is Jamerson there?'

'No, he's *not*, so why don't you just run along like a little good *freak* that you are?' said Bella rudely, and scowled hard at him and went to close the door.

Jamerson, who was stood behind her in the hallway, shoved Bella out the way and opened the door. 'Back off, Bella, leave my mate alone,' he barked.

'Oh look, it's the little geek coming to his rescue. How sweet,' said Bella, laughing in a squeaky voice, and gave a wry smile. She crossed her arms and bobbed her head from side to side and continued her tirade: 'The little GEEK and the little FREAK, what a lovely little pair of love birds you make!' pointing her finger at each one of them.

'If you don't back off I'm telling Mum,' Jamerson snarled whilst looking up to her.

'Go ahead, she knows I'm right. You two are pathetic, I don't know why I'm wasting my valuable time on you,' Bella said, and flicked her straight hair over her shoulder and began to walk off towards the living room.

'Well good, go away and do ya make-up, troll,' Jamerson said, retaliating.

Out of nowhere, Bella whipped her head around the doorway and said, 'Bite me' and snapped her teeth together like a crocodile and made Jamerson jump, and then slowly disappeared again.

Jamerson ushered Joseph in and closed the front door. 'Sorry about that, Joey, you know what sis gets like, she only does it to get at me. She thinks 'cause she's older she owns the place, she does my frigging head in. C'mon, let's go upstairs before she comes back again,' he said and nodded his head sideways.

Joseph followed closely behind Jamerson, watching him stomp up the stairs on purpose to annoy Bella. When he reached the top of the landing, the warmth of the house hit him like he was in a sauna and he felt a little flushed. He followed Jamerson into his bedroom and gently pushed the door closed behind him. He slipped off his coat and placed it down onto Jamerson's bed and sat down on the edge of it. Jamerson threw himself into his worn black and red gaming chair and began to spin around in it like a fool. He pushed it across on its wheels to his gaming station and casually picked up a bunch of games and started to read the titles out loud, carelessly throwing each one that he didn't want to play over his shoulder. 'What shall we play, Joey? Devil's War, Apocalypse of the Bone Cruncher, Dragon's Chamber, Uprising of—'

'If it's okay I'll just sit here and watch you play. I'm not really in the mood, mate,' said Joseph, cutting him off.

'Suit yourself,' Jamerson replied, with a shrug of his shoulders.

Deep in thought about the evil eyes he had just seen in the trees, Joseph leant forward to rest his elbows onto his knees and anxiously rubbed his hands together. He began to chew his bottom lip, watching Jamerson load up the game and said to him, 'Hey, Jamerson, can I ask you something?'

'Yeah, sure, anything mate,' replied Jamerson chirpily.

'Do you ever feel like you're being watched?' asked Joseph with concern.

'Yeah, all the time,' replied Jamerson nonchalantly.

Joseph quickly straightened up from his hunched position and said, 'YOU DO?' sounding utterly surprised.

'Yeah, Mum's always watching me,' said Jamerson and

raised his eyebrows. 'I can't even go to the fridge at night time without her knowing and banging on the bedroom floor shouting for me to get back to bed,' and he rolled his eyes.

'No, stupid, I never meant that, I meant . . . huh, never mind,' said Joseph, and shook his head and pressed his lips together, thinking he should never have bothered to ask in the first place.

Jamerson shrugged his shoulders and spun back around to grab his controller.

Annoyed, Joseph unintentionally glanced across the bedroom and spied Jamerson's pet iguana in the tank, leapt to his feet and marched quickly across. 'Hey, Brutus has gotten bigger, mate, what the hell have you been feeding it?' he said, and gently tapped on the glass as it sat perched up on a branch.

'Oh, you know, the usual, vegetables, cabbage, cucumber, all that kind of stuff – burgers,' calmly replied Jamerson, and turned his eyes to him.

'WHAT! BURGERS?' Joseph replied, shooting him a darting look, stunned.

Jamerson began to laugh hysterically and rocked back and forth in his chair and almost fell out of it. 'I'm only playing with you,' he said, rolling with laughter. 'You should have seen the look on your face when I said burgers!'

Joseph rolled his eyes and shook his head at him. 'Burgers,' he said, turning back to face the tank and gave a little sigh. 'Wish I still had my iguana, though, which Dad gave to me.'

'What did happen to yours, Joey?' asked Jamerson.

'It got sick, and without Dad being around I didn't know

what was wrong with it, so I ended up giving it away to Charlie's Pet shop,' Joseph said with a sad look on his face.

'Well, at least you took it to the right place. Charlie's is the best. That guy seems to know everything about animals. I think mine probably needs to go on a diet, to be honest with you, Joey, but HEY, big and round, the girls love the hound, know what I mean, Joey?' said Jamerson, as he stood up from his chair and circled his hips with both hands held behind his head.

Joseph looked round and began to giggle at him being foolish. It wasn't very often that he found himself laughing but he recognized that Jamerson did try his best to crack jokes all the time to lighten his mood. 'You know I miss him,' he said, and stooped his head, thinking of his father.

'Yeah, but you can always get another one, Joey,' replied Jamerson.

'I can never replace my dad. What are you talking about, you idiot, it's not like—' said Joseph angrily, yelling at him.

'I never meant your dad, Joey; I was talking about your iguana, the IGUANA! You can always get another iguana, that's what I meant,' Jamerson quickly interrupted with a shocked look upon his face.

Joseph felt his face turn red with embarrassment. 'Oh. Sorry, mate, I thought you meant my dad,' he said and turned his head sheepishly to the side.

'It's okay, Joey, I understand, but you need to chill out more. I know you miss your dad. My dad took it pretty hard too, you know, them being best friends an' all. That's why he finished as a fireman, said he couldn't cope, said he wished he could have done something – you know, to save him. You know you always got me, though – right, best friends?' said Jamerson and smiled.

Joseph nodded with a sorrowful look upon his face. 'Yeah, best friends,' he said unconvincingly, but never meant for it to sound the way it did. He saw Jamerson get up out of the chair and walk towards him for some peculiar reason, which made him feel slightly unnerved. Then suddenly he felt Jamerson wrap his chunky arms around and hug him. He felt awkward that he couldn't find it within him to return the kind gesture and instead placed his hands on Jamerson's hips to create a little space between them. 'Okay. Thanks for that, mate,' he said, feeling restless, and patted him on his hip to let go of him.

'No problems, mate, anytime you feel you need a hug, just—' said Jamerson.

'Listen, I got something I wanna show you,' interrupted Joseph, and he picked up his coat from off the bed and pulled out the envelope. Gently he slid out the photograph and flipped it over to the other side to the riddle. 'You're pretty good at solving puzzles and riddles, seeing as you're always on your gamer all the time. What do you think this means?'

Jamerson looked surprised, taking the photograph from Joseph, and began to mutter the message to himself. 'Okay, so where's the key and what's it for, Joey?' he replied.

'That's what I want to know,' replied Joseph 'There wasn't any key left for me,' he said, raising his eyebrows with a baffled look.

Jamerson flipped it over and stared at the photograph. 'Well, that's clearly your dad, but who's the other guy, and who's the mad hatter? Sounds like an evil villain from *Batman* or something?' he said, chuckling.

'My dad told me years ago it's what my gran used to call my granddad because he was crazy apparently,' replied Joseph and rolled his eyes.

'Oh. And that's him in the photo, is it?' asked Jamerson.

'Uh-huh, and that in his hand is what he's referring to – my so-called destiny, I think – but I don't know what it is either,' said Joseph, pointing to it.

Once again, Jamerson flipped over the photograph and stared at the riddle. 'Huh, well he's definitely crazy, that's for sure; look, he's even spelt *devine* wrong. *Are you hungry, Joseph, look for a fork at Talgar,*' he said out loud. Suddenly Jamerson's stomach rumbled loudly.

'What was that?' asked Joseph, staring at Jamerson, whose face had turned crimson.

'Oops, looks like I'm a little hungry,' replied Jamerson with embarrassment and rubbed his grumbling stomach. 'Say, Joey, what's Talgar?'

'That's where my granddad use to live with Gran, and where she still does, I think,' replied Joseph.

Jamerson walked back and forth in his bedroom, playing with his hair while staring at the riddle, then out of the blue he clicked his fingers together and his eyes lit up. 'I got it! Hey, Joey, you know how I love food so much,' he said with a big grin.

'You got that right,' said Joseph, and rolled his eyes and began to think about food himself after hearing Jamerson's stomach rumbling. 'So what's your point?'

'Well, sometimes I use a fork and sometimes I don't, you know me, Joey, I like to get my hands in there and—' said Jamerson, going off on a tangent.

'Get to the point, would you, knucklehead!' interrupted Joseph, growing impatient.

'Oh yeah, sorry, well, there must be a fork somewhere, like on a sign or something distinctive,' said Jamerson excitedly, like he had cracked Morse code.

Joseph paused for a moment to think and then said, 'Yeah, you could be right, but how does that fit in with the rest of the riddle?' he said, turning to him again.

'Well, it says it's at Talgar, so if you find the fork you might find the key?' said Jamerson and shrugged.

Joseph shifted his eyes to stare blankly at the floor and became deep in thought. *That's a good point, but how the hell am I supposed to get there? It's miles away, and Mum can't drive and I certainly wouldn't trust her even if she could.*

'You alright, mate?' asked Jamerson.

'Uh, yeah fine, listen, I'm gonna shoot off home now,' said Joseph, and took the photograph from Jamerson and placed back into the envelope.

'But you've only just got here,' Jamerson groaned and flapped his arms in a huff.

'I know, mate, but Mum doesn't know I'm over here and I wanna make sure she's okay,' he said, eager to leave.

'Aww, okay,' replied Jamerson begrudgingly. 'But you'll call for me in the morning for school, won't you?'

'Sure. Say, Jamerson, is there any chance I can . . . you know, lend some money off you, I'll pay you straight back soon as—' said Joseph.

'Look, Joey, I'm here anytime you need me, okay,' interrupted Jamerson, and strolled over to the other side of his bed and picked up a square tin and yanked it open. 'Here you go, mate, this is all that I've got,' he said, handing him the money.

'Are you sure? That's a lot of cash which I—' said Joseph with a surprised look upon his face.

'Joey, you'll pay me back one day, I know you will,' replied Jamerson, and patted his friend's shoulder. He turned around and grabbed Joseph's coat off the bed and threw it at him. He pointed to the door and said, 'Here you go, freak, now be gone with you, get out of my house before I set my nasty, growling, boy-eating troll sister on you,' and held his hands up like claws and pulled the meanest of faces at him.

Joseph raised his eyebrows and smiled. 'Jamerson, you need help.'

'I heard that!' an angry voice said on the other side of the bedroom door. Suddenly the door flew opened and Bella stood in the doorway with her arms crossed and face screwed up while she leant her full weight on her back leg with attitude.

Joseph nervously turned around to see whose the voice was, realized, and snapped his head back to face Jamerson. 'I'm off, mate,' he said with wide eyes.

Jamerson's face turned red. 'Arrgh, sis, I wasn't talking

about you, honest, I was just talking—' he said.

'Shut your face, fat boy, or I'll shut it for you,' yelled Bella back at him.

Joseph stooped his head as he headed for the door and tried to slip past her, but she blocked the doorway and he felt her barge him unkindly with her shoulder.

'Huh, bye, freak,' said Bella, screwing her face up at him.

Jamerson raised his hand to the side of his mouth and yelled, 'Bye, Joey!' and then smiled awkwardly at his sister.

Joseph scrambled down the staircase like a maniac as fast as his legs would carry him and leapt the last few steps at the bottom. He almost knocked over Jamerson's mother in the process, and darted for the door.

'*Oh*,' replied Nancy, startled as she spun around holding her hands up. 'Goodbye, Joseph.'

Joseph gave a quick glance over his shoulder and said, 'Goodbye, Mrs Hoggle,' and pulled open the door, bolted through and slammed it shut behind him. He stood outside, relieved to have escaped Bella. But then suddenly he realized he had to face what was lurking in the trees at the dead end of the road near his house. Slowly he walked off the driveway and stood in the middle of the road for a moment and stared down his street with apprehension. He swallowed nervously and proceeded cautiously towards his house, which was the last one on the left.

Chapter 7

SEIZE THE DAY

Morning light had not yet risen and the bright stars still scattered in the sky shone down on the quiet suburbs. A mist hovered eerily through the dark streets and up to the house of number 25 Lon Green, where Joseph lived, and seeped through the broken letter box of the front door. Up the stairs the mist climbed and into his bedroom where he lay in bed, tossing and turning. The mist rose up and formed a hand of death and reached out for him.

Suddenly Joseph lunged up in bed, panic-stricken and gasping with his hand placed upon his chest, and felt his heart going ten to the dozen. His eyes darted back and forth in his shadowy room but he saw nothing. Shaken, he quickly leant over and flicked his side lamp on and squinted at the bright light. He sat for a moment, on edge. 'Must have been a dream,' he muttered to himself, still staring around.

He rubbed his tired eyes and glanced at his clock, which read 5 a.m. and he huffed with displeasure. Since the discovery of the photograph and the uncanny riddle, his thoughts had become restless. The same questions hounded him and repeated over and over again, and no immediate answers sprung to mind to fill the frustrating void inside of him. He stared blankly at the bottom of his bed and began to ponder. *Maybe Jamerson's right, if I go to Talgar and find a fork of some kind maybe it will lead me to the key, but I still don't understand what my destiny is . . .*

Casually, he turned his head to the side to gaze at a small picture on the bedside table of his father. 'What would you do, Dad?' he whispered softly to it. He frowned in frustration and felt like the devil and the angel were fighting on his shoulders. 'What to do, what to do?' he muttered to himself. After a few seconds he kicked back the duvet and said, 'Ah, bugger it, what have I got to lose? I could be back home by four p.m. and Mum wouldn't even know I'd been gone. Let's find that key and find out what my so-called destiny is,' and he leapt out of bed to his feet.

Without a moment to spare, he grabbed his rucksack from off the chair in the corner of the room, dumped it down onto his bed, and quickly began to pack everything he might need for his journey. He yanked open the doors on his wardrobe and riffled through the mound of messy clothes, until he found a white long-sleeved top and a black pair of jeans to wear. He quickly got changed. Then he turned to his chest of drawers and tugged at the heavy bottom drawer filled with junk. He rummaged through in search for his black bobble hat and accidentally stumbled across his slingshot. 'Ah, my black widow, I forgot I had that!' he said to his surprise, and reached in to fetch it, finding his bobble hat underneath. He slipped the hat on and leisurely strolled back to his bed while pulling back on the rubber band of the slingshot to check its elasticity, then threw it inside the rucksack along with a bag of ball bearings.

The floorboards creaked as he knelt down and slid his hand under the bed and fingered for the envelope. He rose to his feet, carefully placed it inside his rucksack and sat down anxiously on the edge of his bed. Uncertainty began to shroud him and he turned to stare at the bright numbers on the clock displaying the time 5:30 a.m. He rubbed his legs with his clammy hands and wondered whether he was making the right decision. *C'mon, Joey, get it together!* he thought to himself.

His eyes shifted a little to the left and he took a final look at the photo on the bedside table, before he sucked in a deep breath and blew it out. He then reached down for his beaten-up trainers and quickly placed them on. As he rose to his feet, he slung his rucksack over his shoulder, grabbed the money from the bedside table and stuffed it into his jeans pocket. He looked around his room as if it was going to be the last time he would see it, before he leant over and switched the lamp off.

He waited impatiently for his eyes to readjust to the darkness before he headed for the door. His heart beat a little quicker than usual as he crept across the landing and approached the staircase. Slowly and quietly he descended. The sound of the creaky steps grated on him and caused him to grit his teeth.

Finally he reached the bottom and sighed with relief. As he was lifting his shabby dark-grey duffle coat from the hook, suddenly he heard his mother groan. Joseph felt his heart skip a beat and snapped his head around to see her lying on the sofa. He hadn't noticed her as he came down the stairs and normally when the TV was off it was an indication that she had gone to bed. He watched nervously as she turned over on the sofa to face his direction and went back to sleep. On edge, he held his breath too frightened to let it out for risk of the noise it might create and swallowed down hard. Standing in the shadows, he apprehensively stepped forward and took a final look at her lying motionless and breathing heavy. 'I'll be back soon, Mum,' he whispered softly, and quietly scarpered off towards the kitchen.

The large window over the sink allowed just enough light to pass through for him to see, as he emerged and tiptoed across the kitchen floor. Quietly he placed his rucksack down onto the kitchen table and then quickly slipped on his coat. Staring at the internal garage door, tremendous nerves filled him inside, which supressed the hunger pangs he had felt upstairs in his room. He gripped his rucksack from the table and anxiously drew in a deep breath through his nostrils and let it out shakily, and leant his weight down onto the handle.

A gust of cold air whipped past him into the house. His hand wandered for the light switch and fired up the strip light. With unease, he stepped inside and prayed nothing else was likely to be lurking, and quietly closed the door. Stepping sideways behind the car he saw the monkey wrench where he had dropped it and quickly scooped it up. He turned to place it down onto the workbench and as he did so he saw a torch. Curiously he began to fiddle around with it and repeatedly press the ON button but it didn't seem to work, so he gave it a quick shake and a tap in his palm. He looked into the lens to check for bulb damage and foolishly pressed the button again and blinded himself. Dazzled by white flashing stars he stumbled about and blinked repeatedly to try and see. 'Huh, stupid torch,' he said to himself, feeling like an idiot. He dumped his rucksack down and threw the torch inside.

Joseph swung around to face the car and with one fell swoop he whipped back the white cover and threw it to the ground. A huge grin spread across his face to see his father's old Jaguar sat proudly in all its glory. He took a moment to admire and remember what it meant to his father, and held a long stare. The shiny chrome spoke wheels and chrome bumpers dazzled his eyes as the light bounced off them. Slowly he ran his fingers along the long, sleek, sloping backside of the car, which was finished in stunning racing green paintwork, all the way to the chrome handle of the driver's door. He stopped and pressed the button with his thumb.

Instantly he was struck by the overwhelming distinctive smell of the green leather seats which collided with the smell of the beautiful crafted walnut dash. The smell was a wonderful reminder and he felt like it was only yesterday rather than years ago that he last sat in the car. Carefully he slid down into the cushioned seat that resembled something more like a living-room sofa than a car seat. He beamed with joy as his hands caressed the overly large black steering wheel, and he began to have flashbacks of fond memories of sitting in the driver's seat pretending to drive the car as a young boy, and how excited he would get when he played with all the buttons on the dash.

Once again he started to fiddle about with all the buttons. To his delight and to his great surprise he saw a black leather key-ring with the word Michael written upon it, with the key placed into the ignition. Euphoria overcame him and his hands began to shake. He turned the key over but the car simply grumbled away. A little annoyed, he clenched his lips and teeth together and tried once again. But again the car simply groaned. His patience was beginning to wear thin and he began to turn the key over and over and over again. The sound of the engine whining irked him and he was starting to lose his temper with the car. 'C'mon, you *stupid* car, *work*, why won't you *work!*' he fumed and banged the steering wheel with his hand.

The car continued to groan, when all of a sudden it finally roared into life. Black fumes bellowed out from the exhaust pipes and quickly began to fill the garage with smoke as it choked and spluttered. Joseph sat, thrilled by it firing up, but grew concerned by the noise of it rumbling away like a farmer's tractor and leapt out immediately. Instantly he began to choke on all the smoke, covered his mouth quickly and stumbled towards the garage door. Frantically he twisted the handle, which wouldn't budge at first, then the lock clunked, and he thrust it up over his head. The fresh morning air swept into the garage to his relief and he stumbled out and fell helplessly to his hands and knees, coughing hard repeatedly and gasping for air. His watery eyes burnt tremendously, like after chopping raw onions. He scrunched them shut and picked up the cold snow with his hands and pressed it against his lids to cool off. Out of breath, he heaved himself back up onto his feet and stumbled about for a second, feeling lightheaded, before he ran back inside to fetch his rucksack. He opened the car door and threw his rucksack across onto the passenger seat, leapt back into the driver's seat and slammed the door shut.

'Okay, what do I do, Joey? What do I do? Think, think, think, what did Dad show me?' he said, panicking and began to press the pedals. The engine roared as soon as he pressed down hard on the accelerator pedal.

'Okay, so the other one must be for the brake pedal,' he said to himself. He pressed the accelerator pedal again, expecting the car to move forwards, but to his disappointment it just revved and didn't budge an inch. Baffled by it, he gazed around, looked down and saw the gearstick with the word Drive. He thrust it forward into position and quickly dropped the handbrake. Overly keen, he slammed the accelerator pedal down hard to the floor and to his utter astonishment the car launched out of the garage like a rocket. Joseph gasped and clung to the steering wheel for dear life as the car bounced off the driveway and onto the road, heading for the neighbouring wall. He shut his eyes and hit the brake pedal with both feet as hard as he could, which caused the car to skid across the road and grind to a halt.

Shocked, he huffed and puffed uncontrollably and said to

himself, 'Wow, that was a close one, Joey,' and swallowed hard. Sheepishly he turned around to see if anyone was watching from their houses and gave a sigh to see the street silent and still. His shaky hand pulled the stick out of Drive and he moved to get out. On edge, he stood eyeing his front window and felt relieved that the light hadn't been switched on. He crept quietly back to the garage and sneaked inside. Quickly he flicked the light off and ran to the front and gently pulled down the garage door. Joseph gazed across to the car as it chugged away in the middle of the road. A quick glance to his front door and then to his right, and he sprinted as fast as he could back to the car. He leapt inside and whipped the seat belt across him, cranked the gearstick into Drive and carefully pressed down on the accelerator pedal but inconsistently. The car kangarooed forward bit by bit and slowly he manoeuvred it around the mini roundabout and drove up the road.

As the car continued to bunny-hop down the street without the headlights on, a grin spread across his face. 'Nothing to it, this driving lark!' Joseph said proudly to himself, and eased back into the cold soft leather seat. He stared at Jamerson's house smugly and said, 'Ha! Who's ya Tonto now, hey, Jamerson?' But momentarily his concentration lapsed and he struck one of the parked cars, smashing his chrome wing mirror clean off. Shocked, he swung his head around and stared out through the rear window to see the wing mirror tumbling down the road behind him, along with the other parked car wing mirror dangling down the side of the door by its wires. He turned to face forward again with a look of shame. 'Sorry, Dad,' he said, clenching his teeth, and slowly trundled off down the road.

Chapter 8

EGGETTS AND MUFFLES

The wonderful morning sun began to rise and creep slowly beyond the Black Mountains shrouding the sleepy village of Talgar, deep within the valley. Beams of streaking orange light gradually pierced through the heavy dark clouds that spread across the countryside. One by one, the street lamps in the village gradually switched off, and villagers steadily drew back their curtains to their frosted windows ready for the day ahead. The cold snap from the wintry conditions whipped through the streets and didn't faze the cheery people as they went about their business. The sense of happiness and strong community spirit cloaked the people as each person that walked by greeted one another with the utmost respect, and some who were more acquainted stopped to chat.

Steadily plodding along the winding country road, Joseph held up a host of motorists behind him with his slow pace. One by one they overtook, honking their horns aggressively, then were taken back with surprise to see such a young driver as they passed by. Joseph ignored them all and stared trans-fixed at the road ahead. He felt too afraid to look elsewhere out of fear of damaging his father's pride and joy any more than he had done already. Doubt began to occupy his mind as to whether he was on the right road. Though he had travelled along it countless times with his family when he was younger, it felt different to him this time around.

In the distance up ahead, a road sign drew nearer and nearer, until it eventually became clear and close enough to read and said: *Welcome to the Sleepy Village of Talgar*. Elated to see the sign, Joseph continued to stare at it as he went past and the car began to veer onto the other side of the road towards the oncoming traffic. A car heading towards him began to flash its lights and blast its horn abruptly to alert him. Joseph swung back around and gasped and his eyes lit up. At the last second, he swerved the car back onto his side of the road and missed the other one by the skin of his teeth. The sudden jolt of the steering wheel began to snake the car from side to side, and he held his breath and fought to gain control until eventually he straightened up again. Tensed up and white as a ghost, he held the steering wheel in a tight grip and slowly exhaled and eased himself back into the seat. No sooner than he had passed the road sign, a black crow landed on it with its evil, red glowing eyes. It ratcheted its head around and watched him travelling up the road and began to squawk loudly.

The picturesque countryside gradually became less visible leading into the village. The road soon began to bottle-neck and rows and rows of quaint stone terraced cottages on either side looked familiar to Joseph as he headed towards the town. He smiled to see a row of shops that he recognized as a young boy. He read the signs on each one of them out loud, with a thrill in his voice as he past by.

'Finley's Butchers, Grove's Veg Market, Nancy Gretel Flower Boutique, Portobello's Hairdressers, Leaning Tower Bookstore, oh my God, Gran's favourite shop is still there – Patty's Bakery!' he said. His stomach rumbled like a bubbling volcano at the sight of the bakery shop, and his mouth started to salivate at the thought of how delicious their custard slices were, and how he always opted for white and detested the pink, thinking it was too girly for him.

Joseph continued for a short while, keeping an eye out for anything that remotely resembled a sign with a fork when the road curved slightly to the right. He passed a corner shop on the right called Gobble Sweeties, which he didn't recognize, and suddenly he hit the brakes. The car skidded slightly along the road until it finally stopped. Out of the damp window he gazed up a narrow street that ran alongside the sweet shop to the top, where there stood a colourful building that caught his attention. Intrigued, he turned the car up the road and headed up towards it. He began to pass some colourful terraced cottages, when his eyes began to widen at the sight of a flamboyantly decorated building which stood proudly in the middle of the split road, called Eggetts and Muffles Café. Carefully he pulled the car over, switched off the engine and slumped back into the seat. 'Jamerson was wrong. It wasn't a sign that the riddle was referring too, it was a fork in the road!'

he said, astonished, to himself.

His eyes were mesmerized by the eye-catching vertical yellow and white striped exterior across the top half of the building, and the blue frame below with the name scrolled across it. His mouth began to water, almost close to drooling down his coat, at the sight of food being served through the window, and he clutched his empty stomach and said out loud, 'Well, Granddad, I am definitely not hungry, I'm starving!' and hopped out of the car and briskly walked over to the door.

A short, slightly overweight man with thin, jet-black hair combed backwards and a thick black moustache, dressed in blue trousers, a yellow shirt and with a horizontal blue and white striped dicky bow, placed a full British Breakfast onto the table, to his customer's delight.

'Thank you, Gilbert,' said the old man, his eyes popping out of his head, and he licked his lips like a hungry wolf, with the knife and fork already in his hands.

'You're most welcome, sir,' replied Gilbert the waiter, and briefly closed his eyes, nodding his head to the side with appreciation. 'Is there anything else I can get you?' he asked in a funny accent as though he was imitating a French person.

'I'll let you know soon as I've eaten your *appetizing* food,' said the old man, gawping at the scrumptious food.

Just as Gilbert turned to walk away, the gold bell above the café door chimed. The door slowly opened and in walked Joseph nervously and closed it sheepishly behind him.

'Good morning, young man, how do you do?' said Gilbert chirpily.

'Hi,' replied Joseph in a low tone with his head stooped.

'Please, take a seat and I will be with you shortly,' said Gilbert, offering his hand out to any one of the chairs in the café.

With his eyed fixed to the floor, Joseph quickly and quietly scurried over to a table positioned neatly in the front window, sat down on the wooden chair. He picked up the menu and hid behind it. With the menu stood on its end, he peered over and looked around warily and then lowered his head back down. He pulled out the loose change from his jeans pocket and started to count it, when the sound of a loud cough startled him and he nearly dropped all of it out of his hand. His eyes shifted up to see the waiter stood beside the table staring down at him with a grin upon his face and a pen and pad held in his hand.

'Good morning again, young man, and welcome to Eggetts and Muffles Café, can I get you something to drink?' said Gilbert.

'Umm, just an orange juice, please,' mumbled Joseph.

'And what would you like to eat?' asked Gilbert with raised eyebrows.

Feeling under pressure, Joseph quickly scanned the menu in front of him and read out the first thing that he saw, 'Umm, could I have a breakfast roll?' he replied timidly.

'Most certainly. Coming right up, and if you need anything else, young man, just give me a shout. My name is Gilbert Devine, spelt with an E, not an I, in Devine,' he said and held one hand to his chest.

Joseph's ears perked up at the sound of the name and his eyes widened. He nodded and watched Gilbert zip off like a fly behind the counter, which had a very large and old, disused wooden till displayed on top of it. He scurried up some steps and out of sight. Joseph sank back down behind the menu, deep in thought about the waiter's name, and tried to marry it up with what he already knew. *Well, I'm hungry, sat in a café in the middle of a forked road, the waiter's surname is Devine, so obviously Jamerson was wrong about Granddad in the way that he spelt it. Surely I must be in the right place to find the key?* He stared blankly at the menu whilst biting his bottom lip. The wondrous smell of food which hovered around the café wafted his way and made his stomach rumble.

Curiously he peered over the menu and marvelled at the delightfully decorated and eccentric-looking café, with its extremely high bookcases dotted all around filled with no end of books. The dark grey swirled wallpaper, tastefully fused with all the multi-coloured striped chairs and white table-cloths, presented a warm and comforting feeling like you were sitting in a cosy house rather than a café. Before he knew it, Gilbert had arrived back at his table with a tall glass of orange juice, and he happily smiled as he sat it down in front of the menu then rushed off again. The moment Joseph set his eyes upon it, he swiped it from the table and gulped it back like there was no tomorrow. The rush of coldness flowing deep inside caused him brain-freeze momentarily, and he plonked the empty glass back down on the table with a thud.

Joseph accidentally let out a small belch, which caused two

little old ladies to turn around and glare at him. He blushed and held his hand to his mouth then ducked back down behind the menu again, feeling embarrassed. A couple on the other side of the café yelled goodbye to Gilbert and left the money for the bill on the table and headed for the door. Joseph watched them leave and make their way down the street until they were out of sight. Unintentionally he glanced across to his father's car and noticed there was something sat on top of it. He wiped the steamy window and leant in closer to get a better look. Suddenly he felt his stomach tighten with knots as a beady red-eyed crow perched on top stared back at him.

'There you go, young man, one breakfast roll – Bon Appétit!' said Gilbert and thudded the plate down onto the table and removed the menu.

'Oh, good God,' said Joseph, as he leapt out of the chair with fright from the noise, unaware that Gilbert was beside of him.

'Apologies, I didn't mean to scare you,' replied Gilbert with sincerity in his voice.

Joseph, on edge, didn't say a word, and instead turned his attention to look back at the car, but the red-eyed crow had vanished. Unnerved, he began to bob his head everywhere through the window looking for it.

Gilbert stood with his one eyebrow raised. 'Is everything okay, young man?' he asked, and then coughed. 'YOUNG MAN!' He raised his voice.

Joseph slowly turned to face him with a troubled look to see Gilbert stood with his hands clasped in front of him. 'Oh yeah, I was just looking to see what the weather is going to be like, as I'm off to see someone,' he replied, thinking of an excuse.

'Oh, and does that someone live around here then?' replied Gilbert.

'Oh yes, not far from here,' Joseph said with his mouth full of food as he quickly began to tuck into the roll like a vulture.

'And what is this mysterious person's name, may I ask?' said Gilbert.

Joseph felt somewhat reluctant to say his grandmother's name, knowing she wasn't the real reason why he was in Talgar, and he hesitated to reply as he continued to devour his food. 'Umm, Mary,' he muttered.

Gilbert had a blank look upon his face. 'Fairy, what an unusual name to give someone, but mythical and—' he replied.

'No, not Fairy – Mary,' interrupted Joseph as he chewed.

'Argh, Berry, like the fruits of the earth – a gracious name too,' said Gilbert.

Joseph grew frustrated and swallowed a load of unchewed food and coughed and choked. 'No, MARY!' he said out loud. All the other customers in the café turned their heads around and scowled at him, and he shifted uncomfortably in his chair.

'Oh, my humble apologies, young man, my hearing is not quite what it used to be. Let me think: Mary, Mary, Mary,' said Gilbert stroking his thick moustache. 'Ah yes, Mary Butterfield, and may I say what a splendid, fine young woman she is. I can see why you have chosen her as your—'

'I don't know who you're talking about, sorry,' interrupted Joseph again with a shrug of his shoulders.

'Oh, I must have her confused with Mary Farage,' replied Gilbert, and shifted his eyebrows inwards.

'Nope, I don't know who that is either,' Joseph said, shaking his head from side to side.

Gilbert narrowed his eyes. 'Oh yes, Mary Cullun,' he said.

Amused, a grin started to form at the corner of Joseph's mouth from the guessing game. 'Nope,' he said.

'Mary Serotine?' asked Gilbert.

'Nope,' replied Joseph once again.

'My, my, I'm running out of Marys who would fit the bill for a strapping young man like yourself. There's only one other Mary I know, and that is Mary Van Pearce, but she is not of your age,' said Gilbert and huffed.

'That's her!' replied Joseph with a surprised look upon his face.

'What! Don't you think she is a little old for you? I mean, each to his own and this being the twenty-first century and all, but—' said Gilbert.

'No, silly, she's my grandmother,' giggled Joseph.

'Oh, I see, how foolish of me,' replied Gilbert, and slapped his forehead and began to mutter in a language that resembled nothing like French. 'My sincerest apologies. How could I not see,' and shook his hands together like he was praying for forgiveness or something.

'You know her, do you?' Joseph said.

'Why yes, I most certainly do. Do you mind?' said Gilbert

and pulled out the chair to take a seat at the table. 'She and Cyril used to dine here all the time over the years, especially for afternoon tea.'

'Does my gran still come here?' Joseph asked keenly.

'I'm afraid not. Ever since Cyril passed away, God rest his soul,' said Gilbert and placed a cross upon his body with two fingers. 'I suddenly saw less and less of Mary, until one day she stopped coming here altogether,' and he lowered his head.

A sad look came over Joseph and bowed his head to the side and thought, *I never did know the reason why Granddad passed away. Mum never mentioned it, or maybe she thought she couldn't tell me because she was in a bad way herself after losing Dad.*

Gilbert raised his head with a big smile and said, ''Ere, I will say this about your grandmother – she was such a charismatic woman, always cheerful and witty, and always wore—'

'A PINK FLOWER BROOCH,' they both said simultaneously together and laughed.

'I bet she'll be glad to see you,' said Gilbert and wagged his finger at him.

'Oh really, why is that?' asked Joseph dubiously.

'Well, she never used to stop talking about you when she was in here, or Cyril for that matter, and when they weren't bickering, of course,' said Gilbert, and rolled his eyes and leant back into his chair and folded his arms.

'Why were they bickering?' asked Joseph, very intrigued to know.

'Because your grandfather was crazy, that's why,' replied

Gilbert, laughing his head off, 'and I don't mean that in a bad way either, so please do not be offended when I say that.'

'Yeah, I've heard that before; the mad hatter, Gran used to call him,' said Joseph and raised his eyebrows as though he was bored of hearing it.

'Ah yes, but do you know how she came to call him that?' asked Gilbert, leaning forward on the table and turning his head sideways slightly.

Joseph edged his head back as he did not have the foggiest notion. He stared blankly at Gilbert, shook his head and gave a shrug. 'Uh-huh,' he said.

'Well, it was here, of course!' said Gilbert excitedly and slapped the table and extended his arms out to the place.

'I, I don't know what you mean,' replied Joseph, looking totally confused.

'Your grandparents used to sit at this very table, and one day when they were sat here, they were having an argument about the Black Baron, and your Grandfather Cyril claimed he had found the key to the secret location!' said Gilbert with large eyes.

'But I thought that was just a myth,' replied Joseph with a slightly screwed-up face.

'Well, if you side with your grandmother on this, then yes, as she didn't believe him either and told him he was crazy as the mad hatter in the book that he was holding in his hand, which was the book he often read while he sat here – the one up there,' said Gilbert, pointing behind Joseph.

Slowly Joseph turned his head around to see the bookshelf

behind him, and there amongst the other books, all stacked neat and tidy, was the one called The Mad Hatter that Gilbert pointed to. His eyes lit up and his thoughts began to run wild. He wondered whether the book had anything to do with the riddle and casually turned back round to face Gilbert, pretending as though the book didn't mean anything to him. He calmly asked, 'So why did he want to find this place?' He watched Gilbert turn his head suspiciously to the side to check to see if any of the other customers were listening, then lean in closer to him.

'A few days after the argument between your grandparents, Cyril came in here alone – which was unusual for him – and we began to talk about this and that but mainly we talked about the Black Baron and all the lost treasures. I said to him that with one piece of that treasure I could retire for life and quit this business for good. But your grandfather wasn't concerned with any of it, which I found very strange. When I asked him why, he simply replied that he was only concerned with one thing, one piece of treasure that has never been found,' said Gilbert, and he looked out of the corner of his narrowed eyes at the customers.

'So what is it?' said Joseph curiously.

Gilbert turned his eyes back to stare at Joseph. 'A dagger!' he whispered.

'A dagger?' Joseph snorted and wrinkled his nose.

'SSHH, keep your voice down,' said Gilbert, waving his hands at him. 'That dagger your grandfather mentioned is priceless, and was the very one that got stolen from the British

Museum by the Black Baron and was never recovered! When I was a young boy, my parents immigrated to London, and when we lived there they took me to visit the British Museum. It was there I saw the dagger, but at the time I didn't know it was a replica until your grandfather told me it was.'

'But what did he want with a *dagger?*' Joseph said with a puzzled look upon his face.

Gilbert casually leant back into the chair. 'Well, that's something he didn't tell me, I'm afraid,' he said with raised eyebrows.

Unexpectedly the gold bell chimed against the door and a couple entered and sat down on the other side of the café. Gilbert turned his head to look and said, 'Well, I'd best be getting back to work, as they say, a woman's work is never done but a man works from sun to sun. It was a pleasure to meet you, Joseph. Make sure you say hello to your grandmother for me, won't you?' He rose to his feet and extended his hand to shake.

Stunned, Joseph looked at him surprised and stuttered, 'How do you know my name?' and shook his hand.

'Well, why wouldn't I? You're the prodigal grandson that your grandfather kept telling me about,' said Gilbert and gave him a wink. 'Remember, do say hello to your grandmother for me,' and he gave him a gentle pat on his back.

Joseph nodded and smiled awkwardly. He kept his eyes fixed on Gilbert as he walked off towards the counter and waited impatiently for him to go up the steps. The moment he was out of sight, he eased up out of his chair and inconspicuously turned around to face the bookshelf. Casually he pulled the book out and quietly sat back down. He threw a quick glance to the other customers to check that they weren't watching him. Calmly he began to turn the pages in the book. A quarter of the way through, he turned one more page when his mouth dropped open with utter shock. A hidden compartment revealed itself, with a gold pouch laid inside.

He looked up at the customers before he slyly slid out the pouch and held it down in his lap. Nervously he opened the drawstring and peered down inside to see a key and a small folded piece of card. A surge of excitement overwhelmed him and jubilation shone in his eyes. He wriggled his fingers down inside and pulled them both out. He stared curiously at the brass key for a moment, which was the same size as his palm. His attention then turned to the card which had three horses' heads printed on the front, and slowly unfolded it to see a message written inside

'*A happy moment captured in a frame; to find me, go to the place of three of the same!*' he whispered to himself. A vacant look came over him, and he closed the card back down and stared long and hard at the printed front. Then all of a sudden, his eyes started to grow large and he said under his breath, 'I know where he wants me to go.' Once again, his suspicious eyes scanned the café, before slipping the card and the key back inside the pouch which he then tucked inside his coat pocket. Quietly he stood up and placed all of his change down onto the table, closed the book and slipped it inside his coat too and made a swift exit for the door.

The doorbell chimed and a moment later Gilbert re-emerged, wiping his hands on a tea towel and trundled down the steps and looked around the café. He turned his head and stared through the overly large window and saw Joseph getting into a car. He strolled over to the window and watched him drive off down the road, and then turned his head to the bookshelf to see *The Mad Hatter* book missing. He smiled. And slowly his eyes drifted upwards to the top shelf where a solid gold frame stood of a picture of him and Cyril sitting in a fishing boat together. His eyes drifted back to the window and quietly he said, 'Good luck, Joseph!' He turned and walked away.

Unbeknown to Joseph as he chugged along in his father's car, the red, evil eyes of a crow perched on the café's rooftop were watching him. The crow gave a squawk and flew off into the air, then began to follow him.

Chapter 9

AN UNHERALDED GIFT

Joseph's face turned green as he bounced around like a pinball, travelling along a narrow, beaten track covered in snow. Just when he thought the lane couldn't get any narrower, thick overgrown hedges began to scrape the sides of the car. He winced at the horrendous noise, which sounded like the car was being sliced open. Eventually the lane widened again and the sound stopped, to the relief of his ears. Out of nowhere, an opening emerged not far away on the left-hand side. His eyes narrowed with suspicion. He drew closer and saw a white painted wooden sign attached to a splintery wooden post which was fixed to a stone wall. It gently swayed at the slightest breath from the cold wind.

'The Three White Horses, I'm here, I'm here!' he said, bursting with joy and started to jump up and down in his seat like a buffoon, and accidentally banged his head on the inside of the roof. 'OWW!' he yelled, rubbing his head. He pulled the car over onto the cobbled drive and sat back and stared at the sign for a second, then turned his head to gaze down the sloping gravel driveway at his grandmother's cottage, lying low down just beyond the trees. It looked every bit as charming, nestled amongst the snow. Intently he watched as the grey smoke lightly puffed away from the chimney stack. His hand wandered inside his coat pocket and he pulled out the pouch, and then the key. He held it up between his fingers and whispered to himself: 'Okay, Granddad, I'm here; let's see why, shall we?' and he unzipped the side of his rucksack to tuck it inside.

The cold air pressed against his face the moment he stepped out of the car. He took a deep breath and felt the harshness of it travel down his throat. He slung his rucksack over his shoulders and proceeded down the driveway with slight uncertainty. Absorbed in his thoughts, he wondered what his grandmother might say, given how long it had been since she last saw him. A distinctive sound came out of the blue and stopped him dead in his tracks. His head snapped around and to his dismay he saw a black crow perched on top of the cottage sign. It cawed repeatedly, then ceased and turned its head to stare at him with its burning red eyes. Joseph was becoming concerned by frequently seeing these ghastly things and worryingly began to step backwards. Quickly he gathered momentum until he couldn't go any faster than his legs could carry him, and turned awkwardly and paced quickly towards the house, whilst he glanced back over his shoulder. He stopped at a flight of steps, which led down to the porch. He looked back to see the crow had gone.

Joseph sighed with relief and turned to stare at the quaint cottage and smiled. 'Looks like the place hasn't changed much,' he mused aloud. Swiftly he made his way down the steps to the front door and raised his hand up to knock, but hesitated. 'Wait a minute, what am I doing, what am I going to say to her? Oh hi, Gran, it's me, your grandson who you never see; just thought I'd call 'cause Granddad been leaving me some crazy riddles. What happens if she can't remember me or doesn't want to see me and tells me to go away?' he said, talking to himself, and slowly lowered his hand.

Out of the corner of his eye he saw something move through the sash window. Curiously he wiped the frost from the glass and pressed his face up against it and peered through nosily into the kitchen. Though doubtful, he faced the door again, paused to suck in a deep breath and exhale, and gently tapped it. His nervousness grew as he anxiously waited and once again stared through the window but saw no sign of anyone inside. He promptly knocked once more but with a bit more of a clout.

'Alright, alright, hold your horses, I'm coming,' said an elderly voice on the other side of the door.

Surprised to hear the faint voice, Joseph took a nervous step back and swallowed. He watched a shadowy figure emerge from behind the glass of the door then suddenly it swung open inwards. Shocked and unable to utter a single word, he stood and stared at the little old lady with short silvery, white hair in a dusky pink knitted cardigan and matching brooch glaring back at him with suspicious eyes.

'Joseph,' she said softly. Her bottom lip began to quiver and the muscles in her face began to relax from the scowl she held.

'Hi, Gran,' Joseph replied sheepishly and grinned awkwardly.

'Oh, good heavens, my dear Joseph,' said Mary, and immediately stepped out from the porch to wrap her arms around him.

Joseph's eyes glazed over. His clammy hands slowly released the tight grip he held around his straps and gradually he placed his arms around her frail body. He closed his eyes and felt an overwhelming happiness fill him inside that he hadn't felt in such a long time.

'Oh my dear, dear, Joseph, I have missed you so, so much,' said Mary, with tears in her eyes, and she moved to place her hands upon his face. 'Come in, come in, we can't have you standing out here in the cold,' and ushered him in through the front door.

Warily Joseph stepped inside and slowly made his way into the kitchen area and stopped by a pale orange-tiled worktop counter. A sense of unreality and delight all rolled together came over him as he gazed around, when suddenly he was struck by a wondrous smell wafting through from the living room. With great pleasure he sniffed the smell of the burning logs that he could hear faintly crackling away in the background.

Mary quickly closed all the doors one after another and stood in the kitchen and stared at him. 'Oh, Joseph, it is so good to see you! You don't know how happy I am,' she said, and hugged him again before fussing with him and brushing down his coat. 'Well, come on, you're no stranger to this household, Joseph. Take your coat and hat off and let's have a good look at you, my dear boy,' she said and stepped back.

Joseph felt reluctant to, but knew how domineering she could be, and slowly slipped off his rucksack and set it down on the floor, then took off his coat and draped it over his rucksack and bowed his head with embarrassment.

'No need to be shy around me, Joseph, and the hat too,' said Mary in a commanding tone of voice.

He removed his bobble hat from his head and dropped it down on top of his coat. He began to brush his hair down before he straightened up to his full height as though he was on show and smiled bashfully.

'My, my, haven't you grown since the last time I saw you, and into a handsome young man too!' said Mary grinning. 'And hasn't your hair gone real thick, just like your father's,' she said, gently stroking it. 'Here, why don't you go and warm yourself in front of the fire and make yourself comfortable, and I'll fix us a nice pot of tea and bring in some of those Jammie Dodgers that you like.'

A broad smile appeared upon Joseph's face while he nodded. Before he stepped one foot through the doorway of the living room he was taken aback by the heat of the open fire. At first it was a little uncomfortable, as he had forgotten what it was like to be exposed to such warmth, but he soon adjusted and felt drawn to it. He stood and marvelled at the enormous brick surround that spanned practically the whole breadth of the living room, with its magnificent solid dark oak mantelpiece sunken into the brickwork. Calmly he strolled over and ran his fingers across the brickwork and gently touched all the old antique brass horseshoes that hung upon it.

'Don't get too close now, Joseph, I don't want you burning yourself now, do I?' said Mary, standing in the doorway between the kitchen and the living room.

Her words were so familiar. It felt like it was only yesterday that she would say the same thing to Joseph. He smiled and replied, 'I'm okay, Gran,' and continued to walk the breadth of the fireplace to the right. He stopped to look attentively at an old brown leather single armchair. 'You still got Granddad's armchair?' he said, and lightly touched it with his fingertips.

'Some things don't change in life, Joseph, and some things never leave us either,' Mary replied with a sigh, and turned and walked away.

A great sadness filled Joseph as he stared at the doorway and slowly lowered his eyes to the floor. He began to reminisce about his grandfather sitting in the armchair with him sat upon his lap. Casually he walked over and plonked himself down on a beige double-seated sofa that was pushed up against the staircase and gazed around the room. Everything was exactly how he remembered it as a boy, from the beautiful old wooden beams that ran across the ceiling, with two of them going directly into the fireplace surround, the greenish patterned carpet which had diamond shapes etched into it, to the little lamps attached to the fireplace surround at either end. He took great pleasure spending time at his grandparents' house, and slumped back to indulge in the ambience of his surroundings. He became engrossed in the dancing, naked flames.

The sound of his grandmother softly humming in the kitchen pleased him and caused him to roll his head in the direction of the doorway to listen closely, when his eyes unknowingly drifted over to a sideboard on the back wall. Slowly his head edged from the sofa and his eyes began to widen with surprise to see the same identical photograph that he had brought with him, mounted in a rustic gold frame. Quickly he rose to his feet and briskly walked over and snatched the frame from the sideboard and stared suspiciously at the faded picture. 'That's strange, why would Gran have the same photo here . . . unless of course . . . ?' he muttered to himself while deep in thought. He threw a darting glance over his shoulder to the kitchen doorway and flipped the frame over and began to unpin it. Gently he lifted the hardboard to expose the picture and his eyes lit up instantly to reveal another message written upon a piece of paper sellotaped to the back of it.

Strike with my hand, cause no harm,
My face encased with beauty and charm,
I never grow old, year upon year,
Listen closely, what do you hear?

A nonplussed look came over Joseph's face after reading

the message quietly to himself and he was ruminating on its meaning, when the sound of his grandmother's voice startled him and broke his concentration.

'Here we go, my dear,' Mary echoed from the kitchen.

Panicking, Joseph ripped off the piece of paper and stuffed it into his jeans pocket and he frantically fumbled with the hardboard as he tried to clip it back together.

Gran waddled into the living room and sat a silver tray down onto a coffee table positioned in front of the fire. She turned to face him and narrowed her eyes, slightly tilted her body to the side and asked, 'Is everything alright, dear?'

Finally Joseph clipped down the last pin down and swung around, looking flushed. 'Oh yeah, fine, Gran, I was just admiring the photograph, that's all,' he said, grinning and holding it up to show her.

'Oh, that blessed photo,' said Mary grudgingly.

Joseph looked at the picture, confused. 'What do you mean, Gran?' he asked.

'Higgledy piggledy, Joseph, we can talk about that thing later. Right now, I want to hear all about you. Now come, sit,' said Mary in a bossy tone of voice as she sat down.

Joseph looked at the photograph once again before placing it back down on the sideboard with an accidental thud, and he strolled back to the sofa. He watched her hand unsteadily pour the tea from her beautiful crafted white china pot into the cups and politely asked, 'Would you like me help you with that, Gran?'

'No, no, it's quite alright, dear, age comes to us all. I've managed for some years without your grandfather around. I think I'm doing pretty okay for myself, don't you think?' asked Mary, smiling at him.

Joseph smiled back and began to rub his hands together nervously, hoping he hadn't offended her, but knew that she was a cast-iron lady and the boss of the house when his grandfather was alive – and still was. He turned away to stare into space and mull over the piece of paper in his pocket and wondered whether or not to ask her about it.

'Are you okay, Joseph?' Mary asked, while pouring the milk.

'Hmm, oh yes, Gran, I was just thinking to myself, that's all,' he replied.

'So tell me, how did you get here? It's such a long way to travel, Joseph, especially in these cold conditions?' said Mary.

Caught off guard, Joseph pretended to cough and placed his hand to his mouth. He quickly began to rack his brain as to what he could say and grew flustered. 'Oh . . . I, um, drove here. Oh look, my favourite biscuits, Jammie Dodgers!' he said, and picked up a biscuit and nibbled on it.

'Oh, I didn't think you were old enough. My, how time has flown – look at you, all grown up. Your grandfather would have been so happy to have seen you if he was alive, oh I do miss him and your father too. How is your mother doing, by the way?' said Mary, picking up her saucer and quickly dunking a biscuit into the tea before it went soggy.

'Um, she's doing okay . . . I mean, she has some good days,' replied Joseph with a glum look.

'Come now, my darling Joseph, you're talking to your grandmother. How is she really doing?' asked Mary.

'To tell you the truth, Gran, not so well. I've tried my best to help her but—' Joseph paused before he could finish and bowed his head sorrowfully.

Mary's face started to sink. She placed her tea back down onto the coffee table and put her hand on his arm and gently rubbed it. 'I'm so sorry, my dear Joseph, I didn't mean to upset you. You know your mother loves you very much, don't you? It's just she hasn't moved on like the rest of us. She's gotten herself into such a pickle that she doesn't know how to get herself out of it. She loved your father dearly, as did we all,' she said.

Joseph's bottom lip quivered. 'It's okay, Gran. I just haven't been able to talk to anyone about it, that's all,' he said, and inhaled a deep breath and let it out again.

Mary smiled through stiff lips. 'Here, I'll tell you what, fetch me that photo,' she said. She picked her glasses up from the coffee table and put them on. She took the photo from him. Her head tilted slightly back to stare through the bottom of her glasses and she gave a sigh. 'Ah, two such fine men to walk God's earth, it's such a pity that neither of them are here today to see this remarkable young man sat in front of me,' she said, and tilted her head downwards to look through the top of her glasses at him with a smile. 'Do you know the story behind this photograph, Joseph?' she asked.

Joseph shook his head from side to side. 'No, Gran, I don't,' he replied.

'Well, from what I can remember, as per usual your father and Granddad would be out fishing, spending time together; and on this particular day, your father caught a big fish. The two of them were very competitive when it came to fishing, you know, Joseph, and your grandfather taught Michael everything he knew. In fact, suffice to say, the reason why your father excelled at everything was mainly because of your grandfather. I will give him credit where credit is due, he was an extremely clever man, and very mischievous too, always inquisitive about everything and wanted answers to everything! *Huh*, it was the very reason why I named him the mad hatter after the book because of all the crazy things he would come out with and say to me. I suppose that's what you get for marrying an archaeologist – they seem to think they can unlock the world's secrets,' Mary said and waddled her head.

Joseph sat wide-eyed and engrossed by her every word and asked eagerly, 'Do you know what Granddad is holding in the photo, Gran?'

'That, Joseph, is something of a mystery to me. I have been puzzled for many years by what it was, but whenever I broached the subject he simply replied saying it was a piece of junk he found lying around and threw it back into the lake. Needless to say, I questioned him no further, but it did always keep me wondering,' Mary replied, staring at the photograph. Her bottom lip started to quiver and she quickly removed her glasses and dropped them down onto her lap. She turned away to stare at the window. 'Oh, silly me,' she said, and reached for the tissues to wipe her eyes.

'Sorry, Gran, I—' stuttered Joseph.

'Oh, don't be so silly, Joseph, there's no need to apologize; it isn't your fault. It's just, the reason why the photograph carries so much of a burden to me, Joseph, is because, it's the very last photo of them alive together,' Mary said.

Joseph paused to think about what he wanted to say next, without causing her further distress, and then said, 'Can I ask you something, Gran?'

'Of course you can, my dear, what is it?' replied Mary.

'Well, could you tell me what happened to Granddad and how he died?' he asked nervously.

Mary looked at him blankly and said, 'Did your mother not tell you?'

Joseph shook his head. 'No, she didn't,' Joseph replied softly.

'Oh. Well, let me see. I awoke one night to a loud noise, to find Cyril was not in bed and quickly called out to him, but he didn't answer. Worried, I began to search all over the house but I couldn't find him anywhere. Then I suddenly noticed the front door was unlocked. I went outside and made my way around to the front of the house and found the garage door was wide open, which was very peculiar, to say the least. As I stepped closer to the garage I saw something large and dark inside on the floor. It was only when I was at the entrance to the garage that I realized it was Cyril. I yelled at him, "Good gracious me, what do you think you're doing? Get up off the floor this instant and stop being so silly." But Cyril didn't respond and just lay there on the ground. I told him, "Cyril Van Pearce, if you do not get up off the floor right this minute, you'll find yourself sleeping in the spare bedroom," but he didn't move. That's when I realized there was something wrong and quickly rushed over to him. I kept calling him while I cradled him in my arms but there was no response – nothing. My arm felt wet but I couldn't see why as it was dark. All I could do was to hold him in my arms and cry for him to wake up, but at that point I realized he had passed away and there was nothing I could do. The coroner said that the main cause of his death was a heart attack, but also said that he had sustained a small but deep laceration to his head. When I spoke to the police they said there was nothing suspicious surrounding his death, but I couldn't disagree more,' said Mary.

Joseph's eyes narrowed at her last words and said, stuttering, 'Why . . . what do you think happened to him, Gran?'

Mary paused before replying. She stared hard at the photograph in her hand then turned her eyes towards him with a serious look upon her face. 'I think he was murdered, Joseph,' she said.

'MURDERED!' replied Joseph, shocked. His eyes grew large and his stomach tightened at the sickening word. 'How? Why do you think that?' he asked, gravely concerned.

'Because a week later, late one evening, I was boxing some of Cyril's things away when the lights suddenly tripped inside the house. I quickly went and fetched the torch from the kitchen drawer and headed to the garage through the internal door to locate the fuse box. As I was shining the light inside,

I accidentally stepped on broken glass, and when I stepped back I noticed it was white. I had no idea where it had come from until I looked up and saw the strip light was broken and a tiny bloodstain was on it. Now I rarely go into the garage, Joseph, and the only person that did was your grandfather, so it made very little sense to me: why would your grandfather be fixing a broken light in the garage at that time of night? There were no ladders or stool or anything out for that matter that he could have been standing on when I found him, and why would he have a laceration to his head when he died and why would a bloodstain be on the light? I didn't see anything that he could have hit his head on, as he was lying in the middle of the garage floor. It was also strange that the garage door was slightly buckled from the inside. Something wasn't right, if you ask me, Joseph, it just wasn't right,' Mary said, and rubbed her chest.

Joseph tried to swallow but his throat had tightened all of a sudden. He was overcome with grief, but then a sudden sensation of anger burnt away inside. 'Did Mum know about this, Gran?' he asked, hoping she didn't so that he wouldn't have to have it out with her.

'No, she didn't, Joseph; you're the first person I have told. I called your mother to let her know your grandfather had passed away, but at the time she wasn't sober on the phone, and that was the very last time I have ever spoken to her.' Mary sighed. 'You'll have to excuse me, dear, but nature calls, won't be a moment,' and she rose from the chair and made her way up the stairs behind him.

Joseph stared at the coffee table, vexed, with his lips clenched tightly together. *Why would someone want to hurt Granddad? He was the nicest person you could ever meet, everyone loved him and spoke highly of him, especially Gran. I'm going to get to the bottom of this, if it's the last thing I do,* he thought to himself. He took the screwed-up piece of paper from his pocket, reread the riddle and then looked around.

'What is it I'm supposed to be looking for, Granddad?' he said under his breath to himself and huffed with frustration. His eyes wandered around the room, when suddenly the grandfather clock struck loudly and caused him to flinch. He glared at it standing at the other side of the room and said, 'Stupid bloody clock,' and shook his head. The chimes echoed to his annoyance and he was trying to block them out and focus on the riddle, when the last line struck a chord with him.

'Wait a minute,' he muttered, and looked up suspiciously at the clock. Before he knew it, he had risen to his feet and stepped quickly over to it. He began to search it up and down and took half a step back and scratched his head. He watched the pendulum swinging back and forth.

'I wonder . . .' he said to himself and carefully opened the magnetic glass door and stopped the pendulum and peered inside to see a small wooden panel at the bottom. Joseph crouched down onto his knees and fingered around, when suddenly he felt the panel tilt. Carefully he removed it and plunged his arm deep down inside. To his surprise, he felt something. Excitement rose as he pulled the unknown object out and sat back, with a look of shock upon his face. His hands shook nervously as he found he was holding a white envelope in his grasp. He stared at his name scrolled across the front: '*To Joseph, Strictly Private and Confidential*' he read. His eyes shifted sharply over to the staircase for signs of Gran, then quickly he tore the envelope open and began to read the letter.

Chapter 10

THE DRAGON'S HEAD MEDALLION

Dear Joseph,

By the time you read this letter you should have grown into a fine young man just like your father, and I will have passed away, praying this letter reaches you in safe hands. I'm sure you're confused and have a million questions running through your mind that you would like answered and I will endeavour to do my very best to tell you what I know, but first let me begin by saying this.

There is so much I would have like to have said and done with you growing up, but the unfortunate events that led to your father's life being cut short changed everything within the family, and we were no longer as close as we once were. Your grandmother and I tried our very best to remain in contact with Cathleen and you, but as you know all too well, the tragic death of your father had a devastating effect upon your wonderful mother. It was clear to Mary and me that Cathleen was deeply traumatized and in turn became extremely possessive of you. Consequently because of her controlling behaviour this drove us away and we lost contact with you – which we did not wish for. Please do not think this letter is about resentment or blame, as it is not. I am merely highlighting the turmoil of your father's death that has brought the family terrible grief and sorrow. We love your mother very much, she was like the daughter we never had, I just wished things could have been different for our family. I felt you should know all of this because we deeply care about you, Joseph, but also you need to be strong because things are about to change quickly for you.

By now you are probably wondering why I have left a trail of riddles behind for you to follow, which has led to you to finding the hidden key and to this letter. The reason for this is as follows. What I am holding in my hand, standing next to your father in the photograph, is one half of the powerful Dragon's Head Medallion. Did your father ever happen to mention to you, Joseph, that I saw a ghost of some kind? Well, I can confirm the hearsay is true. I encountered a white spirit lady named Quindella and she was once the guardian of the medallion up until her death, but now you are the one chosen to safeguard it. Apologies, as I am unable to answer why you have been chosen, Joseph (this is something you'll need to find out for yourself, more than likely the spirit will know?), but what I can tell you is this:

The Dragon's Head Medallion is not from our world, and from what world it comes I have no knowledge of, but it has the potential to ultimately destroy all of mankind if it was to fall into the clutches of an evil creature (which is also not from our world) that is lurking. Have you ever noticed crows watching you, Joseph? Well, these have been watching our family and you for a very long time, and have followed my every move ever since I discovered the medallion. The creature wants to possess its power and will stop at nothing to retrieve it, including killing our family, which leads me on to what I have to say about what I myself have seen.

My encounter with the spirit was forever life-changing. Her ability to flash-forward gave me an insight to terrible events of the future that might or might not occur. These vile events wherein I saw your mother and Mary die by the evil creature can be averted if you choose to accept this as your destiny and become the guardian of the medallion. That might come as a bit of a shock for you to hear and a bitter pill to swallow, but unfortunately, Joseph, there was no other way to say that, I'm afraid.

My advice is, it would be wise of you not to inform anyone, as you could potentially place their lives at risk (which includes your mother and grandmother – the less they know, the better), and why I felt it was necessary to turn everything into riddles in case anything happens and all is compromised. I hope you understand the gravity of the situation and the dangers that surround the medallion. And for those reasons I felt it was imperative of me to take careful steps. This is why I have chosen to hide it in a very safe location which you'll have to find.

If you choose not to go forth and seek it out, then it's only a matter of time before our family's fate will be sealed.

But if you decide to fulfil your destiny, you will need to defend yourself from the evil creature that will no doubt want to harm you. I have therefore hidden something else that will help assist you, which is also of great importance – a dagger! I will explain things in more depth at the next location, but for now, time is of the essence and the creature's patience grows thin. Locate the dagger and solve the riddle below to find it.

Treasure has a trunk, as do I,
I may weep, others may cry,
How to find me, use an eye,
A pig lives in a sty, I live in the sky
God be with thee.
Love
Granddad X
P.S. Love marks the spot'

~

Joseph sat with his mouth open wide, staring at the letter in his hand. He didn't know whether to feel happy or gutted to hear this from his grandfather. Either way, he felt numb and struggled to comprehend what was required of him. 'Gilbert and Gran were right, he is crazy. But why the hell am I chosen, and what the bloody hell does this medallion have to do with me?' he said to himself, gravely concerned. Endless questions flowed thick and fast through his mind, when his thoughts were suddenly interrupted by the sound of the creaky floorboards above his head. His head snapped upwards to listen intently to the sound of his grandmother's footsteps moving across the house. It sounded as though she was heading back. Frantically, he stuffed the letter back into the envelope and shoved it into his jeans pocket and replaced everything as quickly as he could.

Slowly Mary came down the stairs and glanced across the room to see Joseph stood by the window and asked, 'Is everything alright, my dear?'

'Oh yeah, fine, Gran, just watching the snow come down, it's starting to get heavy. I think I'd better be heading off home,' Joseph said, turning to face her but with a look that showed something was weighing heavily upon his mind.

'But you've haven't long got here,' Mary said, making her way over to him and looked at the clock. 'Oh, silly thing, it's stopped again,' she said and shook her head.

Joseph smiled awkwardly.

'Are you sure you don't want to stay? I have the spare room already made up with thick blankets, you know, the one you use to sleep in as a boy,' she said, raising her eyebrows.

'Sorry, Gran, I need to get back home for Mum, but I would like to come and see you again soon, if that is okay?' he said. He saw the disappointment written across her face and felt guilty and frowned.

'Joseph, my dear, you are more than welcome to come here any time,' Mary said, and smiled. She threw her arms around him and gave him a hug, before kissing him on his forehead.

'Go, and make sure you drive carefully.'

Joseph strode across the living room into the kitchen and quickly whipped on his bobble hat and coat and slung his rucksack over his shoulders. 'It was really nice to see you, Gran,' he said.

'The pleasure was all mine, Joseph, it was truly wonderful to see you, and make sure you don't leave it too long to come see me again, will you?' Mary said, tidying his coat for him.

'I won't,' replied Joseph, and made his way into the porch and opened the door. He stepped out into the cold and looked up to the sky to watch the tiny snowflakes fall and settle on the ground. 'Goodbye, Gran,' he said, and gave a little wave as he headed towards the steps.

'Goodbye, Joseph, be sure to pass my love on to your mother for me,' Mary said, raising her voice to him and folded her arms. She watched him trail footprints in the snow up the long driveway and suddenly stop. She smiled as he waved his arm wildly, and casually waved back to him. A tear of happiness trickled down her wrinkled face. Her eyes continued to follow him until he was eventually out of sight. The moment she turned her back to head in, the sound of crows caught her attention. Mary looked around and saw a black swarm quickly dart from out the trees. She glared at them. 'Huh, irksome things,' she muttered to herself and turned around and went back inside the house.

Chapter 11

THE HUNDRED HOUSE INN

The wipers swept back and forth furiously to clear the onslaught of sleet and snow that belted down onto the windscreen.

'This is just what I need right now – bloody lost in the middle of nowhere and can't see for a blind mole's ass out of this window!' Joseph said, ranting to himself inside the car. 'Huh, not to mention I'm supposedly the CHOSEN one who can't even find his way back home. Even that Kansas girl found her way home!' and he angrily thumped the steering wheel with his hand.

Out of nowhere, an enormous creature as black as the night swooped down behind the car. It flew up alongside the car and slammed into the side of it with a BANG! Suddenly Joseph was flung sideways like a rag doll and his head whacked into the driver's door window. The car slid out of control across the blanket of snow on the road and spun around three hundred and sixty degrees and careered off, landing in a hedge on the side verge. Semi-conscious and disorientated, Joseph's eyes rolled into the back of his head. His vision was completely blurred and doubled. Slowly but surely the dizziness eased, and his sight eventually returned to normal but to complete darkness. 'AWWWW!' he cried out, scrunching his face up and he held his hand to the side of his head, feeling a tremendous onset of pain.

In shock, his whole body began to shake like a leaf. He fumbled about to unclip his seat belt, then desperately tugged at the driver's door handle to get out, which was jammed shut. Repeatedly he shoved his shoulder into it, exacerbating the pain in his head further. 'C'mon, you frigging door. Open!' he yelled out, panicking. Finally the buckled door creaked open and fell off its hinges and onto the ground. Instantly a blizzard of snow blew inside. Quickly he reached for his rucksack and stumbled out of the car, but his legs gave way and fell straight down onto the snow face first.

'Oh my God, that's cold!' he said, lifting his face up, and he shook his head. He heaved himself up onto his wobbly legs and he lifted his hood up over his head, but the penetrating snow continued to strike him in the face. He motioned his head from side to side and felt unnerved by the darkness, quickly delved inside of his rucksack and pulled out the torch. Erratically, he shone it around, but saw nothing more than a curtain of snow raining down. Joseph shone the light over to the car and moved in closer to take a look when utter shock came over him.

'Oh my God, what the hell's happened to the car? How

am I going to get home?' he cried out. He stared with disbelief to see the side of it sliced open like it had been cut with a chainsaw. Before he had time to think about what to do next, a creepy chattering sound echoed in the wind, coming from out of nowhere.

Trepidation grew quickly inside of him as he swished the light from side to side and said nervously, 'Who's there?'

He stopped and pointed in the direction of the sound, when all of a sudden, two large burning red eyes appeared in the darkness. Petrified, Joseph started to tremble and quickly began to back away, then turned and ran as fast as he could through the perilous conditions.

He kept looking behind him to see if whatever it was that he saw was following him, but soon ran out of steam and slowed down. The snow showed no signs of easing and the road ahead was now a white blanket. Every step proved to be more and more difficult to take and made it virtually impossible for him to follow any sort of direction. Undeterred, he marched on, knowing he had no other choice than to find a safe haven fast.

The chilling wind blew up the glistening white snow into mini whirlwinds. The trees creaked and cracked and swayed with the eerie winds. Joseph watched them lean over and thought for a second that they looked as though they were trying to nab him. His shoulders slumped from the extra weight of the snow that rested upon him. Tiredly he held his one arm close to his chest to keep warm; the other felt cold and stiff holding the torch. The coldness pounded against his pale, solemn face, causing it to become numb and stiff.

'Help!' Joseph cried out, barely making a sound out of his frozen blue lips. 'Help!' But nothing came from the emptiness that surrounded him. Joseph felt scared. He knew he was in serious trouble unless he got help immediately. With every step he took, sinking deeper and deeper in the snow, great uncertainty weighed heavily upon him whether he was likely to make it out alive. He felt a strange feeling of death cling to him like it was impatiently waiting for him to give up so it could snatch his life away.

'Somebody please help me, HEELLPP!' he screeched. He stopped for a second to catch his breath and panted hard with exhaustion. Hunched over, the bitter cold air was harsh to inhale, followed by an unpleasant feeling of vertigo. The pain on the side of his head unkindly reminded him it was still there as he shook his head to get rid of the dizziness. Suddenly he heard an eerie sound whistle in the wind.

'*Houssse . . .*' it whispered.

'Who – who said that?' Joseph stuttered, thinking his mind was playing tricks on him. His stomach tightened with dread, thinking the evil eyes that he saw had returned. He whirled around panicking and caused himself to become further off balance. He wobbled about like a drunk and bent over to steady himself, placing his hands upon his knees. His heart pounded nervously as he motioned his head from side to side and eventually straightened back up stiffly. 'Hello . . . is anybody there? . . . Can you help me?' Joseph called out in desperation and held his hand out to prevent the falling snow from striking his face.

'Find the *Houssse* quickly . . .' the slurring sound whispered.

'I don't understand. Who are you, what do you mean?' Joseph replied through chattering teeth. His chest wheezed and he shook uncontrollably from head to toe from the bitter cold that ran deep into his bones.

Suddenly the sound of something very large swooped above his head. Joseph quickly ducked down and cowered. He looked around into the darkness through his frozen eyelids, while his surroundings continued to move as though he was on board a rocky ship. The sound terrified him as it swooped by once again and Joseph was convinced that whatever it was lurking out there was going to kill him. Immediately he sprang up and began to wildly leap in and out of the snow to get further ahead. After a few desperate leaps, Joseph began to gasp for air and slowed down to a crawling pace again. His legs felt like dead weights, the back of his hands caused a painful burning sensation like they were on fire from being exposed to the Arctic conditions. He had no energy left and thought about giving up, when a faint yellowish light presented itself in the very distance.

Joseph squinted and felt a glimmer of hope curled up inside and made haste towards the light. He ploughed on through the storm, pumping his arms as hard as he could to keep momentum going. Finally, after every excruciating step, the yellowish light grew brighter and had become close enough for him to make out that it was a building of sorts. Overwhelmed with relief, he powered on, but suddenly found great difficulty in breathing. The surrounding trees and bushes gradually widened and exposed the plain. The road ahead seemed less covered in snow and the large building set back on the right had become more visible to see. Out of breath, his pace slowed dramatically from the sudden burst of energy he had discovered, and he resorted to staggering about like a zombie.

Joseph looked up to see a large, towering old tree at the entrance to the building that had slightly shaded part of the road that led into the car park area. He squinted at the faded red sign attached to the tree, which swung and clanged violently in the wind. Partly covered in snow, the sign displayed the building's name: *The Hundred House Inn.* He glanced across to the inn that was elegantly lit up and noticed how white the exterior was, making it almost invisible as it blended in with the surroundings. He staggered helplessly towards it, but suddenly stopped in between the large tree on the left and a curved stone wall on the right. He heard faint voices of laughter and made one final cry for help. But his frozen chapped lips barely passed a whisper through them. He couldn't find the energy to take another step and felt his life drain from him and collapsed to his knees. His limp body fell helplessly to the ground with a thud and he lay face down in the snow.

Meanwhile inside the old pub, jolly men – some young, some old – bantered away with one another in good spirits. They sat huddled around rickety old tables and wobbly chairs in a quaint bar area. The smell of the old pub, fused with the distinct smell of beers and ales spilt on the floor and tables from countless of glasses over the years, was ingrained for ever. The stale smell that stained the air was not the most pleasing to say the least, but once a few minutes had passed by, the smell was completely forgotten and all that was left was a few jolly countrymen drinking the night away.

'And what makes you think that, Bryn?' said an old man, Ron Gubert, scrutinizing him, while he sat to the left of the bar on the worn vinyl seat, sipping his dark bitter.

'Listen, when I was your age sonny, I—' said Bryn Dower in his broad Welsh accent.

'What on earth are you talking about? You are not even my age yet, you silly old fart!' old man Ron said, interrupting him, while the whole pub began to roar with laughter from his quick wit.

Bryn's face began to turn crimson with embarrassment. 'That's not what I meant,' he replied. He tapped the arm of Adam Churn with the back of his hand to gain his attention at the bar. 'Err, Adam, tell them, tell them how I used to—'

'Oh, leave me out of it, I'm not getting involved!' Adam quickly replied.

'Huh, well it's true, it's as true as the moon shines in the sky at night,' said Bryn and crossed his arms with a huff.

Old man Ron held his pint up to his mouth to take a sip and said, 'Well, we'll just have to take your word for it,' and grinned behind his pint.

Basil Scott, the landlord of the Hundred House Inn, stood behind the bar pulling a pint for Adam. He rolled his eyes, shook his head and gave Bryn a smile. The last drop of beer was poured into the glass and carefully he placed it on top of the counter.

'That'll be two pound, Adam,' he said in a mild Scottish accent, and took the money from him. He turned around and placed it in the cash register. Out of the corner of his eye he saw his wife, Ariana, walking towards him, rubbing the backs of her arms.

'Hey, handsome, I think we might have to shut up shop early tonight, hon,' Ariana said, slipping her hand up the back of Basil's shirt.

Basil shuddered. '*Good heavens*, yer hands are freezing, woman! Get off me!' he said, wriggling like a worm to break free of her and stepped away. 'And why is that, we've barely been open two hours?'

'I've just been out the back and the snow isn't letting up and the conditions are getting worse by the second. I don't want to have to be responsible for the punters and find ourselves snowed in and having to put them all up for the night, especially old man Ron. I think it's best we send them all home now before the night draws in,' said Ariana.

'Yer know we need the money right now. Things are really tight, we've barely taken a bean this week,' replied Basil, and ran his hand through his long, curly black hair.

'I know we do, and we'll manage, like we always do, but the last thing I want is for these guys to get completely off their trolley drinking beer, fall down drunk on their way home and freeze to death. And who's going to end up in the papers then, hey?' she said, and raised her eyebrows at him. Slowly she moved her cold hands towards his face and touched his thin black moustache and then caressed his face.

Basil shivered again and quickly moved to grab her hands and place them on his chest. He stared into her blue eyes. 'Aye, I see ya point, but they're not going to be happy about this,' he said with a sigh and clenched his lips together.

'They'll be back soon enough. You've known them long enough, hon, to know they're creatures of habit, remember,' said Ariana, and kissed him on the cheek. She eased away and held a smile for a second or so and turned around and walked away.

Basil stroked his trim face with his hand then placed his hands on his hips. His cheeks puffed out as he blew out through his lips and bowed his head. He turned to face the bar and picked up the tea towel, threw it over his shoulder, leant his hand down on the bar and said, 'Okay, guys, listen up, I've just spoken with Ari and—'

'OOOOOHHHHHH!' they all said in harmony together and interrupted him before he could finish.

'Hey, *Scotty*,' shouted out Donald Stewart, pretending to impersonate his Scottish accent, 'never mind the kilt, I want to know, does Ari lend her yer *troosers* when she goes out?' and he started chuckling.

All the punters burst out laughing uncontrollably, knowing very well what Donald was implying, and began to spill some of their beer all over the tables and floor and then started to chant and mock him. 'Scotty, where's ya troosers, Scotty where's ya troosers, la-la-la-la, HEY, la-la-la-la, HEY!'

Unable to keep a straight face, Basil smiled, shook his head and threw the tea towel at Donald. 'Ha, ha, very funny, laugh it up, I'll ban all of *yers* if yer carry on,' he said, giggling with them while pointing and swinging his finger back and forth at them all. 'Now listen, the snow is getting worse outside, and I ain't got room for all yer drunken bums to stay the night, so drink up, ladies, yer going home ta yer wives, the bar is CLOSED!' he bellowed out.

'Huh, my wife would be glad for me not to come home,' said Bryn, and he swigged back the last mouthful of beer and placed the empty glass back down on the bar.

'Aye, and I bet it is because Ethel enjoys the peace, that's why!' replied Basil, chuckling to himself. He picked up Bryn's empty glass and turned away to place it in the dishwasher.

'Oh, the cheek of it, right, well on that note, I'm off. I will see you lot again!' Bryn said, getting off the bar stool, and made his way to the front door. He lifted his heavy green wax jacket from the coat hook and slipped it on. He pulled out his grey flat cap from his coat pocket and slung it over his bald head. The second he opened the old wooden door a fierce blast of wind and snow came hurtling into the pub and pushed him backwards. Quickly he placed his hand onto his head to save his cap from blowing off, and slammed the door shut again.

'Heavens almighty!' he said, wiping the snow from out of his eyes.

A sudden silence filled the room as they all sat and stared

at him for a brief moment, then all burst out laughing again at the sight of him covered in snow.

'Hey, Frosty, think you better come back inside and *chill* out,' piped up Sam Pike and laughed hysterically.

'Ha ha, very funny, sonny Jim, just remember I watched you when you were a little boy running off scared and crying while you got chased away by one of my little piggies on me farm,' Bryn shot back and gave a wink to the others.

Sam's face dropped with embarrassment and suddenly he became quiet and sheepishly turned to the others to see if they were looking at him.

Bryn shook off some of the snow and proceeded towards the door again and braced himself as he opened it. The harsh blizzard blew hard against him as he traipsed across the car park to the right. He squinted and held on dearly to his flat cap with his hand. He bowed and tilted his head to the left as the snowflakes struck his face, when he saw a faint light on the ground next to something small and dark. He stopped in his tracks and sheltered his face with his hands to take a closer look. His eyes narrowed but he was unable to make out what it was.

Bryn trundled towards it and the dark shadow became a lot larger than what he initially saw. He took one step closer and stopped and gasped, realizing it was a body on the ground. Without hesitation, he stumbled over as fast as his legs would carry him and slid down onto his knees next to the person.

'Hello, can you hear me? Are you okay, are you okay?' Bryn asked, and then placed his head down to listen to the person's chest. 'HELP!' he shouted out at the top of his lungs.

Without a moment to spare, he slid his arms underneath and hoisted the person's body up into the air and staggered to his feet. Slowly he traipsed under the strain of their dead weight back towards the pub, when suddenly his flat cap blew off into the wind. He scrunched his wrinkled face as the snow drove hard into him. Finally he reached the door out of breath and puffing and began to pound it fiercely with his foot.

Everyone inside the pub who was laughing and joking amongst themselves suddenly stopped. The place fell quiet as they all listened closely to the repeated loud sound of something thudding against the front door.

'What the hell is that?' said Adam and looked to the others.

'Maybe it's the Black Baron searching for his wife and come to kill us all,' joked Sam and giggled to himself.

'Well, don't just bloody sit there, one of you get up and go and see what the hell it is!' boomed old man Ron in an aggressive tone.

'Go see, Sam, you're closest to the door,' said James.

'What, me?' Sam stuttered. He huffed and got up out of his chair and walked over. Everyone sat in anticipation as he grabbed the handle, but suddenly the door flew open and walloped Sam and knocked him straight to the ground.

Bryn burst through the door covered in snow looking like the Abominable Snowman. He stood over Sam and looked down at him. 'What you doing down there, you silly boy, get up and close the door!' he said in an angry tone of voice and stepped right over him.

With a shocked look upon his face, Sam scrabbled to his feet and quickly closed the door and rushed into the bar area.

Bryn staggered in, huffing and puffing, and just as the person was about to slip out of his grasp everyone spontaneously leapt out from their chairs and took the person from him and carefully placed him down onto the floor. Lightheaded, Bryn fell back and landed into one of the chairs behind him, gasping and clutching his chest.

'Who's that, Bryn?' asked Donald, turning to face him.

Bryn could barely catch his breath and said in a sharp tone, 'How the hell should I know? I found him outside on the floor,' and wiped his face and head from the snow.

'Well, is he alive?' said old man Ron, peering over the table.

Adam placed his head down onto his chest and said, 'Barely.'

While they bickered amongst themselves, Basil bit into the sandwich which he had made in the kitchen, heard all of the commotion and walked back to the bar area. 'Aye, what the hell's going on here?' he shouted out, staring at all the punters gathered round in a circle hovering over something on the floor.

'Bryn's found someone outside,' said old man Ron.

'What do mean?' replied Basil with a look of confusion, and placed his half-eaten sandwich down onto the counter. He swiftly walked through the side door of the bar into the pool room and made his way around, moving one or two of the punters out of the way so he could take a closer look. 'Who the hell's that?' he said, looking at them all.

'That's what I keep trying to tell everyone – I don't know. I found him outside lying face down on the ground,' said Bryn.

'Well, is he alive?' asked Basil.

'Breathing,' said Adam, looking up at Basil. 'What should we do, Scotty? Shall we call an ambulance?'

'Huh, yer gotta be joking, right? Yer won't get an ambulance out here, not in these conditions; they'll never make it!' replied Basil, and he shook his head.

'So what do we do?' said Donald.

''Ere, someone give me a hand to take 'im upstairs. We can't leave 'im down 'ere on the floor,' said Basil, crouching down to grab the legs, while Adam grabbed underneath the arms. 'Someone get the door next to the bar in the lounge, would yer?' He shuffled backwards and then swung around to let Adam take the lead through the narrow door. They clambered through and immediately climbed the steep, creaky stairs to the left. Halfway up, Basil began to yell at the top of his voice, 'Ariana, Ariana, come quick!'

As they reached the top and walked onto the landing, Ariana rushed out of one of the rooms with a shocked look upon her face and said, 'What's going on, what have you done!?'

'What do yer mean, what I have done? Here, Adam, this way,' said Basil, shimmying to the left on the landing and through a door tucked just behind the bathroom wall. Basil entered into a bedroom but didn't stop and kept going towards another door and through into another bedroom and up a set of steps and into a larger bedroom. ''Ere, put 'im down,' he said, and spun around to put the feet at the end of the bed first.

Ariana swiftly entered into the room behind them both and briskly walked over to the bed and placed her fingers on the person's neck. 'Okay, well, he's alive, that's a relief, so what the hell's happened?' she said, and stared hard at Basil.

'Don't yer look at me like that, woman, I have nothing to do with this. 'Ere, tell her, Adam,' replied Basil, turning to him.

'Basil's right. Bryn left to go home and found him lying outside,' said Adam, gasping.

'See. So what do yer think we should do, Ariana? There's no way an ambulance would get out here if we were to call them, with the storm,' said Basil. Ariana swung around and marched out through the door, leaving Basil stumped by her behaviour and yelled out, 'Now where are yer going?'

'Off to call Mrs Dumfries,' Ariana shouted back.

'WHAT? Betty, yer mean?' said Basil, screwing his face up.

'Yes,' replied Ariana.

'What for, we haven't got a dead horse 'ere!' Basil shouted back.

'If you've got any better ideas, Bas, I'm all ears,' Ariana said in a frosty tone and stormed off.

Chapter 12

AN UNEXPECTED GUEST

Joseph gradually half opened his heavy eyes to the blurred sight of a small orange glow. His vision soon cleared and strangely he found himself staring bewildered at a small flame gently flickering away behind the glass of a brass oil lamp. His body ached and his mouth was parched. He tried to swallow, but his throat was too dry. He felt confused. All that he could vaguely remember was something that resembled death chasing him. Then the penny suddenly dropped and he realized it was a dream and he was now somewhere unfamiliar.

He rolled his head nervously against the soft pillow to his left. His eyes shifted back and forth. Panic overcame him and he clambered to sit upright in the bed. The quick shift of movement caused a grizzly headache to appear. He scrunched his eyes shut from the pain and held his hand to his forehead. He felt a great big lump.

'Aww, that's sore,' he said, gently caressing it with his fingertips.

He looked across the room and stared at the window that was a picture of darkness. The harsh winter's breath pressed up against the thin pane of glass, which was partly frosted. It was all that stood in the way of the cold entering in. The chill from the room caused goose pimples to spread across his body. He shivered. The unsettling darkness unnerved him and so did his unfamiliar surroundings. He pulled the duvet and thick woollen blanket up close to his chest.

'Where the hell am I?' he said under his breath.

His mind drew a blank. But then something else grabbed his attention the moment he glanced down.

'Wait a minute, these are not my clothes . . .' he said, fretting to himself and holding his arms out to stare at the over-large pyjamas. 'Where's my clothes, and where's the letter?'

Panic-stricken, he flung himself up from his slouched position and looked all around the room.

'Oh no, my rucksack is missing as well. I've been robbed!' His heart began to race wildly. He freaked out and kicked back the duvet, which exacerbated the headache even further, and he slowly lowered his feet down onto the cold wooden floor. The floorboards creaked under his weight as he slowly rose to his feet.

Out of the blue, footsteps thudded along from behind the bedroom door. Joseph snapped his head around to his left to look. Fear dwelled in his eyes and they began to widen. Then the thudding stopped and a heavy knock sounded upon the wooden door. Joseph flinched and quickly swung his legs back onto the bed, as he wrestled with the duvet and blanket to pull them back over him. He yanked them high up onto his chest and cowered behind them. Anxiously he watched as the handle slowly began to turn and the door opened outwards. As soon as the person came into view, a look of complete astonishment fell upon him. A beautiful young girl with flowing long brown hair and shimmering olive skin, that looked flawless in perfection, emerged holding a grey tray in her hands with her head slightly stooped. The girl carefully made her way up the couple of steps in front and entered into the room. The second she looked up she gave him a warm smile.

'How are you feeling?' she said in a well-spoken, soft tender voice.

Joseph gawped at her. His mouth fell open, along with his eyes that grew wide as saucers. He stared at her blinding smile that could light up the world and blinked several times or so, thinking he was dreaming. Not a single word passed his dry lips, and instead he pulled the blanket up even further so that it covered his mouth with bashfulness. An awkward silence fell between them momentarily. Joseph sensed the girl was slightly abashed herself by the way she tightened her lips and shifted her eyes from side to side.

'O–kay,' she said and raised her eyebrows, 'well, I suppose I'll go first then. My name's Erin – Erin Scott, and you are?'

Still hypnotized by her entrancing smile, Joseph continued to stare. 'Joseph,' he mumbled through the blanket.

'Well, it's nice to meet you . . . err, Jos-eph, did you say?' said Erin and wrinkled her nose. 'Anyway, I hope you're hungry. I've made you some food, well . . . actually my mother has made the homemade soup, it's fresh today. Roasted tomato, but I've cut you some thick warm crusty bread and put some melted butter in the dish for you anyway. Oh, and there's a packet of sea-salted crisps in the other dish as well and a hot chocolate drink. Where would you like me to put it for you?' and smiled through her gleaming white teeth.

Joseph shifted his eyes from left to right timidly and gave a slight shrug of his shoulders. He continued to hold the blanket high up over his mouth as if for protection or something.

'Okay, well I'll just pop it down over there on the chair and you can eat it when you're ready,' Erin said, and proceeded to walk across the front of the bed and carefully placed the tray down. As she straightened up and turned to face him, their eyes locked and she bit her bottom lip. Causally she tucked her straight hair behind her ear and said, 'Well, if there's anything else you need just give me a shout, okay?'

Joseph was lost for words and barely managed a nod in response. His eyes followed her as she walked back past the bed and out through the door. A huge grin spread across his face and he sighed like he had just fallen in love, though he didn't know what that felt like. It was a wonderful feeling nevertheless, and he slowly released the duvet from his sweaty grasp and lowered it down.

'She's beautiful,' he said under his breath. All of a sudden his dreamy thoughts were interrupted by the smell of delicious food wafting around the room which sent his stomach into a hunger frenzy.

He crawled out of the bed to fetch the tray and gingerly

placed it down on the duvet. His mouth watered with delight at the delicious food. Without hesitation he snatched the bread from the side plate and like a wild beast bit a huge chunk out of it. He barely chewed it at all and swallowed it straight down before turning his attention to the bowl of soup. With one fell swoop he picked it up and gulped it down, forgetting all his table manners and dumped the empty bowl down onto the tray. In no time at all, Joseph had devoured everything in sight and felt extremely satisfied with himself by letting out a loud burp. He fell back on the bed, full as an egg, with half-closed eyes as if he were punch drunk. He grinned happily and closed his sleepy eyes and drifted off into a slumber. Suddenly there was a loud knock on the door again. Startled by the sound, Joseph leapt up with fright and knocked the tray clean off the bed and sent it crashing down onto the floor.

Erin briskly entered, smiling, with clothes neatly folded in her arms and said, 'I have your clothes here—' but stopped short to stare at him.

Joseph, who was in a frozen state of shock on all fours on the bed, saw her smile slowly disappear. His eyes followed hers down to the floor to see the tray upside down, along with the cutlery strewn all over the place. Her raised eyebrows caused him to swallow nervously. The second he saw her motion towards the cutlery he frantically scrambled to the edge of the bed and carelessly fell off, and landed onto his back with a bang. 'ARGHH!' he yelled out, bashing his head.

Erin placed the clothes down onto a small chair near to the bathroom door and rushed over and crouched down beside him. 'You okay?' she said, tucking her hair behind her ear.

The pain subsided and Joseph eased open his scrunched eyes to find Erin leaning over him with a cheeky smile. He felt her arm scoop under him along with a sudden rush of blood to his head as he got up and sat back down on the bed. Vigorously he rubbed the back of it while Erin placed everything back onto the tray and moved it out of the way.

'Are you okay?' she asked again, turning to face him.

Abashed, Joseph didn't know where to look. 'Yeah, I think so,' he said, scrunching his face up and tightening his lips. Strangely he still felt her staring at him and looked up to see why.

Erin coughed and moved her eyes to the side. 'Ummm, you have soup around your mouth,' she said.

'Oh,' Joseph replied, blushing, and wiped it away with the back of the pyjama sleeve and smiled awkwardly.

Erin turned away to pick up the clothes and said as she swung back around, 'I've come to give you your clothes back. You were probably wondering where they were, but they're all washed and dried and smelling fresh, courtesy of Mum, here you go,' and held them out to him.

Joseph's face fell. Almost instantly he felt an awful feeling of dread rise inside him and immediately leapt to his feet and aggressively snatched them from her, which caused her to flinch.

'Oh, well, a thank you wouldn't go amiss!' Erin said in a sharp tone.

Joseph ignored her comment and threw the clothing

down onto the bed and began to frantically riffle through the pockets in search of the letter. He grew anxious and felt sick to his stomach at the thought of it being lost or shredded in the wash and started to shake.

'Where is it? Where is it?' he repeated out loud.

'What are you doing?' Erin said in a calm tone.

Joseph became cagey at her question and responded, 'I'm looking for something.'

'Well, I can see that, but what is it you're looking for?' she said.

'Never you mind!' Joseph replied in a sharp tone.

'Huh,' Erin said, raising her eyebrows and pouting. She rested her hands in the back of her jean pockets and brushed her fingers against something. 'Oh, I forgot to give this to you,' she said, pulling out an envelope.

In a shot Joseph turned his head to face her and sighed with relief. 'Where did you get that from?' he said.

'Mum always makes sure she checks the pockets on *all* clothes before she washes them, *especially* as Dad is renowned for leaving stuff in his – here,' said Erin and extended her arm out to him.

Joseph's face turned crimson taking it from her. 'Thanks,' he said with a sheepish smile.

'That's okay, must be something important because for a second there you looked *pret-ty* panicky,' said Erin.

Joseph tapped the letter nervously in the palm of his hand. 'Nah, not really, just a letter from my grandfather, uh, I mean my late grandfather, that's all,' he said, playing it down and shrugged his shoulders.

Erin frowned. 'Oh, I'm sorry to hear that,' she said.

'It's okay, he's been gone a few years now so—' Joseph replied and lowered his eyes.

'Even so, it's still never nice losing someone close to you. What did he die of, if you don't mind my asking?' she said, slightly tilting her head to the side.

Joseph paused briefly to look away and began to have flashbacks of his grandmother and the word 'MURDER' repeating over and over again coming out of her mouth. He took a deep breath as the word got faster and faster until it eventually exploded in his mind. His breath staggered out before turning to look back at Erin with an answer. 'Oh, ummm, he had a heart attack,' he murmured.

'Oh, that is sad,' said Erin, and gently rubbed the side of his arm.

Joseph rubbed the area of his arm where she had rubbed him, pressed his lips together and half smiled. 'Say, you haven't seen my rucksack by any chance, have you?' he asked.

Erin clicked her fingers and darted out of the bedroom into the room next door, and hurried back with it in her hand. 'Here you go, one of the locals fetched it in from outside,' she said cheerfully, handing it to him.

'Thanks, I was beginning to think I'd lost it,' said Joseph.

'How you feeling now, anyway?' said Erin.

'Apart from the lumps all around my head, much better after food. Where am I anyway?' asked Joseph.

'Don't you know? You must have really hit your head hard.

This is The Hundred House Inn!' said Erin.

'Oh,' he said.

'This is one of the world's oldest pubs and has been in our family for five generations. It was handed down to my mum by her father. But business has slowed right down and Mum and Dad are having a tough time at the moment with it. They're thinking about selling up and moving to Scotland where Dad is from originally, but I don't want to go; I'm happy here – it's my home. Plus there's still so much of this wonderful country I want to see and explore, don't you think so?' Erin said.

'Uh-huh,' Joseph replied, nodding just to agree with her while he stared at her mesmerising pearl blue eyes that sparkled, and thought how beautiful they looked.

'So how old are you, Joseph?' Erin asked, tucking her hands in the back of her jeans pockets and resting back on her leg.

Joseph felt the lie already pass through his teeth before he had spoken the words. 'Oh, I'm seventeen this year,' he replied with confidence, hoping to impress her.

'Oh really, funny that, 'cause you look a lot younger,' Erin replied with narrowed eyes.

'Yeah, everyone says that to me,' he said sheepishly. 'What about you, how old are you then?'

'Oh, I'll be eighteen at the end of the year,' said Erin.

'Cool. So how long have I been here, anyway?' Joseph asked.

'You've been out of it for three days—' said Erin.

'WHAT?' Joseph said, shocked, cutting her off. He turned white and felt his colour drain from his face as he expected the answer to be a couple of hours. '*Three days* – you are kidding me, right?'

'I'm afraid not. One of our local drinkers found you outside and brought you in, then Mum called Betty right away and she came to your rescue. Said you were suffering from a bit of hypothermia and we just needed to keep you wrapped up warm. You started to come around this morning, so I thought I'd see if you were awake and bring you some food up this evening. It could be a lot worse, like you could have frostbite, *then* you would have been in serious trouble. You should count yourself lucky to be alive. We get terrible winters up here, plus you could have easily died out there. By the way, what were you doing out there anyway?' Erin said.

Not wanting to tell her the truth, Joseph stooped his head to stare at the floor. 'Oh, I was umm . . .' he said, thinking what he could say, then thought of something else and raised his head and said, 'Who is Betty, anyway?'

'Oh, she's our local vet. Mum called her straight away as there was no way that emergency services would have got out here. She's been in and checked on you on quite a few times, which reminds me,' Erin said and stepped forward quite close to him.

Joseph became unsure of her intentions and nervously leant his head slightly back, when he caught a waft of her wonderful sweet perfume. It was enchanting and alluring and gave him an exhilarating rush of butterflies in his stomach that he'd never felt before. For a split second he thought that she was about to kiss him so he scrunched his eyes shut with anticipation. Then to his unexpected surprise he felt her warm hand press gently against his forehead.

'Yep, your temperature's fine,' said Erin and casually took a step back again.

Joseph opened his eyes to see her smiling at him. His heart was going ten to the dozen. Confusion traipsed through his mind, whether he wanted her to kiss him or was more scared that he wouldn't have known what to do if she did, and he began to rub the back of his neck, abashed.

'Betty asked me to check to make sure you don't get a fever or anything,' she said with a casual shrug.

'Nope, no fever here,' Joseph said and quickly stroked his forehead for reassurance and gave an awkward grin. 'Say, I thought vets deal with animals, anyway?' and gently eased himself down and sat slouched on the edge of the bed.

Erin sat down beside him but held a straight posture. 'Yeah, they do, but she was the closest thing to a doctor around here,' she said calmly.

Joseph bounced a nod then turned to look away and stare into space. His thoughts made him feel anxious and he didn't realize he was rubbing his hands together. For a moment he forgot about Erin sitting beside him until the sound of her voice aroused him from his thoughts and he flinched.

'Are you alright, Joseph?' Erin said with her head cocked to the side.

'Uh?' said Joseph, turning to face her.

'I asked you if you're alright?' Erin asked in a soft tone.

'Yeah, yeah, I'm fine,' he said and leapt to his feet, agitated by his thoughts and then began to look around for a clock. 'What is the time anyway?'

'I think it's about nine,' Erin replied, rising to her feet.

'Really?' he said and gave a yawn and a stretch.

'Okay, well I'm gonna leave you to it, but—' said Erin.

'Wait, that wasn't hinting for you to leave,' Joseph stammered, interrupting her.

'It's okay, I think you should get some rest anyway, but if you feel up to it later you're more than welcome to come downstairs to meet everyone,' said Erin.

Downhearted, Joseph smiled out of the corner of his lip. 'That would be nice,' he said.

'Okay, great. Well, I'll guess I'll leave you to it then,' Erin said and gently tapped the side of her hips and rubbed them with her hands. She strolled towards the bedroom door with a slight sway, proceeded down the steps and gave him a passing smile before she closed the door quietly behind her.

Joseph fell back onto the bed and placed his hands together onto his chest and sighed happily to himself. He stared at the big white ceiling above and a huge grin spread across his face.

'Well, Joey, she's definitely out of your league, that's for sure. Can't believe she works in a pub, you'd think she would be a model or something. Huh, stupid me, thinking she was going to kiss me, not that I would have minded, I just needed a bit more time to prepare if she did, you know, hold her in my arms and look deep into her eyes. AARGHH, what are you talking about, you idiot? She'll never kiss you, so forget about it!' he said, talking to himself and flung himself upright in a huff.

Joseph twisted around and slouched against the headboard and crunched his legs up towards his chest, opened the envelope and began to read the letter again. A lump formed in his throat and a sudden flurry of emotions rolled in on him like a wave as he neared the end. Once he had finished he bowed his head and closed his eyes briefly for a moment before swinging his arm out to the side and placing the letter onto the table.

Down the bed he shuffled himself and curled up into a tight ball and stared into the flame of the lamp. As he lay upon the pillow, thoughts of his mother began to trouble him. It was the longest he had ever been away from home, or from her for that matter. Though in essence it only felt like a couple of hours, still he couldn't get his head around the fact he had been gone for three days. It was worrying, but moreover he felt worried on his mother's behalf, as she did not know where he was. There was no way of contacting her to let her know that he was safe and well, as the house telephone had been cut off for years. Nor did she have a mobile. The situation was causing him a great deal of upset and anxiety, and in turn he felt dispirited and more alone than ever. He tried to seek comfort in his grandfather's kind words, but they were hampered by what he had to say about his mother and grandmother. The thought of losing them both to an evil creature put the fear of God into him and caused a chill to run up his spine. There was also the other problem of what his grandmother had said about his grandfather's death. He felt obliged to find out what happened to him.

By now Joseph felt mentally burnt out by his unsettling thoughts, not to mention the fact that his body was aching and he felt physically drained. He gave a sigh and clenched his lips before whispering quietly to himself: 'I will find the medallion, Granddad, and stop this evil creature, and I will find out what happened to you, for Gran's sake,' and he let his tired eyes gently close and carry him off into a deep sleep.

Chapter 13

CONFESSIONS

Erin slipped her flowing hair behind her ear, picked up the sharp bread knife and sliced the bagel in half and placed it down onto a small plate. Cheerfully she smiled and hummed to herself as she set about preparing breakfast in the kitchen. Over to her right, she saw her mother out of the corner of her eye, washing the pots and pans at the sink. Her mother kept turning her head to look in her direction while she continued to hum happily.

'Well, someone's in a good mood this morning. Have a secret admirer, do we?' said Ariana.

Erin knew her mother could be a bit of a tease when it came to boys and decided to remain tight-lipped. 'No, don't be so silly, I don't know what you're talking about,' she replied and threw her a glance. She tried to contain the smile that slowly grew across her beautiful full lips and continued, 'Is it against the law to be happy?'

'Of course not, my dear, nothing gives me greater pleasure

than to see my beautiful daughter in love,' said Ariana, grinning.

'What, *IN LOVE?* Steady on, Mum I think you're getting the wrong end of the stick here,' Erin said, screwing her face up.

'Oh, really, so . . . who's the breakfast for, because I don't see any customers in yet?' asked Ariana.

Erin paused. 'Well, it's for our staying guest, of course. I thought he might still be hungry, judging by the fact he only came around yesterday and has been out of it for the last three days, so I'm going to take him up something to eat. Just showing our good hospitality at the Hundred House Inn, *that's all*,' she said, placing everything onto the tray.

'*Oh*, well, ain't he the lucky one to have breakfast in bed, huh, I can't remember the last time your father ever did that for me. Well, he's definitely better looking than that ex-boyfriend of yours, I'll say that, what's his name again – the one with the big mole on his face?' said Ariana.

Erin rolled her eyes and huffed. 'Douglas Bottle, Mum,' she said, not amused that her mother had brought his name up once again.

'Oh yes, good old Dougie. Do you still see him at all?' Ariana asked, and looked at her.

'No, thank God. Last I heard he had a new girlfriend so I'm *WAAAY* out of the picture now,' replied Erin with relief.

'Well, from what I've seen of the boy upstairs, he looks more your type anyway, but I'm not so sure if he could handle you?' said Ariana with a wry grin.

'*Excuse* me, I'll have you know I'm just a confident lady and your misinterpretation of me is merely insignificant,' replied Erin, waddling her head.

'Ooh,' said Ariana and raised her eyebrows. 'Well, you look like you could be the lovely couple to me, I can hear it now,' she said, and stopped what she was doing to tilt her head back and close her eyes.

'What are you doing?' Erin said, looking at her baffled.

'Can't you hear it, sshh, listen?' said Ariana.

Erin screwed her face up at her. 'Hear what? There's nothing to hear!' she said, getting annoyed.

'The wedding bells, of course!' said Ariana, and began to laugh out loud.

'Ah, Mum, don't talk rubbish,' Erin said, and threw a piece of sliced tomato at her, which just missed and splashed into the water. 'Anyway, he would have to ask me out on a date first, and who's to say I would accept?' she smirked, raising one eyebrow, and she picked up the tray from the stainless steel worktop and began to walk off.

'Oh, before you go, baby, pop the TV on for us, see if it's working. It's been out the last couple of days because of this weather – thanks, dear,' said Ariana, and then began to sing to herself.

Erin pushed the button on the small television which was fitted to the wall, and promptly left the kitchen. Carefully she balanced the tray as she climbed the steep stairs, turned and swiftly passed all of the guest bedrooms until she finally reached the last door. Conscious of her appearance, she placed the tray down and looked in a small mirror hung upon the wall. She ran her fingers through her hair to shake it up, then gently rubbed her well-defined cheeks, before she lastly gave a wide grin to check her teeth were clean and ran her tongue across the front of them. With a quick smile to herself, she turned back to face the door and gave it a gentle knock and collected the tray.

'Joseph? It's me – Erin, I brought you up some breakfast,' she said brightly.

She waited patiently for a few seconds and decided to knock again. Concerned, she pressed her ear up against the cold door to listen but heard nothing. She motioned for the handle. 'Joseph?' she said, pulling the door towards her, and she poked her head round warily. She entered and looked around suspiciously to see the quilt thrown back and the curtains drawn.

'Where is he?' she said quietly to herself. The sound of running water caught her attention and she looked to the bathroom door to see it was shut. She shrugged and carefully placed the tray down onto the bed and niftily moved around to the other side and tore back the curtains. The morning light flooding in made her feel good about the day ahead and she smiled as she gazed out through the window. Swiftly she collected the other cutlery and was heading for the door when the flickering oil lamp caught her eye.

'Oh, it must be out of oil,' she said to herself and placed the tray down near the door and marched over to it. She turned it off and scooped it up by the handle and swung back around, carelessly knocking a piece of paper to the floor. She leant down to pick it up and went to place it back onto the table again, but hesitated. The bold words written across addressed to Joseph made her curious. She threw a nervous glance to the bathroom door to ensure it was shut and placed the oil lamp back down and sat down quietly on the edge of the bed and began to read the letter. Her heart weighed heavy with sadness reading through and she held her hand to her mouth. Her eyes began to glaze but as she continued on, her feelings quickly changed and her eyes grew large as disbelief came over her. She reached the final part when all of a sudden the bathroom door swung open to her surprise and out sauntered Joseph with his head slightly stooped.

The moment he raised his head he jumped back with fright. 'By God, Erin, you scared the living daylights out of me!' he said, holding his hand to his chest.

Erin instantly leapt to her feet and froze like a statue. She didn't know what to say. She knew she had been rumbled the second she wiped away a single tear that broke away and trickled down her face. Instead she pointed to the breakfast, hoping it would help her situation. 'I've brought you up some breakfast, thought you might be hungry,' she said, and smiled awkwardly.

Joseph looked to the food. 'Thanks,' he said. Then his eyes narrowed. 'Are you okay?' he asked, with his head slightly turned to the side.

Erin nodded unconvincingly and bowed her head with shame and slowly brought her hand from behind her back to reveal the letter.

Joseph lowered his eyes. 'Is that my letter?' he asked.

Erin nodded. 'I'm sorry, Joseph, it fell on the floor and—' she stuttered.

Joseph's face turned red. He marched over and interrupted her by snatching it out of her hand and said in a raised voice, 'What do you think you're doing? That's private.'

Erin flinched. Her lips began to quiver and her eyes began to glaze over again. 'I'm sorry, but—' she said.

'Leave,' Joseph said, pointing to the door.

'But—' said Erin, fighting to find her words.

'Now!' Joseph said.

Erin barged passed him, scooped up the tray and stormed out, hearing the door slam behind her. The floorboards echoed from her heels as she thundered along through the guestrooms. When she reached the landing area she clanged the cutlery tray down onto the sideboard and burst into tears. She covered her face with her one hand and leant against the sideboard with the other and continued to sob for a brief moment. But her surroundings made her consciously aware that someone might see or hear her, especially as the landing area was large and sound travelled easily through the pub, so she quickly wiped her face and blew it dry with her bottom lip. She sucked in a deep breath and blew out to gain her composure. She picked up the tray and headed down the stairs as though nothing had happen. The sound of her parents bickering echoed up the narrow bar area from the kitchen and caught her attention when she reached the last step. Concerned, she peered around the corner to eavesdrop on their conversation and strangely heard them arguing over Joseph. She listened closely.

'I'm telling you, Bas, the police are appealing to the public to know the whereabouts of this woman's son,' Ariana said with her hands placed upon her hips.

'How can yer be so sure, Ariana? Did yer see a picture of the kid?' replied Basil as he leant up against the stainless steel worktop while wiping his hands on a cloth.

'No, I missed it. I had my back turned as I was washing the saucepans, because they certainly won't wash *themselves*,' said Ariana.

'Don't be like that, hon, yer know I can't be in two places at once, in the boiler room and washing dishes, can I, so what else did they say?' asked Basil.

'They gave a description and how long he had been missing,' said Ariana.

'Which was?' replied Basil, swirling his hand around to prompt her.

'A young boy aged fifteen with brown hair, tall, slim build, and has been missing for three days, which matches everything to him upstairs. All I'm saying is, if Erin was missing, wouldn't you want someone to report it to the police to know she was okay? I know I certainly would,' Ariana said and crossed her arms.

'*Okay, okay*, if yer feel that strongly about it, let's contact them. But it might be worth having a chat with him first when Erin's not around, and yer need to be careful what yer say to him, Ariana, as he might take off, and we can't hold him hostage here – it'll look like we kidnapped him otherwise!'

Basil said, raising his eyebrows.

Erin had heard enough and clenched her lips together angrily. 'That bloody little liar,' she muttered quietly to herself. Before she knew it, she had raced back up the stairs and reached the top and dumped the tray back down on the sideboard. She continued to mutter to herself as she stormed back towards Joseph's room and without hesitation gripped the handle and flung the door open and barged in furiously.

Joseph, who was sat on the floor next to the bed with his knees up to his chest and his head rested upon them, became startled and lifted his head sharply. A worried look instantly fell upon him the second he espied Erin's angry face. It reminded him of Bella. 'Erin,' he said nervously and quickly leapt to his feet like a frog. 'Erin, look, I just want to apologize about—' but was instantly cut off by her.

'Too right, you need to apologize – you bloody lied to me!' Erin fumed.

Joseph swallowed. He could see by the look in her eyes that she was extremely rattled and he proceeded to tread carefully. 'What do you mean?' he replied sheepishly.

'I'll tell you what I mean, *you* are only fifteen!' said Erin, pointing to him.

Joseph lowered his eyes and sighed. 'How do you know?' he replied quietly.

'Because right now your face is all over the goddamn TV as a missing person, and the police are out looking for you – that's how I know. Right now my mum is about to phone the police about you,' said Erin and crossed her arms.

Joseph's face fell and he felt his stomach tighten into a knot. 'Oh no,' he said in dismay and sat down on the edge of the bed. He leant over and rested both of his elbows on his legs and held his hands to his head.

'So what else have you lied to me about, then?' said Erin.

'What does it matter to you, anyway?' replied Joseph in a sharp tone.

Erin walked over and crouched down in front of him. She rested her hands on his arms and tilted her head slightly to the side, stared into his eyes and said, 'It matters because I want to help you, but you need to be straight with me. You seem like a nice person, Joseph, but I can't do anything if you don't tell me what's going on.'

'Well, you read the letter, didn't you, so you should know,' Joseph said bitterly.

'Yes, I did, which I am truly sorry for and can't apologize enough, but it doesn't explain what has happened before you ended up here and became a missing person,' said Erin.

Joseph sighed. 'You wouldn't believe me even if I told you,' he said with a shrug of his shoulders and frowned.

'Try me,' replied Erin and half smiled.

Joseph proceeded to tell her everything from the beginning up to the point of where he met Gilbert. He went on to explain how he never believed Gilbert's story about the Black Baron and thought it was a myth, when Erin kindly interrupted him.

'The Black Baron is certainly not a myth,' she said.

Joseph became intrigued by the reassuring sound in her voice and his eyebrows narrowed inwards. 'Oh, and how do you know?' he said.

'Because everyone in the whole village knows the story, and if I've heard it once I've heard it a million times in the pub from all the punters. It's all they ever go on about,' said Erin, rolling her eyes.

'Well, all I've heard are the rumours in school that he was a pirate who stole lots of treasure,' said Joseph.

'Not quite,' said Erin. 'He definitely stole but he was by no means a pirate.'

'Oh, so what was he then?' asked Joseph, curious to know.

'He was a fighter pilot,' replied Erin.

'A fighter pilot?' he said, screwing his face up. 'Well, that doesn't make any sense. How can a fighter pilot be a person who steals treasure?'

Erin briskly walked over and closed the door quietly and then sat down beside him. 'Look, have you ever heard of Philippe Inmans?' she asked.

'Nope, who's he?' Joseph replied, shrugging.

'Well, apparently he was the best French fighter pilot to ever exist who fought during the Great War,' said Erin.

'Great, but what's the history lesson got to do with the Black Baron and stolen treasure?' said Joseph.

'Everything – have you ever heard of Edith Willow as well?' she asked.

'No,' Joseph promptly replied, shaking his head.

'Right, *well*, Edith Willow was supposedly this beautiful slim English woman with a blonde curly bobbed haircut and glistening white skin, who worked as a nurse during the

Great War. It was said that she was the most gorgeous woman any man had ever laid eyes on, with her trademark bright red lipstick that she would kiss every injured soldier on the forehead with. All the soldiers would say that it was a pleasure to be injured just to see her, but there was a dilemma for every soldier who fought for her affection. She was head over heels in love with Philippe Inmans who she had never met.

'Now, like I said, apparently this guy was the best fighter pilot to have ever existed during the Great War and by some miracle, and lucky for them, because the British were allies with the French, their two paths crossed. Anyway, once they saw each other, they fell madly in love, but found the distance between them a burden, seeing each other infrequently which drove them crazy. Then one night Edith was working late when news spread around camp that Philippe had been shot down during combat and been killed. As you can imagine, she was devastated and supposedly had a breakdown over his death and ended up resigning from her job shortly afterwards. After that, no one knew where she went. She just seemed to have disappeared off the face of the earth, and then all the rumours started to circulate that she committed suicide because of Philippe. But here comes the big twist.

'Some years later, a black plane was spotted in the skies flying across the far reaches of the west part of Great Britain that looked similar to that of a war plane, but it suddenly vanished. Then some locals started yapping that they would hear a plane land somewhere in a field, but many times they would trek through in search of it and come away empty-handed. This apparently went on for years, until one day a farmer named Boris Hamblin was out walking his dog named Lady across a field a little further away from his holding than usual, when Lady suddenly darted off into the woods. Boris went chasing after her for quite some time until he found her barking at something on the ground by a huge tree, and when I say huge, I mean the trunk was supposedly bigger than a house! Boris kept calling Lady to heel but she wouldn't listen and continued to bark. In the end he had no choice but to go and fetch her, but as he drew closer, guess what he saw?' asked Erin.

Joseph shrugged. 'I don't know,' he replied.

'A *man* leaning up against the tree,' said Erin.

'A man?' Joseph replied, wrinkling his forehead.

'Yes, a man, but wait. Boris quickly ran over to check to see if he was alive, but it was too late – he was stone cold dead from where his wrists had been cut. But do you know what else Boris noticed?' said Erin.

'Go on,' said Joseph, feeling sceptical about the whole story so far.

'The dead man had a fighter pilot's jacket on!' said Erin, raising her eyebrows.

'Really?' said Joseph, surprised.

'Uh-huh, but listen there's more. Immediately after, the police were called and they came and searched the whole area, and as they searched west of the woods they found a field where they noticed large tyre marks embedded in the ground. They followed the tracks that led up to a large steel gate, and as they passed through they continued to follow them all the way up which led to an overly large barn and a stone cottage to the left of it. The police decided they wanted to see what was in the barn and as soon as they pulled the doors open, do you know what they found?' said Erin.

'I don't know – more dead people?' replied Joseph sarcastically.

'Nope, they found a black fighter plane with small writing on the tail wing saying the *Black Baron!*' Erin said, beaming.

'*No way* – are you serious!?' said Joseph, growing very intrigued.

'Deadly serious, but wait, I haven't finished yet. The police decided they weren't going to take any chances and called for backup so they could search the cottage. When backup arrived they broke through the front door and found it was a complete mess inside, but they were gobsmacked about what else they found,' said Erin.

'What else did they find?' he asked eagerly.

'Tons and tons of valuable items that were worth a *fortune*. Apparently the house was littered with priceless artefacts, expensive vases, famous pictures, gold, diamonds, pearls, all inside there, you name it, but do you know what else they found – loads of pictures of Philippe Inmans and Edith Willow together, dotted all around the house! Turns out they'd weren't dead after all and had been living in the cottage all along, until his body was eventually found by Boris, of course. But the police reckon that Philippe had faked his death and stolen the military plane, and used it to fly across the continent stealing precious items, then returning and landing it in the field close to the woods where he was found, and Edith Willow was helping him. They made so much money that they were able to buy the cottage with all the surrounding land, but not all the items were recovered, and *apparently* the police reckoned that he had hidden some of it in a secret location. But to this day they still don't know where Edith Willow went, as they never found her, and why Philippe took his own life. Over the years many stories have gone through the mill that Philippe killed her because he wanted all the loot for himself or she ran off with another man and he couldn't bear it, taking his own life etc. But regardless of all the stories, one thing remains, and that's that people daren't go walking through those dangerous woods or go to the cottage which belonged to him, as they believe it's haunted,' said Erin.

Joseph felt blown away by the story and turned to stare at the floor and became thoughtful until Erin gave him a nudge.

'So what do you think?' said Erin.

'Yeah, it's definitely a crazy story, that's for sure,' he replied.

'So, c'mon, you still haven't told me how you managed to wind up here,' said Erin.

Joseph hoped she would have forgotten, but continued on with his story. 'So after I found the letter I felt I needed to leave Gran's quickly just in case anything might happen to her, but I got lost driving back and I—' he said and purposely sped up his sentence over the driving part.

'Wait a second, go back to what you just said,' she asked.

'Needed to leave Gran's quickly,' said Joseph, knowing what she was trying to get out of him.

'Yeah, keep going,' said Erin.

'I got lost driving,' Joseph said, wincing, and waited for her reaction.

Erin stood up like a shot and held her hands to her head in shock. 'Oh my God, Joseph, what were you thinking, stealing a car? No wonder the police are searching for you!' she said, and started to pace back and forth.

'Well, that's not technically true. I didn't steal the car because it was my father's, which was given to him by my grandfather as a wedding present, but anyway, my father said that it would be mine one day when I was older,' said Joseph, trying to justify his actions, and he watched her continue to pace like a madman.

Erin stopped and said to him, 'But the police are not going to look at it like that. So let me get this straight, you took your father's car, found a key, drove to your Gran's, and then you got lost on the way back and the car is now – where?'

'Well, that's what I was getting to before you interrupted me. When I got lost I ended up on a road in the middle of nowhere in the pitch black and pelting snow, then something suddenly hit the side of the car and I lost control and crashed into the side of a hedge. When I got out and looked at the car, it was totally *wrecked*. All the side of it was caved in with a huge slice running down the middle like something sharp had cut it open. I didn't know what to do. But then I saw something with huge red eyes staring at me in the blizzard, which I couldn't make out, and it scared the life out of me, so I made a run for it. After that I don't remember much except I woke up here,' Joseph said and shrugged his shoulders.

Erin sighed. 'So is there anything else I should know about?' she said, and placed her hands on her hips.

Joseph felt reluctant to tell her what his grandmother told him about the death of his grandfather, but then thought he'd told her everything else so he might as well. 'There is one small thing,' he said and lowered his head.

'Oh God, I'm not going to like what I'm going to hear, am I?' said Erin, and held her hand to her forehead.

'When you asked me about my grandfather and how he died and I said it was a heart attack, that's not entirely true. Gran reckons he was murdered,' said Joseph, feeling as though the word had left him with a bitter taste in his mouth, and he saw her expression change to that of a woeful look.

'Oh my God, Joseph, that's terrible, how did that happen?' Erin asked.

'I'm not entirely sure. But whatever this medallion is that my grandfather wants me to find, I reckon it will lead me to finding out how he died,' said Joseph. He leant forward to rest his elbows on his legs and drooped his head and sighed heavily.

'So what are you going to do now?' asked Erin.

Joseph thought long and hard about the question before replying. 'I need to find the dagger he mentioned, that's what I need to do,' he said.

'But what about your mother, won't she be worried about you? I know my mother would,' said Erin.

'My mother's an alcoholic. I'm surprised she's noticed I'm

missing,' Joseph replied in a snappy tone. He did not mean to react the way he did.

Erin walked over to the bed and sat down. 'I'm sorry to hear that, Joseph. Looking at it, this probably wasn't the best place you could have stayed in, hey?' she said, and nudged her shoulder into him.

Joseph turned to her with a sombre expression and half smiled through tight lips and stared into her glistening blue eyes and said, 'I don't have a choice, Erin. If I don't find the medallion, my mother and grandmother could be in great danger. I can't let that happen.'

Erin paused and stared at him and then said, 'Well, if that's the case, I'm coming with you.'

'Wait, what! Whoooa, no, no, no, you're certainly not. I'm doing this alone,' Joseph said and shot up to his feet. He marched over to his rucksack, scooped it up and dumped it down onto the bed and began to pack.

'Look, the way I see it, you're gonna need my help,' Erin replied, rising to her feet.

Joseph stopped to look at her blankly. 'Oh, and how do you figure that out one out?' he said.

'Because the police could show up at any time and you need to get out of here fast, and I've got a car and you haven't, so unless you're planning on running everywhere, I can get you to wherever it is you need to go. The way I see it, you have two choices: one, you either let me come with you, or two, I'll run downstairs right now and call the police myself,' said Erin and crossed her arms.

Joseph dropped his head, shook it and sighed. 'Well, looks like I don't have a choice in the matter, do I?' he said and rolled his eyes at her. 'Okay, well, Miss *know it all*, how do you propose we get out of here then without getting caught?'

'Simple,' Erin said and walked across the bedroom and opened a door to the left of the bed. 'Voilà!' she said and swung her arm, inviting him to walk through.

Stunned, Joseph's eyes grew wide. Dubiously he made his way through and looked down an unlit set of stairs and wondered where they led to. 'I didn't know this was here. I thought it was just a cupboard or something. Where does it go?' he asked, leaning over the wooden balustrade, peering down.

'The staircase leads down behind the kitchen and into the restaurant area of the pub. Guests who stay here tend to use it when having breakfast, but otherwise it never gets used,' Erin said and shrugged.

'So what's the plan then?' Joseph said, turning to her.

Erin gave a devilish smirk and said, 'Here's what we're gonna do . . .'

Chapter 14

THE GREAT ESCAPE

The old part of the Hundred House Inn was cold and smelt damp where Joseph was standing on the small, dark landing space. The worn carpet that led down the unlit stairs had been trodden on over numerous years and gave off an unusual old musky smell, which was very unpleasant to say the least. He pulled a face of disgust at the stench, but focused on what he had to do to get out. 'I hope you're right about this, Erin,' he grumbled to himself and swallowed nervously. He took a deep breath to calm his nerves, readjusted his bobble hat and took his first step down.

The steps creaked as he slowly descended. When he reached halfway, arriving onto another landing area, he made a U-turn and continued down. His eyes locked onto the door at the bottom and he started to have doubtful thoughts. *What if she's lying and has really gone off to call the police on me? What if this is all a trap and the police are waiting behind the door?* Thinking more about his negative thoughts than what he was doing, he suddenly missed a step and was sent tumbling down and crashed into the door. 'OWWW!' he cried out, lying helpless in a heap upside down at the bottom.

For a second he couldn't move as he was in too much agony, then he slowly wriggled himself across the tiny floor space and used the bottom step to heave himself up. He leant over, resting both his hands on his knees and gasped for air, feeling the wind knocked out of him. His face strained, turning bright red as he straightened up and winced from the pain. 'AWWW, my back!' he said, holding one hand to the lower part to comfort himself. The shock from the fall took the sting out of the nervousness he had felt, and without thinking he flung the door wide open and hobbled out like an old man and collapsed down onto an old rickety chair to catch his breath.

He gazed around apprehensively at the old-fashioned room filled with old tables and chairs, brass trinkets attached to the wall, shoddy carpet and discoloured netting in the window. For a second it reminded him of home, apart from the distasteful smell that still seemed to linger from the stairwell. He glanced across to the corner of the room to see an opening in the form of an archway and slowly rose to his feet. Hobbling over, he stopped at the foot of it and poked his head around warily. 'There's the window, like Erin said. Let's hope she's outside waiting for me and not the police,' he said dubiously to himself.

Unexpectedly, and to Joseph's surprise, the dining-room door flew open and in marched Ariana. His eyes flashed open to see her and he said under his breath to himself, 'Oh no!' and in a shot scarpered into the next room, headed towards the window and hid around the corner. Pressed up against the wall, he held his breath and felt his heart racing as he listened to Ariana humming to herself and fumbling around in the dining room.

Ariana swung around from where she had placed a large tray of cutlery down onto a side table against the wall, and stopped to look at a chair that was out of place. 'Hmm, strange, no one ate in here yesterday,' she said to herself and then shrugged and shifted the chair back underneath the table. She was heading towards the dining-room door when out of nowhere a clanging sound echoed from the other dining room and stopped her dead in her tracks.

Her head shifted to stare at the archway. Slowly she made her way over to it and peered into the room. 'Hello?' she called, her eyes darting back and forth. She shrugged and went to walk away, when another sound appeared but a lot quieter and nothing like the first noise. Ariana turned back again and with narrowed eyes. 'Erin, Bas?' she called out as she entered the room. She headed towards the window and the moment she turned the corner she stopped suddenly with a surprised look upon her face. 'There's my mop and bucket!' she exclaimed, and scooped up the fallen mop and bucket from the floor. 'That bloody Scottish git telling me it's lost, wait till I see him,' Ariana said to herself, and strolled off with it in her hand.

Outside, next to the exit door, Joseph shivered with his back pressed up against the wall of the building. He sneakily peered through the frosted glass of the door and caught a glimpse of Ariana walking away. He straightened up and blew his hot breath into his hands, rubbed them together and turned the other way to look up the car park. 'Hurry the hell up, Erin, I'm gonna freeze to death out here!' he said to himself through chattering teeth.

Meanwhile, Erin stood in her bedroom in front of her mirror and quickly reapplied her make-up before she turned around and frantically began to search for her car keys and mobile phone. 'Where are you – you stupid thing, ah, there you are!' she said to herself, finding them hidden underneath a pile of clothes on her bed. She threw them into her handbag along with her make-up and darted over to her cupboard and threw open the doors and pulled out her denim jacket. Quickly she slipped it on and flicked out her hair that was tucked behind her ear, and then ran over to the window to check for signs of the police. 'Good, they haven't been called yet,' she said to herself, and spun around and marched to her bedroom door. In a hurry, she flung it open wildly and stormed out onto the landing with her eyes slightly lowered to the floor and walked straight into her father.

'WHHOAAH, steady on, sweetheart, yer almost bowled me over there!' said Basil as he stumbled backwards with his hands held up.

'Oh, sorry, Dad, I didn't see you there,' replied Erin.

'What's the rush anyway?' said Basil, and placed his hand upon his hips.

'Oh, I'm heading into town, I made arrangements to meet

Jess for a coffee and I'm running late,' said Erin.

'Oh, okay, well I won't keep yer a moment, I just wanted to know if yer would work tonight because—' asked Basil.

'Sure thing, whatever, Dad, anything to help out,' Erin said, interrupting him, as she tried to slide past.

'Ah, great hon, thanks, I'll see yer later then,' said Basil, and threw a wave to her.

'Yep, see you later,' Erin said as she rushed down the stairs. She reached the bottom in no time at all and spun quickly to her right and went to lean her weight against the door to push it open, when it unexpectedly flew open and she fell through.

'Hey, steady on, darling, you almost hurt yourself there,' said Ariana, while she held the door with one hand and the mop and bucket in the other.

'Well, you moved the door and I missed it!' replied Erin, and huffed and threw her handbag over her shoulder.

'Where you off to anyway?' asked Ariana.

'Off into town to meet Jess for a coffee and I'm running late,' replied Erin. 'Do you want anything while I'm there?'

'No, I'm fine thanks, hon, just remember – drive carefully. The snow might be melting but the roads are still dangerous to drive on,' said Ariana, raising her eyebrows.

'I will,' replied Erin as she headed towards the front door.

'And say hello to Jess for me,' shouted Ariana.

'Will do,' replied Erin, and slammed the door shut.

Ariana huffed and shook her head before she walked through the side door of the bar. Into the kitchen she strolled and dumped the bucket down and looked across the work surface. 'Damn it, I'm out of cooking oil,' she said to herself, and quickly ran back to chase after Erin. She got outside and turned right into the car park, but Erin's car had already gone. Ariana huffed and turned around to head back inside, when she looked up and suddenly froze. She stared at Erin's car. It had stopped at the other end of the car park and Joseph was opening the passenger door.

Erin unintentionally glanced in her rear-view mirror and then quickly turned her head around to look through her rear window and her eyes widened. 'Oh no, it's my mother, quick, get in, get in!' she screamed at Joseph.

Joseph turned his head and looked Ariana square in the eyes. As she began to run towards him and cry out, he quickly lunged inside the car and slammed the door shut and shouted to Erin: 'Go, Go, Go!'

'NO, NO, NO, ERIN, WAIT, STOP, PLEASE STOP!!' Ariana yelled out at the top of her lungs. As she got closer she suddenly slipped on a patch of black ice and fell straight to the ground.

Erin slammed the gearstick into first, pressed down hard on the accelerator and accidentally wheel-spun the car out of the car park and onto the main road. She glanced out of her window at her mother on her knees waving her arms, but then looked straight ahead and carried on going.

Ariana stumbled to her feet holding her knee and limped back to the main entrance, when out of nowhere a swarm of squawking crows flew overhead. She looked up for a split second and continued towards the doors and burst through, screaming repeatedly for Basil at the top of her voice.

'What the hell's the matter?' Basil said, arriving behind the small bar.

Ariana began to cry and muttered to him, 'It's Erin. She's gone, SHE'S GONE!'

Chapter 15

THE HUNT

Sitting in the passenger seat, white as a ghost, Joseph held his breath and clung for dear life onto the handle above the door like he was on a white-knuckle ride. He felt his heart was beating as fast as Erin was driving as they zoomed down the country road at speed. He threw a quick glance in the wing mirror and saw nobody was behind or even following them and he turned his head slightly to look at Erin. 'I think you need to slow down,' he said in a shaky voice. His stomach shifted and began to rise up in his throat with the sensation that he was going to throw up at any second. 'Erin, stop the car!' he said, panicking, but she remained silent with her eyes firmly fixed on the road ahead.

'ERIN, STOP THE CAR!' Joseph boomed, which caused her to flinch and swerve sharply into a layby ahead and hit the brakes hard. They both jolted forward against their seat belts as the car slid across the gravel for a few feet until it finally came to a halt.

Shaken up, Joseph frantically reached for his seat buckle. The acid was beginning to burn the back of his throat like hot Tabasco sauce and he quickly flung open the door and pounced out. He only managed a couple of steps across the frosted ground when suddenly the vomit came pouring out of his mouth uncontrollably. His face strained and he turned a beetroot colour. The second he stopped vomiting he gasped for air to fill his depleted lungs.

Erin leapt out and ran over to him. 'Are you okay?' she asked, placing her hand on his back to comfort him.

'Get off me!' Joseph yelled, shrugging her off as he straightened up and stumbled back. 'What the hell's wrong with you? You could have got us both killed, driving like that!' he said and wiped his mouth with the sleeve of his coat.

'I'm sorry, I just thought we needed to get away as fast as possible,' Erin replied, and frowned.

Joseph hated spitting, thought it a disgusting habit, but felt he had no choice but to clear his mouth from the awful taste and spat out what remained onto the ground. 'Do you see anyone chasing us?' he asked angrily, pointing his arm in the direction of the road they had just travelled.

'No. I know, and I'm sorry – what more do you want me to say? I got scared as soon as I saw my mum. You know it's not every day I go running off with someone,' Erin replied, and placed her hair behind her ear and folded her arms.

'Well, I didn't ask you to come, remember!' Joseph snapped back thoughtlessly and felt the guilt from his words curl inside of him, but he was too angry to let it show.

'Do you know what, screw you, Joseph, I haven't gotta listen to this crap,' Erin said, and stormed off back to the car.

Joseph clenched his teeth and aggressively kicked the sparse snow on the ground and then placed his hands behind his head and took a couple of consecutive deep breaths to calm himself down. He licked his dry lips as they tingled from the cold and stared across the open field that lay white in front of him. His throat felt on fire and the aftertaste was not the most pleasing to say the least. But that didn't bother him half as much as what he had said to Erin. He sighed with regret and let his thoughts wander off.

In the meantime, Erin climbed inside the car and slammed the door shut. She yelled to herself and propped up her elbow against the door and stared out through the window. The sound of her mobile phone beeping made her jump. She reached down to retrieve it and stared at the screen to see ten missed calls from home. Her thumb hovered over the callback button, when all of a sudden the passenger door flew open and Joseph climbed back in. She turned to him as she discreetly slid her phone down the side of the door compartment.

'Look, before you say anything, I just want to say I'm sorry, I didn't mean what I said, it was just the heat of the moment,' said Joseph and lowered his eyes.

'I'm sorry too. I didn't mean to make you throw up with my crazy driving. Friends?' said Erin, and held her hand out for him to shake.

Joseph shook her hand and said, 'Friends' with a happy smile.

'So how do you feel now?' asked Erin.

'Yeah, okay, but you are one crazy driver, that's for sure,' he replied and raised his eyebrows.

'I know I am, even my driving instructor used to tell me that. He was always going on at me to *SSLLOWW* down, then one day he had a seizure because of my driving and died,' Erin said and bowed her head.

'WHAT! Are you serious? That's terrible,' said Joseph, feeling scared for his own life.

Erin shoved his arm. 'Got you!' she said and burst out laughing.

'Argh, what? That's an awful joke to play. I really did believe you,' said Joseph, grinning.

'My driving instructor isn't dead; if anything he thought I was an amazing driver, but admittedly he did think I drove a little *too* fast. I passed first time and I only had eleven lessons as well! Obviously it helped that my dad used to take me out to practise though,' said Erin.

'I don't think my father would have been best pleased knowing I've trashed his beloved car, that's for sure,' said Joseph.

'So what do we do now?' asked Erin.

Joseph paused before replying, '*Well*, I need to find the dagger, and going on what Gilbert said to me, I've got this feeling that the Black Baron is the answer to finding it, but I don't see how it fits in with the riddle,' he said with a puzzled look.

'Where's the letter?' said Erin.

Joseph raised himself up from the seat and pulled it out from his back pocket. 'Here it is,' he said, holding it up.

'Do you mind if I take a look please?' asked Erin.

'Seeing as you asked this time, no, I don't,' said Joseph, smiling, and handed it to her. Patiently he waited for her to read it and gazed at her intently while she brushed her fingers through her long hair, and he let his pleasant thoughts of her carry him away . . . until Erin suddenly turned her head to him and broke his reverie. He grinned awkwardly and quickly looked out of the window instead.

Erin blew out her cheeks. '*Wow*, that's a lot to be lumbered with all of a sudden, isn't it, guardian boy?' she joked cheekily, and gave him a wry smile.

Joseph rolled his eyes. 'Tell me about it,' he said.

'Magic medallions and daggers, scary creatures, *you* the chosen one, I *mean*, what do you make of it all?' asked Erin.

'Well, it all sounds crazy, that's for sure, but I don't see what my grandfather would gain by making it all up either,' said Joseph.

'Love marks the spot,' Erin muttered to herself.

Joseph started to grow impatient and began to fidget. He started to fiddle around with his bobble hat and then the door handle. He could see she was deep in thought but he wanted answers now or for her to at least have an idea what it could mean. 'Look, we're getting nowhere fast and the longer we sit here trying to figure this out, the more worried I am about my mum's and my gran's safety. I say we go and look for the Black Baron's location.'

'What, you mean go to the cottage?' Erin said, creasing her forehead.

'Yeah. That's exactly what I mean,' replied Joseph firmly.

'*Whoa*, steady on, cowboy, are you serious? Didn't you listen to what I said to you back at the pub? That place is *haunted!*' said Erin.

Joseph could hear the nervousness in her voice, but felt he didn't have time to worry about silly ghosts, as time was ticking and they needed to get a move on. 'Look, how far is it from here?'

'By car, about fifteen minutes or so,' replied Erin.

'And do you know how to get there?' asked Joseph.

'*Yeah, of course*, I've driven past it many times with my parents *and* on my own,' replied Erin, screwing her face up.

'Well, great, what are we waiting for then?' Joseph said, and eagerly pulled the seat belt across the front of him and buckled down.

'You're kidding me, right?' said Erin.

'Do I look like I'm kidding? Look, you said you wanted to help me, so help, and take me there, otherwise just point me in the right direction and I'll walk from here,' said Joseph, staring at her with a serious expression.

Before they could continue their discussion, out of nowhere a crow suddenly came crashing down onto the bonnet of the car. They both jumped out of their skins with sheer fright and swung their heads around aghast to see a crow twist its head to stare at them with its red eyes.

'Oh my God, what the hell is that?' Erin blubbered.

Joseph held his breath in shock for a second before he said, 'Erin, start the car!' in a commanding tone.

Strangely the crow raised its head and began to squawk, and then out of the blue many more crows landed down on top of the car and began to bang on it with their powerful beaks, which together sounded like a rain of bullets being fired at the car from inside.

'START THE CAR NOW!!' Joseph yelled to Erin as he cowered down into the seat.

'I'm trying!' Erin yelled as she repeatedly turned the key over until it eventually started. The wheels spun on the gravel and caused dust clouds to kick up and immediately the crows dispersed and took off into the air.

They raced down the road again, and once more Joseph clung on for dear life. 'Remember, Erin, take it easy. I don't want to be throwing up again,' he said.

'I know, and I'm trying, Joseph, but what the hell are those creepy-looking birds doing?' said Erin.

'I wish I knew; they seem to be following me everywhere I go,' replied Joseph as he nervously swallowed and pressed his head up against the window to stare up at the sky.

'Do you see them anywhere?' Erin said as she quickly glanced across to him.

'No, I think we've lost them,' he replied with relief.

Erin turned to look ahead again, when her eyes suddenly began to grow large at the sight of something large and black in the sky that was fast approaching towards them. Erin screamed as the creature swooped down and faced the car head on.

Startled by the deafening sound of Erin's scream, Joseph swung his head around with utter shock and disbelief. Fear flashed in his eyes at the scary sight of razor-sharp claws pointing towards them and he said, 'Holy—' But before he could finish his sentence, at the last second he felt the car swerve sharply and narrowly miss the creature's claws by inches as it swooped past. The sudden jolt caused the car to snake across the road and then sent it sliding sideways to the right towards an embankment that had a three-foot drop.

Everything moved in slow motion for Joseph as he glanced across to Erin to see her wailing, but weirdly he wasn't able to hear her. He watched helplessly as she whacked her head against the driver's door window, and they both suddenly shifted sideways inside the vehicle from the force of it entering into the ditch. They flipped over time and time again until the car finally came to rest on its roof, nestled in amongst the trees.

Suspended upside-down, held in by his seat belt, Joseph slowly opened his eyelids. He felt enormous head pressure from the instant rush of blood running to it and turned to look across at Erin, to find her in the same position but motionless with her arms and all her hair draped downwards. 'Erin, wake up, WAKE UP!' he yelled, panicking as he struggled to unclip his belt. The second he hit the button he was sent crashing down onto the inside of the roof. Frantically he crawled across and shook her by the shoulders and said, 'ERIN, ERIN, WAKE UP, WAKE UP, PLEASE DON'T DIE! PLEASE DON'T DIE!'

Erin groaned as she gradually came to. She stared at Joseph to see him the other way around and shrieked, 'Joseph, JOSEPH, get me out of here, get me out of here!'

'It's okay, Erin, I got you, I got you, just calm down a minute while I get your seat belt,' said Joseph.

As soon as the button clicked, Erin instantly collapsed down on top of him in a heap. She wrapped her arms around him tightly and began to sob on his chest.

Hesitantly, Joseph nervously cradled her in his arms and could feel his heart beat strongly against her head. 'It's okay, Erin, we're okay,' he said in a soft voice, trying to reassure her while he gently stroked her hair. Strangely his nose began to twitch at a strong odour that wafted inside the car. 'I can smell petrol,' he said worryingly. 'Erin, I can smell petrol, we need to get out of here, we need to get of here now, C'MON!'

Quickly he crawled along to the passenger door and began to yank the handle, but the buckled door was jammed. 'C'mon, goddamn it, open!' Joseph yelled and began to kick it repeatedly as hard as he could. The door finally swung open. 'Quickly, Erin, you first!' He watched her slither along on her stomach like a snake out onto the frozen grass and stumble to her feet. Halfway out himself, he realized he had forgotten his rucksack and slipped back inside to fetch it.

Erin turned around, holding her head, and said, 'Joseph, what are you doing?'

'My rucksack's still in here!' Joseph shouted as he wriggled along to the back of the car.

Erin looked up to see the front of the car slowly starting

to catch fire and she started to scream hysterically. 'JOSEPH, GET OUT! GET OUT! THE CAR'S ON FIRE! THE CAR'S ON FIRE!!'

'Got it!' Joseph said, and quickly crawled back out. He felt Erin grab his arm and swiftly yank him to his feet. They shifted away and stood in amongst the trees from a safe distance to watch the mangled car slowly smouldering. Then suddenly it exploded and burst into flames. Joseph stood and watched, shell-shocked. He couldn't believe what had just happened to them and felt haunted by his grandfather's words in the letter. *This is really happening, something really wants to hurt me,* he thought to himself, and then turned to look at Erin, whose face was streaked from where her mascara had run down it. He watched her tears slowly well up as she stared at the car with a dour expression.

'Are you okay?' Joseph asked with a sorrowful look upon his face.

'Two years it took me to save for that car, two *long* years, now look at it, up in smoke along with my belongings. No, I'm not bloody okay!' said Erin.

Joseph frowned and bowed his head. He couldn't find the words to comfort her and instead slung his rucksack over his shoulders with effort and began to make his way across the frozen grass.

'Where are you going?' Erin yelled to him.

He stopped and turned back to look at her. 'Well, we can't stay here, that evil thing might come back and kill us, plus I still need to find the dagger,' Joseph replied.

'Is that all you care about right now – that stupid dagger? What about my frigging car?' Erin yelled at him.

'Look, I'm sorry about your car, but I didn't do that,' said Joseph with a shrug.

Erin scowled at him. 'That's not the point, you could be a little more sympathetic about it all,' she replied in an angry tone.

Joseph could see the resentment dwell in her eyes and felt it was pointless to stand there any longer than necessary to argue and said, 'I haven't got time for this,' and turned his back on her and headed into the forest along the roadside.

Scrunching up her lips, Erin huffed. She stood for a moment staring at him and then looked around. She shuddered and rubbed the back of her arms, and then motioned to walk in the opposite direction to him and began to mutter to herself as she traipsed through the frozen grass and held her hand to her head.

On edge, Joseph gripped the straps over his shoulders anxiously as he looked around for signs of crows. Out of curiosity he glanced back to see what Erin was doing and wasn't surprised to see her heading in the opposite direction to him. 'Huh, knew she would give up,' he hushed under his breath to himself, and then placed his hands to his mouth to throw his voice in her direction.

'Heading back, are we?' Joseph shouted to her.

Erin stopped with a smirk of satisfaction upon her face, before she swung around and yelled back, 'No, *you* are!'

Joseph's face sank. He looked through the thicket towards

the road and swung his head from side to side and huffed. '*Damn it*, she's bloody *right*,' he said bitterly to himself and clenched his lips hard together. Quickly he turned and jogged along to catch up with her.

'You could have told me I was heading in the wrong direction,' Joseph said, out of breath, as he arrived alongside her.

'*Huh*, you could have been more sympathetic about my car! I loved that car,' Erin shot back at him as she stomped along.

Joseph remained silent. He didn't want any further confrontation with her. It was the longest time he had ever spent with a girl and he was finding it difficult to say or do the right thing, especially to someone as pretty and as confident as she was. Instead he followed along quietly like a little lapdog with his head drooped, and every now and then he glanced up nervously between the treetops for signs of the crows.

Chapter 16

THE BLACK BARON OF INMANS WOODS

Joseph followed closely behind Erin and weaved in and out amongst the trees and branches. The ground was shaded by mighty trees and covered sparsely in wet snow. There was very little wind but the air was bitterly cold. Joseph's nose was bright red. He licked his chapped lips and his eyes drifted skywards with anticipation of the crow's return. 'How much longer till we get there?' he said, throwing his voice ahead to Erin. He waited for her reply but her silence was a clear indication that she was still upset and giving him the cold shoulder. Since they had started walking, Erin had barely said two words to him, which hadn't bothered him up until now, when he saw her for the second time touch the side of her head again and decided to ask.

'Is your head okay?' he asked.

'Not sure,' said Erin.

'Do you want me to take a look at it for you?' Joseph asked, ducking under a branch.

'I'll be fine,' said Erin.

Joseph shrugged at her blunt response before hurdling a fallen tree and continuing for a few more feet when the woodland came to an end. They both stood in the shadows and gazed across a wide open field that inclined slightly and was covered in snow. Joseph turned to Erin to see her clutching her arms around herself to keep warm. He thought about giving her his coat but felt a little embarrassed by its condition, and instead slid off his rucksack and pulled out a light grey hoodie that he had brought with him. 'Here, put this on,' he said.

Erin slipped off her jacket and quickly slung on the hoodie, zipping it all the way up, and placed her jacket back over the top. 'Thanks,' she said and gave half a smile.

Joseph felt a little happier to see her smile, even if it wasn't beaming, and said, 'Don't mention it,' then turned back to look at the field and huffed, 'So where to now?'

Before Erin replied she stared at the field and swivelled her head in the direction of a large opening that was formed between the trees at the very top. 'That's the start of Inmans Woods up there, through that mouth-like opening,' she said, pointing to it.

'Are you sure?' said Joseph dubiously.

'Yeah, I'm sure. You can see it from the roadside just behind the hedging over there. And just across there, somewhere through that opening a path leads to the cottage but I have no idea where. But I still say it's a bad idea,' said Erin and folded her arms and shuddered.

Joseph gazed at the strange opening that did look somewhat

like a huge gaping mouth formed by the trees, before shifting his eyes across to the other side then returning back to Erin, who looked gravely intimidated by the place. He thought it was odd that he didn't share the same feeling as her, and thought it probably had something to do with the fact he felt overly concerned about what could be lurking in the dark sky above them. His eyes scouted back and forth for signs of crows while his worried thoughts preoccupied him. 'Well, there's only one way to find out. C'mon,' he said, and gave her a nudge with his elbow.

They advanced across the unblemished snow, which was surprisingly a lot deeper than Joseph initially expected and covered a lot of ground when he heard Erin call out to him. He stopped to turn around and saw she had halted just a few feet behind with her hands rested upon her hips.

'Are you okay?' Joseph asked, breathing heavily.

'Yeah, I'm fine. Just give me a second to catch my breath,' replied Erin.

Joseph nodded reluctantly. He didn't want to stop; he wanted to keep going because the longer they stood the more exposed he thought they were becoming. He looked around warily and threw a glance behind him at the opening, which only seemed a stone's throw away, and went to utter something to Erin. As he turned back, the sound of crows suddenly appeared out of nowhere. He fixed a startled look at Erin, who said to him, 'Do you hear that?' to which Joseph replied, 'Yeah,' then stared upwards. The echoing sounded near but he couldn't see anything amongst the grim-looking clouds. He whirled around with trepidation and froze in the direction of the road at the bottom of the field. His eyes grew large and fear quickly rose inside him at the sight of an eerie black swarm heading directly towards them. At the same time as he began to back away, he yelled 'RUN, ERIN, RUN!' and turned and bolted.

Erin couldn't keep up and soon fell behind and called out to him, 'Joseph, wait for me, wait for me!'

In no time at all, Joseph reached the opening and ran a few feet inside and stopped. He placed his hands on his hips, gasping, and turned around shocked to find Erin still out in the field. 'Oh no,' he said to himself, and quickly darted back to her. He grabbed her by the hand and pulled her along up the gravel track just in the nick of time as the swarm swooped past and up the field.

Breathless, he placed his hands behind his head and said to Erin, who was hunched over with her hands on her knees, 'That was a close one . . . are you alright?'

'Why didn't you wait for me? I was calling to you!' Erin said, gasping.

'I thought you were right behind me, sorry, Erin,' he replied. The look from her was cold and unfriendly, but quickly changed the moment she straightened up. Joseph saw a look of fear dwell in her eyes and wondered why she was staring at him – but through him – until he swung around and gazed along the gravel track. It was extremely long and very wide, with trees on either side that were tall and uniform all the way up. The evergreens were vibrant in hue and their branches drooped together into the middle, which formed a tunnel effect. It was well shaded from light and barely any snow had touched the ground there. The air didn't feel as cold but the smell of moisture lingered. Joseph thought it was most deceptive from the outside, but he could now see why Erin felt the way she did about the place, as it made him feel quite nervy himself, but he wasn't going to let it show. 'Looks like we got some walking to do,' he said, turning to her, and he jerked his rucksack on his back. Erin seemed oblivious to what he had just said as she kept staring ahead, so he prompted her.

'Erin . . . ?' he said.

'I, I can't go in there, Joseph, I can't,' Erin said, stuttering.

'Erin, I know you're scared, but we have to, we don't have much of a choice. Knowing what's out there, we need to keep going,' said Joseph. Her silence was enough for him to walk over and reassure her by looking her in the eyes and he said, 'Trust me, it'll be fine, I won't let anything happen, okay?' Erin nodded, but Joseph could tell she still had reservations so he held his arm out for her to take a hold whilst he clutched his rucksack with his hands. They walked along the beaten track for quite some time. It appeared to have no end in sight. Joseph grew irritable, and to make matters worse his stomach started to rumble with hunger. He stopped and huffed.

'This is ridiculous, where is it leading to?' he said, flapping his arms. 'We've been walking for ever.'

'I told you, I don't know, I've never been here before,' Erin replied, shrugging, her arms crossed.

Joseph kicked the dirt and a cloud of dust blew up. 'This is a waste of time,' he said, annoyed.

'Look, it has to be around here somewhere; it's not like it was going to be signposted: *This way to the Black Baron's hideout*, was it?' said Erin.

Joseph wasn't impressed with her facetious remark and gave an exasperated sigh, flaring his nostrils. All of a sudden a strong gust of wind blew down the track and almost bowled them completely over. 'What the hell was that?' he said, swinging his head from side to side, expecting to see something.

Erin stared up the track and said, 'Err Joseph, what's that?'

Joseph heard the nervousness in her voice, twisted his head around and then walked a couple of steps ahead to get a better look. His eyes narrowed, but couldn't make out what the peculiar shadow was in the distance. 'I don't know,' he replied in a worrying tone. He turned around and grabbed Erin by the arm and started to walk back the other way, when he saw a dozen or so crows were flying towards them. It stopped them dead.

'Oh no,' Joseph said with a scared look upon his face, and he glanced back over his shoulder at the murky shadow which had now drawn even closer.

'What do we do?' Erin said, turning to Joseph.

Panic-stricken, Joseph looked around and caught sight of a trail that cut through the woodland. 'Here, through there!' he said, and yanked her by the hand.

They scarpered through the forest along the trail, running scared for their lives whilst they brushed against the under-growth, and crossed over a footbridge where a stream had frozen at the edges and was trickling underneath, and continued on a little further until they were met by a steep embankment where huge tree roots grew along the top of the ground. They quickly climbed the roots and reached the top and stopped to gather their breath but were immediately taken aback with surprise. Through the opening of the thicket stood a huge disused wooden water wheel covered in moss and weeds and attached to the side of a dilapidated stone house which was fenced in by a tumbledown stone wall. They both looked at each other, amazed and speechless, before proceeding towards it and climbed over the broken wall.

Joseph strolled along the side and stopped in shock to see practically half the house had crumbled away. All that was left erected was either end, but chiefly the water wheel side. A little sadness fell upon him at the sight of the ruin which was overgrown with weeds and branches and he wondered who might have lived there. Suddenly he heard a distress cry from Erin. A chill ran through him.

'JOSEPH, C'MON, QUICK, C'MON, QUICK!' said Erin.

In a flash Joseph bolted around the other side but saw no sign of her or where she was calling from.

'WHERE ARE YOU?' he yelled at the top of his lungs, fearing something terrible had happened to her.

'Through here!' Erin yelled.

Joseph hopped over the wall and pushed his way through some bushes to find her standing by a dry-stone building in the shape of a hive, smiling like the cat had got the cream.

'God, Erin, you almost gave me a heart attack,' he said, placing his hands upon his knees, relieved that she was okay.

'Never mind that, look!' said Erin.

He straightened up and stared perplexed at the structure with its partially dilapidated roof. Screwing his face up he said, 'What the hell is that?'

'Don't you know?' said Erin.

'No, I don't,' he replied, shrugging.

'Look!' Erin said, pointing.

Joseph followed her fingerline and saw a pig's head made of stone attached to the building just above a small opening.

'It's a pigsty! Erin said.

Joseph turned to Erin speechless at first and then said 'Does this mean—?'

'Uh-huh,' said Erin, wide-eyed, 'I think we may have found the hideout!'

Filled with exhilaration and before he knew it, Joseph sprinted over the wall and crawled through the small hole to get a closer look. 'It's definitely a pigsty, Erin, it stinks in here!' he said, holding his nose.

Erin walked through an opening that had once been gated and then crawled through. 'It's not that bad,' she said, tittering.

'Maybe not for you, you're a country bumpkin and used to it,' said Joseph.

'Ah, poor little city slicker can't handle the bad smell,' Erin said, pouting her lip whilst grabbing his cheek between her finger and thumb and flapping it.

'Get off me,' said Joseph, pushing her hand away and

grinning at her wry sense of humour. 'C'mon, we haven't got time to mess around; we need to find the dagger. Help me look for it.'

'Fine, you search in here, and I'll take a look outside,' said Erin.

'Why do you get to search out there?' Joseph said, frowning.

'Figured the smell would be more up your street,' Erin said with a sardonic smile before ducking back under the opening.

'Huh, the cheek of her,' Joseph said to himself, then sniffed and pulled a disgusted face. He searched all around through every nook and cranny but found nothing and stood scratching his head with frustration. He pulled out the letter to read the riddle again and looked up through the roof's opening and mumbled to himself, '*I live in the sky*' and huffed and shook his head. He climbed back under with a disappointed look upon his face and met Erin outside who looked equally frustrated.

'Anything?' he said.

'Nope, you?' she replied.

'Nothing,' Joseph said, shaking his head and clenching his lips together. 'I don't get it –what are we missing?'

Erin folded her arms and shivered. 'Maybe we need to take a look back at the house?' she said.

'Can do, but I can't see what we're likely to find; the place is a ruin,' Joseph said, and pulled his hood up over his head to keep warm.

'No harm in trying,' Erin said and shrugged.

Joseph followed her down a small slope, which judging by

the fresh footprints in the frozen turf was more than likely the way she had found to the pigsty, and bore right around a group of trees where the ground was flat. As they walked along the level ground for a brief moment, and before they started to go up the incline again, Joseph unintentionally glanced down a track that was overgrown and spotted something at the bottom of the hill amongst the foliage. He did a double-take and then stopped to stare at what it was that almost blended with the trees but was not of the same hue. It appeared a darker tone and larger than the surrounding tree trunks. It aroused his curiosity.

'Hey, Erin,' he called.

Erin stopped, turned and said, 'What's the matter?' and strolled back to him.

'What do you think that is down there?' Joseph said, pointing.

Erin's eyebrows shifted inwards. 'Where?' she said.

'Down there, in amongst the trees,' Joseph said with frustration.

'Well, I don't know what you're looking at, but I can't see anything,' Erin said and shrugged.

'Ah, forget it. Let's just go and take a look to see what it is,' Joseph said, and began to walk down the hill. As soon as they reached the bottom, Joseph thought it was odd, but also wondered why one of the tree trunks had a thick web of ivy roots sprawling all the way up its trunk, whereas none of the others did. But the moment they half circled it, his question was immediately answered when stonework became visible.

'That's not a tree,' Joseph said, shocked.

'No, you're right,' Erin said, staring up. 'It looks like a tower!'

'Why would that be out here in the middle of nowhere?' said Joseph with a puzzled look as he gazed up.

Erin stared at the ground and began to tug at her top lip. 'It all makes perfect sense,' she muttered.

'What does?' Joseph said turning to her.

'If the Baron really did use a plane, then this tower might have been used to help guide him to safety. Which also means—' Erin paused.

'Which means what?' asked Joseph.

'Which also means there's a barn around here, quick – help me find it,' Erin said and started to pull away the branches.

'Remind me again why we're looking for a barn and not the dagger?' Joseph said, feeling confused as he helped shift some of the overgrowth.

'The last part of the riddle said, if I remember rightly, *I live in the sky*. Well, the Baron lived in the sky, metaphorically speaking,' said Erin.

'Oh, I get it, so you think the dagger is in the barn?' said Joseph.

'It could be,' said Erin as she removed a branch. Suddenly a collapsed wooden door was revealed. 'Look, Joseph, I think we've found the barn, but I can't see inside. It's too dark.'

'Hold on,' Joseph said, and quickly pulled out his torch. 'Here.'

Erin took the torch and shone it inside. 'Looks like one of

the sides has completely collapsed,' she said.

'Here, let me take a look,' said Joseph, and he squeezed his way past the door and branches.

'Do you see anything?' asked Erin.

Joseph carefully crept along and shone the torch up to where half of the roof had collapsed down inside. Broken wood was strewn all over and weeds and roots grew up through the ground. He went to turn and yelled to Erin but jumped back with fright. 'God, Erin, don't sneak up on me like that!' he said.

'Sorry,' Erin whispered. 'But I wasn't going to stay outside. This place still gives me the creeps, you know.'

'Well, it doesn't look like there's anything here,' Joseph said, as he swished the light back and forth.

'Wait a minute, shine the torch at the back again,' Erin said.

Joseph swung it back around again.

'There, look, it's a door!' said Erin.

They both climbed under a broken beam and made their way carefully over to it. At the door, Joseph turned the rusted handle but it broke off in his hand.

'*Great*, now how do we get through?' said Erin, pouting.

'Here, stand back,' said Joseph, and raised his foot up high and booted the door as hard as he could.

The door flew open, causing a gush of cold wind to blow past them. Cautiously, Joseph proceeded through, with Erin clutching his arm, and they manoeuvred between piles of broken stones that were scattered on the ground. Joseph glanced around at the unusual circular stone room that they found themselves in. It was covered in snow. It was cold, icy, and filled with a certain amount of daylight, which almost made it feel like they were outside. Joseph shivered. Then he tilted his head upwards and saw the grey sky above.

'We're inside the tower, Erin,' he said to her, surprised. When he didn't get a response he swivelled his head left and right to look for her.

'Joseph, over here, I've found something,' said Erin from behind.

'What is it?' Joseph replied, hopping over a large stone to reach her.

'It's a set of steps,' Erin said, tapping her foot on the bottom step.

Joseph shone the light onto the crumbling stone steps that jutted out from the wall and followed them as they spiralled around. 'Looks like they lead all the way to the top,' he said, staring up. When he turned to face Erin again, panic suddenly overcame him to find she had already started to climb the steps.

'Hey, where are you going?' he called out to her.

'I want to see what's up top,' replied Erin.

'Are you *mad*? It's too dangerous. You can see perfectly from here. There's nothing up there except the sky!' Joseph yelled to her as she went higher.

'That's exactly the point,' said Erin.

For a split second it crossed Joseph's mind to follow her. But his fear of heights stopped him from taking one step further. Instead he watched nervously as she spiralled around and around and rose higher and higher until she was barely visible.

Finally Erin reached the top, tired and out of breath. She grabbed hold of what was barely left of the crumbling wall and side-stepped along carefully on the stone platform. She looked down at the mighty drop below and stared at the light from Joseph's torch shifting around in the dark. 'JOSEPH, I'M UP HERE!' she shouted down.

The faint sound of her voice echoed down the tower and caused Joseph to heave a sigh of relief. He placed his hand to his mouth and yelled back up: 'DO YOU SEE ANYTHING?'

Erin pressed her hand against the wall and went to turn around, when part of it suddenly gave way and fell down inside the tower. 'JOSEPH, LOOK OUT!!' she screamed.

Joseph saw the rocks plummeting towards him and at the last second dived quickly out of the way as they smashed into the ground.

'Oh my God, Joseph, are you okay? SAY SOMETHING?' Erin yelled.

'I'M OKAY, JUST BE MORE CAREFUL, WILL YOU?' he yelled the second he rose to his feet, and he dusted off the snow.

Erin breathed a sigh of relief. 'I WILL. SORRY!' she yelled. Nervously she turned around and the second she did so, her mouth fell wide open. The breath-taking view of the whole of countryside took her by surprise, as it was nothing like she had ever seen before. It made her feel as though she was literally on top of the world. 'Good heavens,' she said to herself. She took a moment to take it all in and watched intently as the sun's rays split through the clouds in the far south. Goose pimples spread across her from the sharp, bitter wind, and sent shivers up her spine. She shook before saying to herself, 'Okay Erin, think, what am I looking for . . . ?'

She gazed around observantly but saw nothing more than the white picturesque countryside. Then out of the corner of her eye she caught sight of a red mark on the inside of the tower wall to her left. Curious, she side-stepped carefully anticlockwise around the platform and stopped as soon as she reached it and crouched down. Her fingertips gently touched the red faded heart that was painted upon the wall and had an arrow pointing up towards the centre of it. 'Why would that be on the wall all the way up here?' she said to herself in a low tone, wrinkling her nose up.

As she rose to her feet she continued to stare at it and slowly raised her head and gazed vacantly at the mist drifting eastwards above the treetops. It parted slightly, and almost immediately her eyes began to widen with amazement at the sight of a tree towering above the rest in the distance. She looked back at the heart and then stared at the tree again and said 'That's it!' Excitement filled her and she turned around and went to shout down to Joseph what she had discovered. But suddenly a swarm of crows came from out of nowhere and attacked her. She screamed and stumbled backwards and screamed as she fell straight over the side.

Joseph heard the harrowing echoes from Erin's scream and

looked up aghast to see a swarm of crows and no sign of Erin. He felt his heart had stopped and yelled at the top of his voice: 'ERINNNN!' Like the wind, he ran back through the barn and out into the open and called her name repeatedly. With his heart in his mouth, he raced through the woods behind the tower and searched frantically for her. All of a sudden, he heard a faint groan coming from the bushes. He raced over and saw her lying flat on her back underneath a pine tree and fell instantly to his knees.

'ERIN, ERIN, ARE YOU OKAY? SPEAK TO ME, SPEAK TO ME!' he said, cradling her in his arms.

Slowly Erin opened her eyes and groaned: 'It's a tree.'

'I know, you just fell through it,' Joseph said in a shaky voice, looking up. Gently he helped her onto her feet and took half a step back. 'Are you okay, are you hurt anywhere?'

'Just a little winded, that's all,' Erin said, bending over and coughing.

'See, I told you it was too dangerous to go up there, but *no*, you wouldn't listen to me, you wouldn't listen, because I'm younger than you,' he said, as he started to pace back and forth while he mumbled to himself.

Erin straightened up and smiled to herself. 'Joseph,' she said.

'What?' he replied, and stopped.

'It's alright, I'm okay, look,' she said, holding her arms out.

Joseph sighed and half smiled. 'So did you see anything up there?'

'That's what I said it was——' Erin said, but paused.

'It was . . . what?' said Joseph, prompting her, when he noticed her bottom lip start to quiver and her face turned ashen. 'Erin, what's wrong?' He turned around to see why she was looking past him and gasped at the sight of an apparition not far away.

Its face was that of a man, and it appeared emaciated. Its clothes hung in rags from its body. And while it swayed unfettered back and forth, causing an uncanny sound, Joseph was clearly convinced that it was staring at them, despite the fact it had no eyes and its eye sockets were black and opaque.

'Oh my God, it's the Bl—' said Erin, but was cut off by Joseph when he placed his hand around her mouth.

'Don't make a sound, just follow me slowly so we can get back to the track,' Joseph whispered in her ear. On tenterhooks himself, he took her by the hand and started to creep backwards when Erin pulled at him.

'Joseph, that's not the way we need to go,' she muttered to him.

Joseph looked at her, puzzled. 'What do you mean?' he said.

'The way we have to go . . . is that way,' Erin said, and nodded in the direction of the ghost of the Black Baron.

Joseph turned to look at the ghost, who evidently was blocking their way, and swallowed.

Chapter 17

EDITH WILLOW

Erin was leaning against a tree with one hand, her other hand pressed against her knee. 'Joseph, wait, wait, I can't run any more,' she panted.

Just a couple of steps ahead, Joseph stopped and jogged back to her. His face was flushed, and he too was panting tremendously as his hot breath collided with the cold air and caused clouds of smoke to cascade from his mouth. 'What are you doing, Erin? We can't stop, we need to keep moving!' he said in a raspy voice.

'I can't, I can't run any more, Joseph,' Erin said breathlessly and slumped down against the tree, resting her head against it.

On edge, Joseph looked around at the dark forest, dreading the ghost's imminent return, and turned to Erin who looked completely drained and was staring at her own shaky hands. 'Are you okay? You're not looking too good,' he said.

'Not sure,' replied Erin.

'You might be in a bit of shock from the fall, judging by the way your hands are shaking like that,' said Joseph.

'I just need to rest for a bit,' said Erin, and held her hands to her chest.

'Okay, two minutes,' Joseph said, dumping himself down beside her. He took off his bobble hat and wiped the beads of sweat from his brow. His hair was damp and limp and steam was rolling off his head like a boiling kettle. He rolled his dry mouth and thought what he'd give for a cold drink right there and then, before licking his chapped lips.

'So what is it we're looking for?' he asked.

'It's a tree,' said Erin, still gathering her breath.

Joseph looked around, stumped. 'A *tree*? But there's millions in here; take your pick,' he said.

'Yeah, you're right, but there's only one Edith Willow tree,' she said.

'I'm not quite sure I understand what you're getting at,' Joseph said, screwing his face up.

'Remember I told you back at the pub about Philippe Inmans and how he was found up against an enormous tree?' she said.

'Uh-huh,' Joseph replied.

'Right, well, that's the tree we're looking for,' said Erin, and relayed to him what she had seen at the top of the tower. 'Here, pass me the letter, and I'll show you.'

Joseph handed it to her.

'Look, the riddle is split into two halves; first, *treasure has a trunk* – trunk also means tree trunk. *I may weep*. A name for a tree is a weeping willow, and Willow also happens to be

Edith's surname. Then the second half is a guide to find the place, how to find me use an eye – the tower is a watchtower to look out from, and lastly *I live in the*—' said Erin.

'Sky!' Joseph exclaimed, finishing her last word and turning to her. 'I get it now. My grandfather wanted me to find the hideout but must have thought he couldn't tell me in his letter, so he told someone he could trust, someone who could nudge me in the right direction, hence why Gilbert told me the story.'

'Exactly, and he must have thought that once you found the pigsty it would be only a matter of time that you would have figured out the rest,' said Erin, smiling.

'But how do we know which way we're heading?' asked Joseph, looking around.

'The tree was located east, which I think is the direction we've been running in,' replied Erin.

Suddenly the silence of the forest was broken by a disturbing rustling sound in the undergrowth. Joseph instantly leapt to his feet and stepped forward, and moved his head from side to side. The unnatural noise grew stronger and became more of a whining sound and swished rapidly in and out of woodland.

'Joseph, what is it, is it the ghost?' Erin asked, leaping to her feet.

'I don't know, but I think we'd better get going,' Joseph replied, feeling his stomach tighten nervously.

The swishing stopped and the noise intensified from behind a tree just a few feet away. Erin grabbed the torch from

Joseph's coat pocket and quickly flashed the light against it and froze.

'Joseph,' she muttered, tugging on his coat.

He snapped his head around in the direction of the light and gasped as the Black Baron floated through the bushes. It stopped momentarily and let out an almighty ear-piercing deathly scream. Before Joseph knew it, Erin had already run off. 'ERIN!' he called, and then he turned back to see the ghost shifting towards him, and he made a break for it.

Joseph ran blindly through the forest after her and stopped briefly and called her name at the top of his voice. Suddenly he heard her scream, which sounded exactly the same as when she fell from the tower, but it seemed to last longer. He made haste in the direction of the noise, fought his way through some branches and glanced through at what appeared to be a clearing. He took one step and fell straight down a steep slope and landed hard onto his back at the bottom. He groaned in agony.

Stunned from the fall, the wind completely knocked out of him, he battled to catch his breath. He tried to roll over onto his side but the pain was unbearable. After an agonizing minute or so, he eventually managed to roll off his rucksack and onto his side, and to his surprise saw the back of Erin just a few feet away. 'Erin!' he called in a raspy voice. But she lay unresponsive. Fearing the worst, he crawled along on his elbows over to her. 'Erin, Erin. Are you okay? Say something!' he gasped, out of breath.

He saw her eyes gradually open and felt relieved. 'Thank

God you're okay, you had me worried there for a second. Are you hurt anywhere?'

Erin tried to move but cried out in pain. 'I don't know, I can feel pain everywhere,' she said, while a tear trickled down the side of her nose and fell off.

'Okay, well don't move for a moment and just rest,' Joseph said, smiling at her, and he held her shoulder.

He looked around and saw a dim glow. It was coming from the torch as it lay amongst the damp leaves on the ground. He crawled over to fetch it, as Erin groaned and eased herself over onto her front.

'Hey, take it easy,' Joseph said with concern.

'I'm okay, just help me up,' said Erin in a strained voice.

Joseph tucked his arms under hers and gently hoisted her up. 'OWWWW!' she cried out.

'Sorry, Erin, where does it hurt?' Joseph asked.

'My ribs,' she said, holding her midriff. 'What about you, though, are you okay?' asked Erin.

'Yeah, I think so, just had the wind knocked out of me, but I'm alright now,' replied Joseph.

The torch flickered in his hand until he gave it a gentle tap in his palm and it stayed permanently on. He shone it around warily, noticing the area was much darker than when they were up at the top of the slope. Slowly Joseph moved the torch beam from his left across to his right but abruptly stopped. At first he thought it was a continuous rock face in front of him with an opening that looked like a huge cave, until he shone it upward and looked with shock.

'Err, Erin,' he said nervously. 'I think you'd better come take a look at this.'

'What is it?' Erin said as she straightened up and slowly staggered over to him. 'Well, what?'

'I'm not sure, but you'd better take a look for yourself,' Joseph said, and handed the torch to her.

Erin followed the light as she shone it upwards and gasped. 'Oh my God, Joseph, it's, it's the tree – we've found it!' she exclaimed.

They both stood speechless, staring at the colossal tree with amazement. They were not able to see to the top of it, nor to see the breadth of it, unless they turned their heads from side to side or stood so far back that they would be virtually climbing back up the steep slope that they had just fallen down.

Joseph looked around the surrounding area and could not believe that even the largest tree that stood nearby was completely dwarfed by it. 'It's no wonder there's not a drop of snow on this ground – what's the chance of anything getting through those massive branches and leaves?' he said, staring upwards.

Unexpectedly he felt Erin thread her cold fingers through his, which gave him a shiver. With his head still cocked back, he turned his eyes to the corner and saw her staring directly ahead. An unexplained excitement and nervousness over-whelmed him, but the fear of rejection weighed upon his mind, knowing he had never been much of a hit with the girls and apprehensively he wrapped his warm hand around hers.

'Joseph,' Erin whispered.

'Uh-huh,' Joseph muttered.

'Can you believe what we have found, I mean, look at it – it's the biggest tree I have ever seen in my entire life and we're standing in front looking like a blade of grass!' Erin said in a low tone.

Joseph went to speak but his throat had suddenly turned dry from nerves and he began to cough as he tried to wet his throat. As he composed himself to talk, Erin pulled away. He watched her leisurely stroll towards the tree and run her hand up and down the bark.

'Come take a look at this, Joseph, it's incredible,' said Erin.

Joseph sighed with disappointment. The warm sense of passion that he had felt faded away instantly, and all that he was left with was an empty feeling. He stepped forward grudgingly. 'It's nothing special,' he said out of spite.

Erin turned to him with a screwed-up face. 'What are you talking about? This tree could be like the eighth wonder of the world! I've never seen anything like it before, have you?' she said.

Joseph gave an apathetic shrug.

'What's gotten into you all of a sudden?' Erin said, narrowing her eyes.

'Nothing, I'm fine. I'm gonna take a walk around it to look for clues,' said Joseph, walking off.

'Okay, just don't be long, will you?' replied Erin.

Joseph searched all around the tree meticulously and arrived back to find Erin gone. Panic erupted inside of him and he spun around shouting, 'ERINNN, WHERE ARE

YOU, ERINN!'

'In here, silly,' Erin said in a dull tone.

Joseph stared into the darkness of the gaping hole in the tree and saw the light bobbing around. 'What the hell are you doing in there?' he said, standing by the opening.

'Looking for clues. Quick, come take a look at this!' said Erin with a sound of thrill in her voice.

Joseph cautiously entered and caught an awful whiff of damp rot that lingered and he held his arm to cover his face. 'Yuck, it stinks in here!' he said, screwing his face up.

'Forget that and take a look at this!' Erin said, and shone the light against the back of the tree.

At first Joseph stared vacantly, when he realized it was a shape of a heart carved into the wood with the letters R I P, E W and underneath the numbers 1935 in the centre of it.

'Love marks the spot,' Joseph said vehemently, turning to Erin, who had a huge grin on her face.

'Or the death of her, that is,' said Erin. 'We must be close.'

'Quick, keep looking,' Joseph said, and ran his hands up and down the sticky bark and worked his way back to the opening. 'There's nothing in here.'

'Was there anything on the outside?' Erin asked, standing on the opposite side.

'Nothing.' He shrugged and walked out into the open.

'Are you sure there was nothing when you walked around?' Erin said, following him out.

'No, nothing, like I said, it's just a great big old, hollow tree,' Joseph said, flapping his arm and looking up at it.

Suddenly the sound of a branch breaking echoed and caused him to snap his head around.

'What was that?' Erin asked, flashing the torch about.

'Not sure,' replied Joseph. 'Quick, get inside the tree.'

Erin grabbed his arm as they both crept backwards. She clenched her teeth together to stop them from rattling. 'Joseph, did you hear that?' she muttered.

'Yeah,' he whispered, feeling his heart racing with fear.

'Joseph, I'm scared,' said Erin.

'Me too,' he replied.

They both stood inside, cowering, a couple of feet away from the opening, staring at the light, when out of nowhere the Black Baron suddenly appeared. It floated at the opening and bellowed a deathly scream before shifting towards them. They both screamed at the top of their lungs with fright and immediately began to backtrack, when the ground strangely creaked beneath them, and all of sudden it gave way and sent them tumbling down a black hole. All the way down they tumbled against the hard surface in the dark until they both landed at the bottom with a bump.

The torch slid out of Erin's hand and across the ground. Quickly she scrambled on her hands and knees to fetch it, when something grabbed a hold of her ankle. She screamed again and began to lash out with her foot until it finally let go of her. With her back pressed up against the wall, Erin swung the torch erratically. The light shone upon Joseph who was rolling on the floor and appeared to be in agony.

'Joseph,' Erin said, scurrying over to him. 'Are you okay?'

she stuttered.

'AWWWWWW, NOO,' Joseph replied.

'What's wrong? Tell me what's wrong, where are you hurt?' she said, holding his shoulder.

'My head, you kicked me in the head,' Joseph said, while he held his face.

'Oh my God, I'm sorry, Joseph, I didn't know it was you who grabbed me. Here, let me take a look,' said Erin, and pulled his hand away from his face. 'Oh, that's not good,' she said, her voice sounding guilty.

'What, what isn't good, how bad is it?' said Joseph, panicking.

'You might end up with a black eye, sorry,' Erin said, clenching her teeth.

'Great, that's all I need. Here, give me that,' said Joseph stroppily. He took the torch from her and staggered to his feet.

'Where are we?' asked Erin.

Joseph shone the light around curiously. 'It looks like we're beneath the tree,' he said, staring with disgust at all the roots and vines growing through the roof and walls, and all the little creatures crawling about.

'I don't know what's worse, being up there or down here,' Erin said, and shuddered.

'I know it feels a lot colder down here,' Joseph said, and shivered. 'C'mon, we'd better find a way out quickly before that thing finds us.'

He flashed the light in the direction of where they had fallen, and then beamed it in the other direction down an eerie, dark, burrowed tunnel that looked no wider than four people abreast and eight feet tall. 'Looks like that's our way out then,' he said, and gulped nervously.

Erin clung to Joseph's arm for dear life as they crept slowly down the tunnel as it gradually descended. She ducked her head repeatedly to avoid all the creepy-crawlies that were scattering along the ceiling and in and out of all the nooks and crannies. Finally they reached the end of the long tunnel and to their surprise were met by a rusted double gate which appeared on the right-hand side of the wall.

'Here, hold this,' Joseph said, passing her the torch. He tugged forcefully at the gate. 'Damn it, it's locked.'

'Didn't you say you had a key?' Erin whispered to him.

He clicked his fingers together. 'Good thinking, Erin,' Joseph said, and unzipped the side pocket of his rucksack. He pulled it out the key, saying, 'Here it is, let's hope this works.' He inserted it into the rusted lock. *CLUNK*, the gate sounded, and gently he pushed it inwards. 'It's open!' he exclaimed, grinning at Erin. She handed him the torch and he proceeded through into a small rectangular area with two huge stone pillars directly in front.

'I don't know about you, Joseph, but this place gives me the creeps,' said Erin.

'I agree,' Joseph replied, feeling his arm starting to go numb where Erin was holding onto him so tightly.

They crept warily between the pillars and stopped dead in their tracks and held their breath. Complete shock and disbelief fell upon them both at the sight of an extraordinary stone tomb situated in the middle of the room.

Erin held her hand to her mouth and hid behind Joseph. 'Oh my good Lord, it's, it's a tomb!' she said, her voice shaky.

Joseph felt nervous and took a careful step back and shone the light over it. 'You could well be right,' he said.

'Do you think it's Edith's?' Erin whispered. Her voice had a hint of excitement to it.

'I'm not sure I wanna know who's inside it,' Joseph said. 'I think it's best we take a look around it first.' He shifted the light, when suddenly and to his astonishment, everything inside the room glittered and sparkled.

'HOLY—' said Joseph.

'Don't you dare,' Erin said, cutting him off.

Stunned, Joseph moved around the side of the tomb, eyeing all the marvellous treasure that littered the room. 'Gilbert was right, it's like Aladdin's Cave in here,' he mumbled whilst he picked up a heavy plate that was pure solid gold.

'Do you know what this means, Joseph? We're rich – we're completely *rich!*' Erin shrieked.

Joseph thought for a moment about what she said and then placed the plate down and sighed. 'No, we're not,' he said, turning to her with a frown.

'What do you mean, we're *not?*' Erin stuttered. 'Joseph, take a look around you, it's ours for the taking. I can buy a new car, my parents can give up the *pub*—'

'If gold and riches is all you're interested in and the only reason why you came along was for your own selfish gain – then go ahead be my guest, take it, take it all and leave!' Joseph said angrily.

'Joseph, why are you being like that?' asked Erin.

'I came here to look for a dagger that will save my family's lives, not look for all of this rubbish!' he said, scowling at her, and then turned around and began to search for the dagger.

Erin stared at the pearl necklace which sparkled in her hand and said, 'You're right, we did come here to find the dagger,' and she threw the jewellery to the ground and began to help him look.

High and low Joseph searched through all of the treasure and precious artefacts and slowly he grew irritable. 'Where the hell is it?' he said out loud in an exasperated voice.

'I'm not having much luck either,' Erin said, holding up a wondrous gold jug that was encrusted with emeralds and she raised her eyebrows.

Joseph stood in the centre of the room and thought for a moment. 'If I were to hide a dagger in a room full of treasure, where would I hide it?' he mumbled to himself. His eyes narrowed as he glanced around and stopped at the tomb.

'I wonder . . .' he said suspiciously under his breath. 'ERIN!'

The booming sound of Joseph's voice caused Erin to jump and drop a china vase which broke into pieces as soon as it hit the ground. 'OOPS!' Erin said, clenching her teeth.

Joseph scowled. 'Come give me a hand please, would you?' he said, and dumped his rucksack on the ground and placed the torch on top, directing the light at the tomb.

'What are you doing?' Erin said, screwing her face up.

'What does it look like – I'm opening the tomb up,' he

replied.

'Well, I can see that, but what the hell for?' she said.

'Because I've looked everywhere for the blessed dagger and the only place I can think of where it might be is in here, now give me a hand, would you?' said Joseph, pressing his hands up against the lid.

'I am so going to hell for this,' said Erin.

They both began to push with all their might, and slowly but surely the heavy stone lid suddenly shifted on the sarcophagus. Red-faced and giddy, Joseph stumbled back gasping and placed his hands on his hips. 'I feel like my lungs are about to explode,' he said, huffing and puffing. 'Here, see what you can find,' he said, scooping the torch up and handing it to her.

Erin shone the torch down inside when suddenly out crawled a large spider. Erin screamed and began to dance around crazily as it crawled down the side and across the floor towards her. 'OH MY GOD, OH MY GOD, GET IT AWAY FROM ME!' she yelled.

Joseph chuckled to himself. 'It's not that scary,' he said, and shooed it away with his foot. 'Here, pass me the torch.' Carefully he peered over the edge of the tomb and shone the light down and gasped.

'What is it, Joseph, what have you found?' asked Erin, and peered over herself, and then turned to Joseph with wide eyes. 'It's her!'

Joseph nodded to her, before he turned to stare down again at the dusty off-white fragile cloth, which looked like it could disintegrate from the slightest breath and carefully was wrapped around the delicate skeleton body. His heart felt heavy with sadness and sorrow, when he suddenly caught a glimpse of something tucked underneath the skeleton's right arm.

'What's that?' he said, bobbing his head back and forth, trying to get a better look underneath the lid.

'Where?' replied Erin.

'On the other side of the body. Here, hold this,' Joseph said, passing her the torch.

'Oh my God, what are you doing?' Erin whispered.

'Going to fetch it,' replied Joseph, and carefully climbed inside.

'This is *so* wrong on so many levels, Joseph. I said I would help you look for the dagger, *not* climb inside of a *tomb!*' Erin said, shining the torch on him.

'You're not, I am!' said Joseph.

'That's not what I meant,' said Erin with a scowl.

Joseph grimaced from the disgusting odour that he could smell as he crawled underneath the lid and began to fumble with his hand underneath the skeleton.

'Hurry up, would you!' said Erin.

'Almost got it!' he said and shifted back over and passed a wooden box through the gap to her, and quickly began to climb out.

Erin had a look of disgust on her face as Joseph leant his weight against her shoulder to hop down and quickly dusted off her shoulder. 'Well, after that, I definitely can say I want to be cremated,' she said. 'Here, finders keepers, as they say,' and passed the slightly weighty box back to him.

Joseph blew the dust off and rubbed it with his hand. A wave of mixed emotions washed all over him as he stared at it with large eyes.

'C'mon, open it, would you?' she said.

Gently he rested his thumb against the pointed clasp in the centre, and with one flip of his thumb it opened. Slowly he lifted the lid back onto its hinges. A stunned look came over him as he stared mesmerized at the most beautifully crafted piece of metal he had ever seen.

'Cor, would you get a load of that!' he said, and held aloft the dagger in his hand with a broad grin.

Erin's mouth fell open. 'Whoa, that's amazing, look at the handle, it looks like it made of gold!' she said.

'It feels really light considering the size of it,' Joseph said, and he watched the light bounce off the blade and dazzle his eyes. He passed Erin the box and carefully ran his finger along a dragon's head that was replicated on both side of the handle and snaked along slightly onto the blade, and continued all the way up to the tip. He carefully touched it, but he still managed to prick his finger. 'OUCH, that's sharp!' he said, shaking his hand, and he placed his finger in his mouth to suck the blood.

Erin giggled. 'That'll teach you never to mess around with knives,' she said, before looking down into the box. She reached in against the red velvet lining and held up something in her hand. 'Look, Joseph, look! It's a scroll of some kind!' she said.

He swiftly placed the dagger back into the box, took the scroll eagerly from her and untied the little bow. Carefully he unravelled it with his fingers and noticed that the paper had a funny feeling to it. His heart began to flutter with excitement as he sat down next to the tomb and cast his eyes over the opening line.

'What does it say?' asked Erin, sitting down beside him.

'*Dear Joseph . . .*' he read.

Chapter 18

THE DRAIGAR DAGGER

Dear Joseph,

Nothing would give me greater pleasure than to know that you are safe and well and reading this letter, but moreover I want to say how proud I am of you for making it this far. To think that you were able to solve my riddle is a great achievement, as not many could have done what you did. You clearly have your grandfather's blood in you.

So where are we? Well, I am thrilled and honoured to say: welcome to Edith Willow's Chamber! I assume that you already know the great mysteries and stories of Edith Willow and the Black Baron (and no doubt Gilbert will have informed you), so suffice to say I will not go into great detail about them, but what I will say is this. However Edith Willow died, one thing is for certain: she was very much loved by Philippe Inmans and he was deeply torn by her loss (which we both can relate to). Why do I say that? Because why else would someone go to such great lengths to build such a remarkable tomb for her.

Normally royalty are found in these types of places and not ordinary folk like you and me (but you are an exception to the rule, of course).

I'm sure you're wondering what role the dagger plays in all of this, and why it is so important that you have traipsed across the country to find it? Well, the dagger that you now have in your possession is called the Draigar.

I can confirm that it was stolen by the Black Baron for selfish purposes from the British Museum during the period of his purloining campaign, and I only gained knowledge of this when I paid a visit to the British Museum. I described to the tour guide what I was looking for and they then kindly pointed me in the direction of the medieval room. As I stood there gazing at the dagger in the glass cabinet, I had a peculiar feeling something wasn't quite right. At that moment an old and slightly overweight security guard who was passing by on his patrol came up to me and told me how it was his favourite one in the whole of the museum, but it was such a shame it wasn't, in his words 'the real McCoy!'

As you can imagine, I was extremely interested to know what he meant by this, so I kindly prompted him (along with the help of a few Jelly Babies, of course) to find out more and it turned out it was the Black Baron who stole it along with other items. He said that the museum was very embarrassed and didn't want people to know that it was a replica on display, and they frowned upon people spreading the word and he could lose his job for telling. I told him that his secret was safe with me and gave him the rest of the bag of sweets to *keep him happy.*

From thereon I made it my mission to find the Draigar, and knowing the legend and the location of Inmans Woods, I set about searching the area. After a few days of hard hunting, and a few run-ins with the Black Baron ghost, I was finally able to locate it. In my professional opinion as an archaeologist I believe that when Edith Willow passed away, Philippe might have thought from a religious point of view that by burying this magnificent dagger with her, he would thus help her pass over safely into an afterlife.

So what is the importance of the dagger? Well, for starters, like the Dragon's Head Medallion it's not of this world, and its former owner was Quindella – the white spirit lady – but now you are its master. I believe there to be a mysterious connection between the dagger and the medallion (something which I felt when I handled it) and judging by the way it has been incredibly smelted it would therefore become highly attractive and valuable to many on the black market, hence the reason for keeping it hidden inside the tomb. But as I stated previously, the most important thing is it will help keep you protected from the evil creature that you might have already encountered?

Remember, Joseph, everything that you are doing is shaping you and preparing you for what you shall become. I will explain everything openly once you locate the Dragon's Head Medallion, but for now I leave you with this:

nec vero vivus nec mortuus usque relinquor;

nil mihi amoris inest, deficit atque dolor.
desunt et foliae, quas quis lacerare soleret;
solus nunc adsto mirificusque viris,
frigidus atque cavus, quibus hic nulla ignis adurit.
aetatemque meam discere non potis est.
me ut regem in solio celebrant proavique patresque:
mirabundus ero semper in ore virum

Be careful, Joseph, and let God be with thee.
Love
Granddad X

~

'P.S. *If you look through the hole, what do you see?'* Joseph finished. His face drew a blank, staring at the scroll in his hand. 'Well, I can safely say I can't speak any other languages apart from English, so I don't have the foggiest of what that says – do you?' he said, turning to Erin.

She moved her head in closer and narrowed her eyes. 'Nope, me neither, but it definitely looks like it could be Italian or even Latin,' she said, turning to him.

They suddenly heard a loud scraping noise behind them and simultaneously they both peered over the tomb. Erin shone the light between the pillars in the direction of the gate.

'Joseph,' she whispered.

Joseph felt a lump form in his throat. 'What?' he muttered out of the corner of his mouth.

'I think we should go,' said Erin.

'Good idea, hold on a second while I get my rucksack,' he said, and quickly rolled the scroll up and placed it back inside the box and crawled along the floor to his rucksack.

The noise drew closer. Erin rose to her feet and began to edge back. 'Joseph, what are you doing? We need to go now!' she said.

'Okay, okay, I'm almost done, okay, let's go!' he said and leapt to his feet.

They both clung to each other and crept backwards nervously past two other stone pillars behind them. The light from the torch ricocheted off the gleaming treasure. Before they knew it, they had their backs pressed up against a cold wall.

Joseph spun around and frantically began to search all over for a way out. 'Damn, we're trapped!' he said.

'There's gotta be another way, there has to be!' she said.

All of a sudden, a cold draught blew upon the side of Erin's cheek. She swung the light to the left and in the corner was a dark shadow where part of the wall seemed to be missing.

'Joseph, this way, I think I've found something,' she said, tugging on his arm. The cold draught grew stronger as she shuffled sideways along the wall.

'Is it a way out?' asked Joseph eagerly.

'Looks like it,' Erin replied, stooping her head down and shining the light up the extremely long and narrow passage-way that looked barely wide enough for them to fit through. 'But I can't say—' she continued, then stopped herself short the moment she swung back around, and she froze like a statue.

The terrified look upon her face caused Joseph to turn his head in the direction of the light which she had cast on the other side and he stared aghast. Between the two pillars on the other side of the chamber, the Black Baron floated back and forth eerily. 'RUN, ERIN, RUN!' he yelled, and pushed her through the hole, followed by the ghost screaming and quickly shifting over the tomb.

Up and up and up the inclining narrow passageway they both scrambled, scraping their shoulders against the walls. As they drew nearer to the top, a shred of light beamed down in their direction giving a glimmer of hope that they could escape.

'It's a way out, Joseph, it's a way out!' said Erin.

'Keep moving, just keep *moving!*' Joseph said, panicking as he glanced back over his shoulder.

They reached the opening, only to find to their dismay that it was blocked by thick heavy roots that grew down like bars on a cell.

'Hold this,' Erin said, passing back the torch.

Joseph watched helplessly as she began to claw and fight her way through and turned sideways on and shone the torch back down the passageway. The ghost lay at the bottom and bellowed out another horrifying scream, sending fearful shivers up and down his spine as it slowly headed up towards him.

'C'MON, C'MON, THAT THING'S COMING!' he yelled at her through chattering teeth.

'I'M TRYING, I'M TRYING!' Erin said. She looked close to tears, when she broke off one of the vines and squeezed herself through the small opening. 'Quick, pass me the torch and your rucksack.'

'Here, take it, take it! Joseph said, trembling as he pushed it through the opening.

Erin shone the torch back through the roots and down the passageway. The ghost was closing in. Erin grabbed Joseph's arm as he tried to squeeze through and began to scream at him. 'C'mon, that thing's behind you, it's behind you!'

Joseph clawed at the ground and just as he was about to pull his last leg through, he felt a sudden jolt and he was being dragged backwards. He spun his head around and his eyes flashed with terror to see the ghost holding onto him.

'HELP ME, ERIN, HELP ME!' he screamed out.

Erin wrapped her arms quickly around Joseph's body and began to heave, when his leg suddenly broke free and she fell backwards onto the ground.

Joseph stared at the ghost who was reaching out wildly with its arm to grab him again. He turned to Erin and yelled, 'RUN, ERIN, RUN!' as he stumbled to his feet. She scooped up the torch and rucksack and darted off through the woods. The moment Joseph got into his stride, his foot snagged on one of the roots poking up and he tripped and fell straight back down again and landed with a thud. He raised his head from the dirt and looked into the forest with despair to see Erin had disappeared, and nervously he turned his head around and watched the Black Baron rise up through the roots. Joseph lay helpless and petrified on the ground as the ghost floated towards him.

He was doomed.

Chapter 19

ENTER THE CROWMAN

With his heart in his mouth, Joseph glanced back over his shoulder fearfully as he desperately fought his way through the branches. He was extremely lucky to have escaped. But he knew the ghost was hot on his heels, as the repeated echoes from its horrendous screaming sounded too close for comfort. In the midst of his own panic, as he ran for his life, he was also concerned for someone else's safety – Erin seemed to have just vanished into thin air.

'ERIN, WHERE ARE YOU? ERINNN!' his voice strained, shouting loudly to her. Razor-sharp thorns snagged at his coat and held him back as he frantically pushed his way through. The woodland suddenly descended. His legs gave way to the soft ground and down he tumbled, out of control, rolling over and over. When the forest came to an abrupt end at a four-foot drop of the embankment, he rolled onto a wet, slippery road.

Joseph lay on his back, out of breath and gasping for air.

He stared at the murky sky, only to see a multitude of crows circling high above. It was clear the danger was far from over. Swiftly he rolled over onto his front, dazed and disorientated, and glanced up the road. The second he did so, his eyes flashed with fright at the sight of a speeding car heading towards him. Rendered helpless and without any time to move, Joseph placed his hands upon his head and scrunched himself into a foetal position, bracing himself for his fate.

~

A bald-headed, middle-aged man was whistling along to his music inside the car without a care in the world, when at the last second he noticed a figure lying in the road. Immediately, he slammed on the brakes as hard as he could. The wheels screeched as they locked up. In the nick of time, he swerved the car around the person. The man clung to the steering wheel for dear life as the car drifted sideways on the icy road. Finally the car came to a halt in the middle of the road to his overwhelming relief. Struggling to catch his breath, the man huffed and puffed erratically as though he was about to have a panic attack, and nervously readjusted his round, thick-framed glasses before he sounded his horn angrily at the person.

Joseph flinched at the loud, startling noise. He looked up quivering and saw tyre marks embedded into the road; the car had swerved around him only a few feet away, and the smell of burnt rubber grated by the tarmac lingered over him. 'I'm alive!' he said to himself, shocked, as he touched his body in disbelief and felt as though he had cheated death by a whisker. Without hesitation, he leapt to his feet and swiftly darted across the road to the other side and onto the pavement. Like a gazelle he ran as fast as his feet would carry him towards a rather old, tall and slim, black and white house. As he glanced back over his shoulder, to his dismay he saw the ghost floating in amongst the trees.

The driver of the car stepped out of his vehicle as Joseph was running past and yelled, 'Oi, you get back here!' while fisting the air in a furious manner, and then turned to puff on his inhaler.

Undeterred, Joseph kept up his pace and didn't waste a second of his time to acknowledge or even look back at the man. He was chiefly concerned about the crows, as more and more gathered in the sky. Just beyond the old house, which had a distinctive Tudor design – half-timbered in black upon its white structure – a descending road emerged. The road appeared to run alongside a stone viaduct but then disappeared underneath it. Joseph caught sight of it and sprinted down the hill to the bottom, where it bore sharply to the right and stopped under the viaduct's arch.

There were two stones bridges: the first passed above Joseph's head, was partially built high upon the embankment and towered fifteen feet or so high, with six huge stone arches, and was used as a railway line. The other bridge, which he was standing upon, passed beneath the railway line through one of the arches, stood a staggering twenty feet high with four arches, and stretched across an open treacherous river that lay deep down within the valley.

Joseph's breathing was erratic, more out of intense fear than exertion. He cradled his throbbing elbow with his hand, where he had hurt it from falling onto the road, and crept forward slowly. He nervously poked his head out and peered up. The mass of angry crows now crowding the sky caused it to appear sinisterly dark. Unnerved, he quickly ducked back under the bridge to hide.

Razor-sharp icicles hung dangerously like knives underneath the bridge, waiting to snap off at the slightest vibration or noise and plummet to the ground and spear him. The floor was wet with melted snow which dripped from the outcrop behind him, creating slush piles all around. The cold, sharp wind from the vast open river whistled through under the arch and whipped against his face, sending shivers up and down his spine.

Though hidden from sight, Joseph still felt vulnerable. He listened on tenterhooks to the crows' repeated squawking. As he eased his hand away from his aching elbow and winced, he saw a red stain had formed in his hand and he raised his arm to look. A small amount of blood had soaked through his coat, but that was the least of his worries. He began to pace back and forth anxiously and bite his nails. 'What am I going to do? What am I going to do?' he muttered. 'Erin's missing with my rucksack, these bloody crows are hounding me, I've got no dagger to protect me – this is great, this is just bloody great! Where are you, Erin? Where the hell are you?'

For a brief moment he stopped pacing and cupped his

cold hands. He blew his warm breath onto them and rubbed them firmly together. His body temperature was starting to drop and he felt cold now. The chill was seeping into his feet, making them ache, so he shifted them up and down to keep warm. He gazed across the stone bridge and decided he had had enough. It was time to come out of hiding and cross over to find somewhere safe to hide out of the cold. Once again he walked nervously to the edge of the arch and poked his head out. To his utter surprise he saw not a single crow in the sky. 'They've gone!' he exclaimed.

Though he remained doubtful, Joseph quickly searched the floor and found a broken branch in the corner. He swiftly moved to pick it up. He moved forward, still keeping within the shadows, and threw the branch as far as possible out onto the bridge. He stepped back and waited.

'Okay, Joseph, looks like the coast is clear,' he muttered unconvincingly to himself. 'Find Erin, find somewhere safe . . .'

He thumped his clenched fist against his forehead in a bid to psyche himself up and regain some confidence, then closed his eyes and took a couple of deep breaths and prayed Erin had made it out of the woods safely. He began a countdown.

'Okay, Joey, on three: one, two – THREE!'

He burst out from underneath the arch like a rocket. As he broke into his seventh and eighth stride, the crows locked eyes upon him and swooped down like an attacking plane. They dived under the bridge and back up again. Before Joseph knew what was happening, the crows had created a huge flying circle formation around him, squawking aggressively. Louder and louder the sound grew as they flew through each one of the arches, around and around like a huge cyclone turned sideways that was about to devour him.

When Joseph was over halfway across the bridge, the crows suddenly shifted direction and shot up high into the sky. Joseph wasn't fully aware of what was happening as his focus was on making it across to the other side in one piece. Three quarters of the way across, and so close to him reaching safety, the crows all of a sudden descended at great speed and did something unimaginable right in front of Joseph's eyes. The crows incredibly morphed into one figure and landed at the very end of the stone bridge and blocked his path.

Joseph tried to stop himself from running, but at the pace he was shifting he was unable to, and he slipped and landed hard on his back. He froze in a state of shock at the sight of what the crows had created. An unearthly, creepy figure, covered in jet-black feathers with a deep purple sheen finish was curled up in a ball, began to reveal itself. Paralysed on the floor, Joseph looked aghast at the immense, terrifying creature ascending in front of him. The half-human, half-crow-like creature began to stand erect, a staggering eight feet tall, with its black muscular body frame covered in feathers lined all down its back, arms, shoulders, neck and head. Its human-like muscular thighs were attached to the bottom part of a crow's legs with four razor-sharp claws on each, and its muscular arms had long finger claws. It was nothing like Joseph had ever seen before in his entire life. To make matters worse, the half-human beaked face with red eyes, gave off the loudest squawk imaginable. It sounded more like a roar from a Tyrannosaurus rex, as it slowly stomped towards him.

'Give it to me,' the creature squawked in a harrowing, deathly voice.

Terrified, Joseph still couldn't move; it felt like his whole body had been welded to the floor even as the creature approached. His face was white as chalk. His eyes were wide open and shining with fear. All of a sudden, he felt one of his trembling arms free up and eventually he began to clamber backwards on his hands and feet, but he was going nowhere fast. His feet continually slipped on the icy floor.

'Get away from me!' Joseph said in a panic-stricken voice.

'Give me the medallion,' said the Crowman, and sounded off another thundering squawk, as it slowly gathered speed.

Joseph lurched over onto his front and made a desperate attempt to get up onto his feet to make a run for it, but as he did so he suddenly felt the creature grab hold of his leg and pin him to the floor.

'AARRGGHH! LET GO OF ME, AARRGGHHHHH-HH!' he screamed out.

The pain was excruciating, unbearable, and nothing like he had ever experienced before in his life. It felt like the creature was about to tear his leg completely off with its squeezing grip. The Crowman pushed its broad chest out and extended its powerful arms out to the side along with its wings. It raised its head towards the sky and squawked repeatedly in victory at capturing him like prey. Joseph continued to scream. Any second now, he thought, he was going to die and be mauled to death and there was nothing he could do to save himself. But to his astonishment, he heard a voice in the distance.

'HEY, BUZZARD FACE!' the person yelled from the shadows of the archway of the railway bridge. Out of nowhere, Erin stepped forward with her body unusually turned sideways. She firmly held Joseph's Black Widow slingshot in her grasp, loaded with a ball bearing and took aim at the creature. 'Get off my friend. NOW!'

The distraction put a stop to the Crowman's triumphant squawk. It stared straight ahead with its glowing red eyes and chattered its beak together.

Erin slowed her breathing to steady her hand as she pulled back on the rubber band with one eye closed. Before the creature could react, she fired off a shot. *WHIIPP* came the sound of the rubber as it released the ball bearing. It cut through the air creating a zipping sound and struck the creature smack on the beak.

'KRRAAAAGGG KKKRRAAAGGG!' the Crowman sounded off. It stumbled back, stunned, and momentarily released Joseph's leg from its grip.

'RUN, JOSEPH, RUN!' Erin screamed at him at the top of voice.

Joseph tried to weave in and out of the Crowman on the ground. It was dazed and screeching. It hopped up and down and flapped its wings in and out, lashing out uncontrollably. Joseph managed to crawl behind the Crowman towards the other side of the bridge and limped to his feet using the right-hand side of the stone wall to aid him. As he was about to make a break for it, he was suddenly struck by the Crowman's wing, which whacked him straight over the side of the stone bridge.

'NOOOOOOO!' Erin yelled. Unconcerned for her own life and fuelled with anger, she ran closer to the creature which had now stopped squawking and looked focused on killing her. Her hand was shaking as she tried to fetch another ball bearing from out of her pocket. She quickly reloaded, aimed, and fired off another shot but completely missed as she watched the creature soar high into the air at speed. It spread its wings before landing thunderously down again on the bridge with a crack only a couple of feet away from her. The bridge shook. Petrified, she staggered back and frantically tried to retrieve another ball bearing from her pocket. Carelessly she tugged too hard and accidentally spilled them all onto the floor.

'OH MY GOD, OH MY GOD, OH MY GOD!' Erin shrieked as she scrambled to her hands and knees, squirming on the floor as she tried to gather up some of the ball bearings. She flinched with fright as she listened to the creature bellow out a thunderous squawk, and glanced around to see it heading towards her. Erin quickly reached out and with her fingertips just managed to grab one of them from the ground. With death only a few steps away, she flung herself onto her back and reloaded the Black Widow.

The Crowman shifted quickly and was now upon her. With the intention of killing, it raised its powerful arm and went to swipe her with its razor-sharp claws. Erin leant against the rucksack, pulled back hard on the rubber band and fired. The ball bearing whizzed out of the slingshot like a cannonball. Suddenly the creature dispersed into hundreds of crows and broke away into the sky, but the ball bearing struck one of the crows and knocked it clean to the ground.

Shaken, Erin quickly leapt to her feet and without a moment to spare started to run across the bridge, but she was stopped by the sound of the injured crow lying on the ground. She walked over and stared into its glaring red eyes. She welled up with anger. She clenched her teeth together and raised her foot up high and slammed it down hard on the crow. 'That's for Joseph,' she whimpered.

The dead crow's eyes turned black and then to charcoal like the rest of it. Suddenly it disintegrated into a pile of ash beneath her foot. Erin stepped back, shocked, and watched the wind mysteriously carry the ashes away. She turned and continued to run down to the end of the bridge, screaming Joseph's name. Leaning over the side of the wall, she looked down and saw a canal below with a footpath to the right of it, which separated it from the river. The canal's waters were black and ran underneath the last arch of the bridge where she was standing, but she saw no sign of Joseph.

'JOSEPH, JOSEPH!' she cried out repeatedly.

With tears rolling down her face, she looked further up the canal and saw a metal pedestrian bridge that stretched out from the embankment high up on the left which crossed over the small canal. It had metal steps which faced her that led down to the bottom, connecting to the footpath. Erin ran like the wind from off the stone bridge and up the steep hill to the right. She reached an opening of the side wall where old stone steps led down to the metal bridge. Without delay, she paced down the steps and onto the metal bridge, crossed over and down the metal steps onto the footpath. She darted down the path and to her relief saw Joseph curled up in a tight ball on the floor, shivering underneath the stone arch.

'Oh my God, Joseph, you're alive, you're alive!' Erin said, falling to her knees. She dropped the slingshot out of her hand. It bounced along the path and into the canal water. She pulled him close to cradle him.

'I thought I'd lost you. Are you okay? Say something!' she said, whimpering.

'C–c–cold,' Joseph stammered.

'How did you manage to get out?' asked Erin.

'C–c–climbed out,' Joseph said, continuing to stutter.

'C'mon, we need to get you somewhere safe and out of those wet clothes fast before you catch your death of cold,' Erin said, holding him tightly as he shook in her arms. 'Can you stand up?'

Erin didn't bother to wait for him to reply. She reached under his arm and hoisted him up as he staggered helplessly to his feet, and she held her other arm around his wet waist. Slowly she walked him up the footpath towards the metal bridge and they steadily climbed the metal steps one by one until they reached the top. Carefully they crossed the pedestrian bridge when he suddenly stopped her.

Joseph turned his head to stare at the stone bridge, then

at the footpath. He was still shaking uncontrollably. 'A couple of metres the other way and I would have been dead!' he stammered through his chattering teeth.

'But you're not, and that's all that matters,' Erin quickly replied, trying to reassure him.

Joseph turned to face her, when unexpectedly he felt her warm lips press against his frozen lips for a split second. A shocked look came over him, followed by a hot flush, which did very little to relieve the coldness and shivering he was feeling but certainly boosted his morale momentarily. He smiled and rested his wet forehead against hers for comfort. The moment his eyelids closed, the Crowman suddenly flashed before him and caused him to gasp. He quickly pulled away and began to shake again.

'What is it, Joseph? Tell me!' Erin said, reaching out to him.

'I'm . . . I'm just freezing, that's all,' Joseph replied.

'C'mon, let's get away from here and find somewhere safe and warm to hide,' Erin said, wrapping her arm around him as they continued their walk across the bridge. 'Hey, where's your bobble hat gone, anyway?'

'Not sure,' Joseph replied, touching his wet head, and he threw a glance at the canal.

'Well, if it's any consolation, you look better without it,' said Erin, smiling.

As they reached the old stone steps, they stopped and turned their heads to glance back at the bridge one last time, and a look of anguish filled their eyes before they made their ascent and sought refuge.

Chapter 20

A PRIEST IS A CORVUS FEAST

Like foxes being hunted, Joseph and Erin scarpered across a vast open field which steeply inclined. The snow was crisp white and unblemished. To add to their problems, the weather had quickly changed and fine sleet had now started to fall again. The day was drawing on and the wind began to pick up and whip horizontally across the field, which caused them a great deal of resistance as they stumbled helplessly along.

Erin had the grey hood tied tightly under her chin. Her pretty face was pale and glum. Everything on her body was beginning to ache; even the lump on the side of her head was still hurting from the car accident. Never in a million years could she have imagined she would have found herself in a predicament where she was on the run, and running scared for her life, and for a split second the thought of giving up and going home crept past her mind. That was until she looked back over her shoulder and saw Joseph, and felt a deep fondness burning inside for him.

'C'mon, Joseph, don't give up, keep going, we will soon find shelter,' she said, but found it difficult to believe her own motivating words.

It was only by a stroke of luck that when she had doubled back in the forest she'd caught sight of Joseph running at speed away from the Black Baron and had been able to follow from a safe distance, otherwise Lord only knows if they would have ever seen each other again. But ever since the moment on the bridge where she thought that she'd had lost Joseph for ever, something had shifted suddenly inside her and an underlying devotion was starting to emerge. Frequently she found herself glancing around to keep a close eye on him, as though she was his protector, because the thought of losing him again would cripple her.

'Keep going, Joseph, keep going, we're almost at the top,' she said, waving her arms encouragingly.

~

Joseph stared vacantly at Erin. Everything around him was shifting like he was on board a ship and made him feel sick. He saw Erin's lips moving in slow motion but couldn't hear a word of what she was saying. His mottled face hidden beneath his hood didn't stop the harsh wind from causing tears to form in his eyes. He felt the coldness bite hard at him and more so from the wet clothes that he wore. They were becoming unbearable to wear and were slowly drying out and stiffening up like cardboard. They rubbed against his skin which felt sore and sensitive. He held his arms tightly to his chest as he shook uncontrollably.

Awkwardly he limped from the relentless pain in his calf, while flashbacks frequently recurred and served as a reminder of the ordeal he had been through. He felt terrorized by them. His heart pounded with great fear so he shook his head to rid them. But they gripped him just like the physical grip that he'd felt from the wicked creature. It was like a plague spreading through his mind that he desperately wanted to break free of, but he felt trapped by the nightmare that he was living.

Giddy and weak, he finally reached the top of the brow of the hill and fell to his knees and sat back on his legs, hunched over.

The hillside was extremely steep and white, and the dark clouds hung so low above their heads that they looked close enough to touch. The air felt thinner to breathe to him, but he thought maybe it was because he felt so drained. He shut his frozen eyelids to stop the spinning and gasped like he was dying.

~

Erin had her hands rested on her hips and was breathing heavily too. She turned her head and panicked when she saw him on the ground and hurried over to him.

'*Oh* no you don't, mister. I'm not having you popping your clogs *here!*' Erin exclaimed, pulling him up.

'I can't go on,' Joseph stuttered.

'Yes you can, and you *will!*' said Erin. She glanced down the hillside through the haze of sleet. In the distance she saw a small hamlet nestled down in the valley. Her stiff face couldn't display a smile at the mild relief she felt inside at the sight of the houses, but her spirit was certainly uplifted which made her feel like she had caught a second wind. 'Look, Joseph, there's houses down there. Maybe someone can help us!' she said, turning to him. Looking back, she saw a large dry-stone wall a little further over to their left which stretched all the way down to the bottom of the field. 'C'mon, we'll use that wall over there to help us down,' she said, and hobbled with him towards it.

As they trekked down side by side, Erin thought it was equally as challenging as going up as she bore the weight of Joseph draped over her shoulders, but as the land slowly flattened out she spied a wooden stile at the bottom and hurried him over to it.

'Here, you first, Joseph, over you go,' she encouraged, pushing against his backside.

The second Erin placed her foot upon the slippery wood she became distracted. The sound of evil squawking echoed all around. It terrified her as it felt near, but she couldn't see where it was coming from when she looked up. Panic rose in her and quickly she climbed over to find Joseph slumped against the wall on the other side.

'C'mon, Joseph, up you get, we need to find somewhere to hide *now!*' Erin said, pulling him by the scruff of his coat.

She dragged him along down the steep and narrow road

which had dry-stone walls running parallel to it on either side. They hobbled around the corner and continued along for a few feet, when to her surprise she saw a sign up ahead that read: *Welcome to the Village of Sorrow. Please drive carefully.*

An unimpressed look came over Erin, but she instantly dismissed it when a large roof with a tower came into view from behind the sign. From their elevated position it caught her attention. Unsure of what it was, she made haste in the direction of it. After some time the road finally smoothed out, much to the relief of her sore feet, and as they strolled alongside the stone wall, the old building suddenly came into full view.

'It's a church!' she exclaimed.

Erin looked left across to the village, which was much further away than she anticipated, and she frowned, then turned to Joseph, who looked like death warmed up, and said to him, 'I don't think you're gonna last much longer. C'mon, this will have to do for now,' and hobbled him through the black steel gates and up the slippery, frozen steps.

Traipsing up the cobbled path, Erin was taken back at the sight of the enormous stone church, with its staggering tower built onto the right-hand side, the slate pointed roof and the huge imposing statue of a man hung from a cross fixed to the wall, positioned centrally above the large oak wooden doors. Intimidated by it, she looked away and saw the sign erected on the grass to the left that read: *Welcome to The Sorrows Church.*

At the entrance she tried the handle but it was firmly

locked and she began to bang upon the door with desperation. 'Someone, help us please,' she cried out.

Close to tears, her emotions were running high, but Erin was determined not to give in and instead propped Joseph up against the door and said, 'Wait here while I go check to see if there's another way to get in.'

Off she trotted across the frozen grass and down the side of the building. She looked up at the huge, curved, stained-glass windows finished in an array of different hues, and gold bars that looked like devil forks attached onto each and every one of them. At the far end she saw a side entrance and quickly shifted into a jog towards it. To her surprise, the heavy door could be pushed open.

'Thank goodness,' she murmured to herself, and spun round and dashed back to tell Joseph.

The moment she turned the corner, she found Joseph curled up in a ball on the floor, shivering to death and said to him, 'Up you get, Joseph, I've found a way in,' and lifted him to his feet. Just then, the sound of crows squawking again startled her. She glanced up to see a dozen or so circling above.

'C'mon, we need to move *now*, those things are regrouping again!' she said, and shuffled him quickly down the side of the church. At the door, a look of dismay fell upon her the moment she pushed it open with her foot and saw another door inside to the right.

'You gotta be kidding me!' she said, forcefully turning the handle, which didn't budge. Anger brewed inside of her. With little room inside of the porch, she took a small step back, raised her leg up high and booted the door wide open. The sound of the door hitting the sideboard behind echoed throughout the church. She quickly hobbled him through and rested him upon the wooden seating area to the right, and ran back and slammed all the doors shut.

'Hang in there, Joseph, I'll be back soon,' she said, striding past him.

The church was just as cold inside as it was outside and it made Erin shiver the moment she took her hood off. Large stone pillars supporting huge stone arches formed tips on each one, with angels and other heavenly statues embroiled upon them, sweeping the length of the church. In between the pillars lay a mass of wooden pews, along with a sea of plush red carpet that ran all the way to the front entrance of the double doors. Erin felt daunted by it, but nevertheless, ran up the nave calling out repeatedly for help. But the stony silence of the church and the echo of her voice was all that she was met with.

She shuddered like somebody had walked over her grave, and fast-paced back towards the chancel, when out of the corner of her eye she caught a glimpse of a door in the far right-hand corner, tucked behind the last stone pillar. She darted over and began to wrestle with the stiff door, and then aggressively began to shove her shoulder into it, when suddenly it flew open and she fell inside the room. She glanced around what appeared to be an office and then rushed over to a double wardrobe near to her on the right. She flung open the doors to see a tartan woollen blanket on the top shelf and clothes hung upon the rail below.

'Excellent,' she murmured, and ran back to Joseph.

Gently she heaved Joseph to his feet and shuffled him over to the office. She sat him down on an old leather sofa near to the door on the left and slipped off the rucksack and winced from the pain.

'Here, this'll keep you warm,' she said, pulling the blanket off the shelf and wrapping it around him, before turning back to the wardrobe and snatching off the hanger a large black, long sleeved button-down top, a pair of large black cargo pants and black Velcro shoes at the bottom.

'Joseph, I know you're freezing right now, but I need you to get out of all those wet clothes and place these dry ones on quickly. I'll wait outside for you while you get changed, okay?' she said, draping the clothes over the arm of the sofa and placing the shoes to the side. Joseph barely managed a nod of his head, he was shaking so profusely, but Erin leant down and gave him a small peck on the cheek and leisurely strolled over to the door.

She stopped in the doorway for a second, glanced back and gave him a smile, before walking out and closing the door behind her.

All of a sudden a rush of emotions hit her like a steam train. She burst into floods of tears whilst she leant against the door and held her hand to her mouth. Her legs felt weak as she stumbled across to the pew and collapsed to the floor in a heap. She buried her head in her arms and sobbed uncontrollably.

Joseph, who heard her cry, limped over to the door and reached for the handle but suddenly hesitated. He stared at it for a moment, numb, and not just because of the cold either. He was suffocated by his emotions and felt a sense of shame fall upon him for everything that had happened. All of his bravery was depleted and he felt exposed and vulnerable. He did not know what he could say or do that would make Erin feel better, or make the situation any easier. Discouraged by his negative thoughts, he lowered his arm back down and limped back to get changed. He wrapped the warm blanket back around him, lay down on the sofa and curled up into a tight ball and closed his tired eyes.

~

The next day, the morning light shone through the church's windows and roused Erin, who had fallen asleep on the pew. She sat up, feeling dazed, holding a stiff neck, and groaned. Her tired eyes glanced over to the office door. It was still shut. It took a minute or two for her to gather herself together, before she rose to her feet, crumpled and cold. She looked around for a sign for the bathroom and saw one at the front of the church to the right. Slowly she made her way over to it with a rigid walk.

A few minutes later she re-emerged, having freshened up. Casually she strolled along the red carpet and down the nave with her arms folded tightly, when suddenly she jumped back with fright as the side door swung open and in walked a short, middle-aged man in a black suit, holding a carrier bag and happily whistling to himself. Erin felt rooted to the floor in shock. Her face sank and her eyes grew wide with concern. She watched apprehensively as the unexpected guest closed the door, and short-stepped his way across the front of the chancel to the office. Her mind drew a blank as to what she could say to stop him, and in a moment of panic she let out a pretend cough to draw his attention, which echoed all around.

The man, clearly startled by the sound, leapt back and stopped dead in his tracks. He snapped his head around and stared directly at her.

The church's deafening silence made chills run up Erin's spine. She swallowed uncomfortably as they eyeballed one another like a western stand-off, and waited anxiously to see who would say something first.

'Hello,' said the man, his voice shaky.

Erin remained mute for now. She was fretting how she was going to explain why she was there, and most of all why Joseph was in his room.

'Welcome to The Sorrows Church. Can I help you, young lady?' the man said in a broad Welsh accent.

Erin smiled awkwardly. 'Hi there, umm, me and my friend were walking by and thought, *oh look*, there's a church, and maybe we should go in, and umm, see what the church looks like, it's a very nice church,' she said, thinking how stupid she sounded.

The man's eyes darted left and right, back and forth, clearly searching to see where the other person was that she was referring to. 'I'm afraid we are closed today and you would normally have to book by telephone to do a tour, but is there anything else I can help you with today?' he said.

'Oh umm . . . no,' replied Erin, clenching her teeth and trying to think of something else to say.

'Then in that case would you kindly see yourself out, please,' the man said abruptly and turned sharply and walked off briskly.

In a fluster, Erin quickly galloped down the nave, frantically racking her brain as she tailed behind him and said, '*Oh*, Mr . . .' But it was too late, he marched up to the office and thrust the door open, walking straight into the middle, and stopped. Erin stood in the doorway, baffled as to Joseph's whereabouts as she gazed around.

'Whose is this?' demanded the man, pointing to the rucksack on the floor.

Stumped for words, Erin began to stutter when the door to her right inside the office unexpectedly flew open and to her shock out walked Joseph.

Joseph jumped out of his skin with fright the moment he looked up and saw the man, and panned his head immediately to Erin, then back to the man again with a look of worry.

The man wrinkled his brow, flipped his eyes back and forth between the pair and said, 'You stand *correct* with regards to the other person you mentioned being here with you, but as to why you are in here, that I do not know, so might I suggest you explain yourselves or must I call the police?' he said in a demanding tone.

'NO!' they both said simultaneously, turning to look at each other then back at him.

'What we mean is there's no need to do that, Mr . . .' Erin said, and paused for his name.

'Father Elias to you,' he said.

'Sorry, Father Elias, I mean there's no need to call the police on us, we're not here to cause any trouble,' said Erin.

'So what is it you are here for, hmmm? And why do you, young man, have my clothes on?' asked Father Elias, turning to Joseph.

Though Joseph's face was still fairly bluish from the cold, it did not stop a tinge of crimson to shine through on his cheeks with embarrassment, and he wrapped the blanket that was draped over his shoulders around him and sheepishly covered up.

'I think I can explain, Father Elias,' Erin said, taking half a step forward. 'What happened was we were out walking through a forest when we suddenly became lost and—'

Joseph rudely interrupted her. 'That's right, then we were following this path near a stream and I tripped and fell in the water and—'

'Then I had to drag him out of the water, Father, soaking wet and he needed to dry off, that's when we stumbled across this wonderful church *with* the door open, of course, because otherwise it would be breaking and entering, Father, and that is illegal,' Erin snorted.

'And I found these nice warm clothes to change into,' Joseph said, cuddling the blanket.

Father Elias sighed heavily and fluttered his eyes. He looked Joseph up and down and said, 'Do you need medical assistance, young man?'

Joseph turned to Erin with a confused look, thinking she might have an answer, but instead she just shrugged at him.

'I'm not sure what you mean, Father Elias?' said Joseph.

'Well, you seem to have a problem with your eye and you look like you're bleeding from the bottom of your leg,' he replied.

Joseph looked down and saw a trickle of blood running onto the side of his shoe. 'Ah, it's probably where I fell in the stream; must have cut myself trying to get out,' he said, acting as though it was nothing to worry about and smiled awkwardly.

Father Elias raised his eyebrows before turning around and strolled behind his desk and casually placed the bag down to the side and pulled out a portable radio from his drawer.

Erin stared down at Joseph's leg and whispered to him, 'Is your leg okay?'

'It still hurts a bit,' Joseph grimaced, and continued, 'but what do we do—?' and cocked his head sideways in the direction of Father Elias.

Sitting down in his chair, Father Elias placed the radio down on the desk and switched it on. He opened the inside of his jacket and pulled out a brown flat case and fingered out his half-moon spectacles and slipped them on, before he gave a polite cough to interrupt them both.

'So is there anything else I can help you with?' he said. His thin lips clenched together.

Reluctant to say anything further, they both shook their heads. Joseph moved to collect his rucksack from the floor and then limped towards the door, but stopped when Father Elias called him.

'Oh, and young man, I would appreciate my clothes back when you have finished with them, WASHED and CLEANED, please,' Father Elias said, lowering his head to peer through the top of his glasses at him.

'Sure thing,' Joseph replied with a frown, and turned back and continued to limp out through the door past Erin who was staring blankly at the floor.

Slowly her head rose and her mouth partly opened as if she was about to say something, when Father Elias spoke out.

'Good day to you both,' Father Elias said, looking down at his book that he was writing in.

Erin bowed her head and turned around and walked out, quietly closing the door behind her. She strolled over to Joseph and sat down beside him and asked again, 'Is your leg okay?'

Joseph had his trouser leg rolled up and was gently pressing against the bruising which was dark and purple and replied, 'It feels painful.'

'Here, let me take a look,' Erin said, and crouched down and rested his foot upon her thigh.

Intently Joseph watched her touch his leg with her warm hands and he felt gooey inside. Half a smile broke out across his face until she touched a sore spot and he jerked back from the pain. '*OWWW*, that's a little sore,' he said.

'Sorry. It's just a little cut you've got; your clothes must have been rubbing against it, but it looks fine except for the bruising,' said Erin.

The moment she looked up at him, Joseph became lost in her eyes. He felt the sudden urge to kiss her and tried to pluck up the courage inside, but his self-esteem was diminished. Instead he smiled affectionately and watched her bite her bottom lip while rolling his trouser back down and then sat beside him once again.

'So what are we going to do now?' Erin asked, tucking her hair behind her ear.

Joseph's reply was hesitant. His eyes were firmly fixed on the floor as he pondered over the question and then heaved a heavy sigh before he said, 'I think we should both go home and call it a day.'

'*What!* Are you *serious?*' Erin said, screwing her face up. 'After everything we've been through and you just wanna give up just like that? Look how far we've come! I mean, seriously, Joseph, are you always this flippant when you make decisions, one minute you want to go trekking the countryside, the next—'

Without hesitation Joseph swung his head and pressed his lips up against hers. The feel of her soft sweet lips caressing his made him feel like fireworks were exploding inside of him with excitement, and after a few seconds of what seemed to him like a lifetime of passionate kissing, he slowly eased away and left her hanging with her eyes closed and lips still pouted. Shocked by his own actions, he watched anxiously as she opened her beautiful eyes and waited for her reaction and swallowed nervously.

'That was unexpected,' Erin softly said.

'Sorry, I—' said Joseph, but Erin quickly interrupted him.

'Don't be, it was nice,' she simpered, and leant forward to kiss him again.

Just as their lips barely touched again, the office door clanged open. They both flinched and pulled away quickly from each and turned to look.

Father Elias strolled out, staring down at a set of keys which he held in his hand and niftily spun around on the balls of his feet and locked the door. With his head stooped, he began his funny short-step waddle. The moment his head raised he jumped back as they both sat staring at him in silence. He crossed his chest with his fingers and began to mutter to himself in his dialect and then said, 'Do you realize how unpleasant it is to keep frightening someone like that, and why are you still here? I thought you'd left?'

'Sorry,' they said one after the other and quickly stood up.

'We were just leaving now, Father,' said Joseph, slinging his rucksack over his shoulders.

Erin, who had her back to Father Elias, whispered through clenched teeth to Joseph, 'What are we going to do about that creature outside that's after us?'

'I don't know, do you think we should tell him?' replied Joseph, looking out of the corner of his eye to see Father Elias looking down at his watch.

'Like he's going to believe us!' said Erin. Her eyes widened at him.

'Well, he's a priest, isn't he? Aren't they supposed to know about good and bad things?' Joseph said, raising his eyebrows at her.

'That still doesn't mean he's going to believe us. *Look*, if we go out there, that thing's going to kill us, *you* know it and I know it, so what are we going to do?' said Erin.

'Well, he's not going to let us stay in here, is he? We'll just have to find somewhere else to hide, or maybe we can ask him to give us a ride home if he's got a car?' said Joseph, shrugging.

'You still want to go home, do you?' Erin asked, and crossed her arms and raised her eyebrows at him.

Joseph sighed and lowered his eyes. 'I just don't want any more bad things to happen to us,' he said, 'or anything to happen to you,' and he raised his eyes to look at her.

Erin smiled and was about to say something when Father Elias interrupted with a cough.

'Do you have everything?' Father Elias said with a hint of exasperation in his voice while he readjusted his glasses.

'Sorry, Father, we won't be a second,' Erin said and turned back to Joseph. Her face was solemn, which he didn't like the look of. 'Joseph, if you give up now you know what could happen to your family. Are you really prepared to take that risk, knowing how close we are? You're clearly destined for something or why else would your grandfather go to all of this trouble in hiding this medallion thing and writing all these riddles? Do you know what my dad always says? He says sometimes you gotta leave something behind to get where you're going in life; you only get one chance, luck doesn't happen twice.'

Joseph sighed, feeling the weight of her words. He felt caught between a rock and a hard place and turned to look away and ruminate over them for a moment. One side of him wanted nothing more than to go home and see his mother who he dearly missed, but he knew the consequence of his actions if he did. On the other hand, he didn't want to let his grandfather down, or Erin for that matter. They both clearly believed in him for whatever reason, which he found foreign, because the way he saw himself, he was just an ordinary teen like any other. But one big problem still remained; amongst all of his troubled thoughts was the Crowman, who had left him very scared.

'Hey,' said Erin and gave him a gentle pat on the arm and half a smile.

They both turned to Father Elias with glum expressions and bowed their heads. Slowly they strolled across the front of the chancel, edging closer and closer to the side door like they were walking to their death-beds.

Joseph's throat tightened, his hands were cold and clammy. He felt Erin slip her warm fingers between his, which was comforting, and turned to her with a dour look when he stopped dead in his tracks, jerking her hand back in the process, and stared at her vacantly.

'What's wrong?' Erin said, and turned around to look behind her and then back at him. 'What is it?'

Joseph stood gazing wide-eyed at a magnificent painting

hanging on the wall behind her and whipped around to face Father Elias, which startled him.

'Father, what is that?' he asked, pointing in the direction of the painting.

Father Elias glanced up and turned to him with a scowl and said, 'Good heavens, young man, you don't know who he is?'

'*No*, I know who he is, *Father*, but what type of writing is that next to him?' asked Joseph and moved closer to point at it again.

'Well, that is Old Latin,' replied Father Elias, staring at the words on the painting.

Joseph's ears perked up and he was eager to know more. He asked, 'Are you able to read Old Latin, Father?'

'I'm afraid not. There is great deal of complexity with the Old Latin language. Though my language, which descended from the Old Brittonic era, was heavily influenced by Latin, and to this day still carries the Latin alphabet and borrowed words, there are still significant differences. I have a copy of the translation of the painting if you want it?' said Father Elias.

'Thanks, Father, but I was looking to get something else translated. Any idea where I could find Old Latin too?' asked Joseph.

Father Elias shrugged his shoulders with open palms. 'I don't know. Possibly, uh, uh the library or something,' he replied.

'A library, of course, why didn't I think of that?' Joseph said, clicking his fingers and he looked at Erin with a grin then turned to him again and asked, 'And where is the nearest library to here?'

'Well, that would be the National Library,' said Father Elias. 'Look, I'm afraid I do not have any more time to stand here answering your questions as I need to be somewhere,' and he stared at his watch.

'Sorry, Father, one more question and we'll go. How long do you think it would take us to walk there?' Joseph said.

'I should imagine quite some time unless you had a car? You would have to follow the road out towards Devil's Bridge,' said Father Elias.

'I'm afraid we don't, Father,' Joseph huffed.

'I tell you what, the library is in the same direction as where I am heading, and *if* we leave now I can give you a lift there, but only *if* we leave now,' said Father Elias, and he motioned his hands for them to go through the door.

'Thank you, Father, that would be great!' exclaimed Joseph.

'What happened to going home?' Erin said, half raising her eyebrows.

'I took your advice. I shouldn't give up so easily,' Joseph said, feeling upbeat.

Father Elias coughed to interrupt their conversation once again and raised his hands and eyebrows.

Joseph turned around and gripped Erin's hand and leant over to her ear. 'Stay close to me until we get to the car,' he whispered, and proceeded towards the internal porch.

His heart began to race and his breathing became heavy as he reached for the outer door handle and pulled it slowly towards him. He peered around and looked up to the sky and turned to Erin and whispered, 'The coast is clear,' and opened the door further and crept out cautiously.

In the trees set back opposite the church, crows sat twitching their heads, observing with their demon-red eyes. The second they caught sight of the two of them, they all began to squawk repeatedly. The sound of them caused Erin to scream and she dived back inside the porch and shoved Father Elias accidentally out of the way. He was about to lock the door, and she bowled him over and ran inside and back up the nave.

Joseph quickly slammed the porch door shut so hard that he caused the handle to break off in his hand and ran over to help Father Elias back up to his feet.

'Are you okay, Father?' he asked with concern.

'What on God's earth are you doing, child, pushing me over like that? How dare you!' fumed Father Elias.

'I'm sorry, Father Elias, I didn't *mean* to, but we can't go out there . . . tell him. Joseph – tell *him!*' Erin said, biting her nails and pacing back and forth in the middle of the nave.

Joseph bowed his head and sighed. 'She's right, Father, something terrible is after us,' he said.

'What are you talking about, who is after you?' replied Father Elias, turning to him.

Joseph looked at Erin and sighed again. He felt lost for words and didn't know what to say or how to speak about the creature without making himself look a fool.

'It's not who, Father, it's what—' he said, but Erin immediately interrupted.

'It's a crow, Father – crows are trying to kill us,' stammered Erin.

Father Elias gave Erin an unfriendly look. 'You're telling me you are afraid of birds, my dear?' he asked, glaring at her, then turned to Joseph again, who shrugged.

'Yes, Father, crows are trying to kill us and there's this creature—' Erin said, but stopped short when Father Elias walked off.

'Where are you going, Father?' Joseph yelled out.

Father Elias stopped and swung around and said, 'I've had just about enough of this foolish behaviour from both of you, and will not tolerate it any longer. I'm going to my office to call the police!' He motioned to turn, but hesitated and slowly shifted his eyes upwards to the church windows.

Joseph and Erin both turned their heads and saw the light from the windows on both sides diminish and grow eerily dark. Suddenly out of nowhere a huge bang came from the main entrance of the double doors and they both jumped with fright. *WHAM!* the doors went again, echoing throughout the church, but this time even louder.

Erin swivelled her head around. She stared wide-eyed at the doors and slowly began to back away.

'What on God's earth is going on?' said Father Elias.

'This is what we were trying to tell you, Father, about the crows,' said Joseph as he nervously looked around.

'Enough of the lies already, young man, you are in the house of the Lord and I will not tolerate any more of them, nor will I tolerate any aggressive behaviour by those you have clearly upset!' said Father Elias and stormed up the nave past Erin.

'Father, don't open those doors, please don't open those doors!' Erin shouted at him.

Father Elias ignored her plea and carried on his march up the nave. Suddenly all the windows smashed like an explosion went off and razor-sharp fragments scattered all over the church. Father Elias fell helplessly to the ground, covered in the shattered glass, as a swarm of crows piled through the open windows and circled high inside the roof rafters.

'ERIN!' Joseph yelled, seeing her on the floor, and he quickly ran over to help her.

Father Elias groaned as he rolled over onto his front and cut his hands to shreds. He stared at the pouring blood when the doors thumped again one final time – *WHAM* – and the next thing they were ripped clean off their hinges. The doors soared past Father Elias on either side and smashed into the pews. The sinister creature pounded the floor with its claws as it entered through the doorway and squawked thunderously.

'My good Lord, it's the Devil!' said Father Elias, and he began to crawl along the broken glass on the floor.

Joseph gripped Erin by the hand and hid behind the last pillar near to the porch door, dropped his rucksack to the floor and frantically began to unclip it.

'What are you doing?' muttered Erin, breathing erratically.

'Getting the dagger we need to protect ourselves,' replied Joseph, shaking.

The floor shook as the creature pounded along towards Father Elias. He turned over and propped himself up on one elbow, trembling as he raised his head upwards and froze. He reached for his cross from around his neck and extended it out in front of him and began to mutter words.

The Crowman slightly tilted its feathered head to one side, then lashed Father Elias with the back of its claw hand and sent him flying through the air into the lectern in front of the chancel.

Out of the corner of Joseph's eye he saw the keys in the internal door and said to Erin, '*Look*, it's Father's Elias's keys, it's got the car keys on them – wait here,' and he slowly began to creep over to the door.

'Hurry, Joseph, *hurry!*' said Erin.

He scurried over and quickly yanked them out. The second he spun around to head back, he spied Father Elias whining injured on the floor, and he straightened up. Without thinking, he began to walk over to help him.

'Joseph, what the hell are you doing?' Erin yelled, and peered around the pillar.

Before Joseph could get to him, the Crowman soared into the air and landed on Father Elias's legs and began attacking him with its razor-sharp claws. Joseph's eyes flashed with horror, when he suddenly felt his rucksack being pulled backwards towards the pillar.

'What are you doing, Erin, what about Father Elias? We can't just leave him!' he said angrily.

'We can't help him. We need to get out of here now!'

screamed Erin.

Joseph clenched his lips and teeth together bitterly. He grabbed her by the hand and ran behind all of the pillars, swinging the dagger wildly above his head as crows attacked them. While Erin ran out, Joseph stopped briefly in the broken doorway and looked back at the powerful creature hammering blow after blow, hearing the mortifying screams. He felt tearful and seething with anger as he squeezed the dagger in his hand and was tempted to go running down the nave to help, when he heard Erin bellow his name, which immediately distracted him.

'Joseph, please, let's go!' Erin called out at the bottom of the path.

Begrudgingly, he turned and ran towards the steps as fast as he could and saw Erin run out through the gates.

A small car was parked outside to the right. Erin fumbled with the keys to press the button on the fob to unlock the doors and quickly jumped in to start it.

'C'mon, get in, get in!' she screamed at Joseph through the window.

Hesitantly, Joseph stood by the passenger door, gripping the handle, and stared back at the church's doorway with grief at the harrowing squawking from inside. He sensed Father Elias was dead and bowed his head sorrowfully before he leapt inside and slammed the door shut and they sped off down the road.

Chapter 21

SSHH, BE QUIET

Joseph's face smouldered with anger. He lost control and repeatedly thumped the dashboard of the car with his fist.

'We should have saved him!' he yelled.

'How could we? You saw the size of that thing attacking him – there was no way of stopping it!' Erin replied.

'You didn't give me the chance to, you just pulled me away!' Joseph snapped.

'*Too* bloody right I pulled you away, otherwise *you* would have been hurt as well. *What*, you wanted to get eaten to death by that evil thing? Be my guest. I'll turn this stolen car around right now, shall I?!' Erin hit back.

Joseph propped his elbow against the door and rested his furious face upon his knuckles. He stared out of the window angrily, and said nothing further, causing an intense silence to fall between them. His eyes glazed over with anger and guilt. *That goddamn creature, how could it kill a priest of all people? Makes me sick to my stomach, the bloody thing. I hate it, I wish it was dead!* he thought, clenching his teeth together.

After a while the crimson slowly drained from his face and his pale complexion returned. He sighed heavily. Out of the corner of his eye he could see Erin was het up as well by the way she ran her fingers through her hair. Calmly he turned to her and said in a low tone, 'I'm sorry for my behaviour. I was out of order. You're right; there's no way we could have saved him without getting hurt ourselves. I – I just wished I could have done something, that's all,' and he bowed his head sorrowfully.

'I know you wanted to, Joseph, and I'm sorry I pulled you away like I did, but I was scared. I didn't want to risk losing you again,' Erin said, and reached over to hold his hand.

He gazed at their woven fingers for a second, then his eyes found their way to her face. The compassion in her words boosted his morale and only made his feelings for her grow stronger. He smiled and stared at her for a moment before the sound of her voice broke his reverie.

'Uh, umm, is everything okay?' Erin said and raised her eyebrows.

'Oh, sorry,' he said, turning away. 'I was, umm, I was thinking you look pretty. I mean, you are pretty, I don't mean I think you look pretty because you, you do look pretty—' Joseph replied, stuttering.

'It's okay, I get it,' Erin tittered with a smile.

Abashed, he tapped the side of his head and turned to gaze back out of the window. *Think you look pretty, huh, she is pretty, you dimwit,* he thought to himself.

'Can I ask you something?' Erin said.

'Yeah, sure?' replied Joseph, turning to her.

'You've never had a girlfriend, have you?' said Erin.

He paused before replying as he became tongue-tied by the awkward question, and a hot flush came over him all of a sudden. 'Oh yeah, I've had a few girl . . . err . . . friends,' Joseph replied, coughing. He sighed, lowering his eyes, and said, 'No, no I haven't, does it really show?'

'Maybe a little bit, but that's not a bad thing. I just think you need to relax more, you know, not be so uptight,' Erin said.

Conscious of her words, Joseph became fidgety in his seat. He wanted to make a good impression so he dropped his shoulders to show he was less tense. That was until he saw a sign ahead with the letter 'D' crossed out from the word Devil's, which then read: *Welcome to evil's Bridge – please drive carefully* which made his stomach tighten up all of a sudden.

'So let me get this straight, we're off to the National Library because you seem to think that the painting on the wall had similar writing to that on the scroll which could be Old Latin, right?' Erin blurted out all in one breath.

'Uh-huh,' said Joseph.

'Okay, so what made you change your mind?' Erin asked.

'You did,' he replied, tinkering with the door handle.

'What do you mean, I did, what did I say?' said Erin and threw a darting glance at him.

Joseph grinned, knowing she was playing dumb. 'You

know what you said,' he replied.

'Do I? Let me see, did I say you were a pain in the ass?' said Erin.

'Nope,' he replied.

'Let me see, did I say you need to smile more?' said Erin.

'Nope, not even close,' Joseph said.

'Well, in that case, I can't remember. It must have just slipped my mind,' replied Erin with a wry smile.

'You said something like . . . your father always says, "You gotta leave something behind to get where you're going because luck doesn't happen twice" or something like that anyway,' Joseph replied.

'*Ah*, so you do listen, I'm *impressed*. And there's me thinking you were just this *irresponsible* city slicker boy from the south,' Erin said, grinning.

Her wry humour made Joseph titter. 'Says she who lives out in the sticks in amongst the hay,' he quickly responded.

He turned to face the road when something immediately caught his attention. 'Look, there's the sign for it!' he said enthusiastically and pointed.

Down the steep road they descended, seeing slush piles of snow pushed up against the kerbs, and they turned left before the library sign and drove up a long stretch of road. Out of the passenger window Joseph gazed, intrigued, at two prominent stone buildings that joined in the middle, covered in a sea of windows, and wondered what they were used for. They quickly passed and a dense assortment of trees, hedging of various hues, red, yellow and green, became visible. Out of the blue, a house emerged, set back in amongst the landscape and painted a pale shade of green. It stuck out like a sore thumb.

'That's weird,' Joseph murmured, as they drove past.

A few seconds later, the house disappeared out of sight, and slowly but surely the trees and hedging became sparse and the country's landscape opened up. Unexpectedly, and to his astonishment, a spectacular grand building appeared out of nowhere on his left and his eyes lit up, when suddenly he was hurled forward.

'Oops, sorry!' Erin said, stopping the car sharply.

He scowled at her before turning back. He saw a set of sweeping steps opposite that led up to the magnificent building, which looked more palatial, with its enormous pillars at the front and small balcony centrally located above.

'There's no way that's a library, that's a palace!' he said, turning to face Erin.

'No, it certainly doesn't look like a library,' Erin said with raised eyebrows. 'Who knows, maybe the royals live there?'

'Forget the royals, I want to live there!' Joseph said, turning back to stare. His eyes sharply shifted upwards to the sky and swivelled back and forth. 'C'mon, let's get in there before those bloody things come after us.' And he quickly hopped out of the car. 'God, it's cold,' he said, shivering.

'Here, put this on,' Erin said, nudging him.

Joseph screwed his face up with disgust at the bright green anorak held in her hand. 'Where did you get that from?' he said.

'It was on the back seat,' she said, nudging him again.

'No way, *seriously*. I feel bad enough wearing Father Elias's clothes,' said Joseph.

'*Fine*, if you'd rather freeze to death like before,' she said, and motioned to the car door.'

'*Argh*, okay, okay, give it here,' he said begrudgingly and slipped it on along with his rucksack.

Erin grinned. 'You look cute,' she said.

'Really?' Joseph said.

'No, really you look like the weather man,' she chuckled, as she began to walk up the slippery steps.

Joseph huffed. 'Thanks,' he said and followed behind her. Up the sea of steps they scurried until they finally reached the top, out of breath, and stood on a stone balcony section.

'Looks like the way in,' said Joseph, panting heavily, staring up at another flight of steps to the top, where an old revolving door stood between the gigantic pillars.

'Great – more steps!' Erin said and rolled her eyes.

'Only a few more. C'mon, let's go and find some answers, shall we?' And he held his hand out to her.

They climbed the last steps, and one at a time pushed their way through the rickety glass and wood revolving door and they were immediately greeted by an overwhelming, grand entrance inside. They both stood staring with their mouths open at the plush red carpet which covered three quarters of the floor that ran away through the heart of the building and led off in various directions. Beautiful dark oak architraves complemented the flawless brilliant white walls and gave the old building both a sense of the modern and an airy feel.

A scruffy-haired man wearing thin-framed glasses, clean-shaven apart from a goatee, sat unusually high up on a chair behind a dark, oak-framed reception desk to the right. He stared beady-eyed at the pair of them and said in a monotonous voice, 'Can I help you?'

Joseph hadn't noticed the man until he spoke and felt a little caught off guard. 'Oh . . . hi, umm, we're looking for help with something,' he said in a timorous tone.

'And what might that something be?' asked the reception man, and dropped his head to peer through the top of his glasses.

'What he means is, we're looking to get something translated?' Erin said, jumping in.

'From what into what exactly?' replied the reception man.

Joseph gave Erin a kind tap with his foot not to say anything further. 'Umm, we're not entirely sure,' he said, and turned to Erin and scowled.

The man puffed his cheeks out, then hopped off his high chair and opened the door to his right. He walked around the side of the reception desk into the middle and wagged his two fingers at them. 'Follow me,' he said, and short-stepped up the centre of the red carpet with his little legs.

Surprised to see that he was a dwarf, they quickly followed behind him. Joseph was paying very little attention to the pace at which he was walking, as he looked around and stared at the building's sheer size and architectural beauty, when he accidentally trod on the man's heel from behind.

'OUCH!' said the man and swung his head around and

glared at him.

'Oops, sorry,' Joseph said, cringing with embarrassment.

They reached the end of the long hallway where it split left and right, and in the middle was a huge wide staircase. The moment they turned left, Joseph threw a glance over his right shoulder and saw a security guard with a dark complexion sitting casually behind a desk.

The man glared at him with his big dark beady eyes. Joseph quickly spun his head back around. But curiously he once again looked back and this time the guard got up out of his chair. Intimidated by the guard's size, Joseph gulped and turned away and chose not to look any further.

The moment they were about to leave the corridor and walk through a set of double doors, the reception man abruptly stopped, about-turned and placed his hands up to halt them both, then casually placed his hands behind his back. 'We are about to enter the reading room so therefore I request that you remain quiet at all times, and respect the others who are there using and enjoying the facility as well – understood?' he said.

They both nodded and followed him in. The second they entered, Joseph heard Erin gasp. He was flabbergasted himself at the sight of the wondrous giant library room. Enormous amounts of light poured through huge windows between the balcony walkways that ran the length of it, and books upon books filled the entire area from floor to ceiling, all neatly stacked in their cases. Caught in the moment, Joseph forgot what he was there for and was oblivious to the reception man calling over to him.

'Psst,' repeated the reception man.

Joseph felt Erin nudge him, causing him to snap out of his trance, and he looked straight ahead to see the reception man standing next to a large, circular reception hub that resembled something more likely to beam him up into outer space. He briskly made his way over with Erin. A little old lady with a wrinkled face and snow-white curly hair sat behind the reception desk and grinned through extremely white teeth as soon as they both approached.

'This is Hilda – she will be able to help you with your enquiry, and remember: Sshh, be quiet,' the reception man whispered to them with his finger to his lips.

'Thank you, Harold,' said the little old lady in a croaky voice. 'Now what is it I can help you with, my dears?'

'We're looking to translate something in here,' Joseph whispered to her as he slid his rucksack off and began to unclip it. He rose up with the box in his hand and wondered why Hilda had not responded when he spoke, and why she was sat with a blank look upon her face. He turned his head towards Erin, who shrugged at him. He leant in a little closer to the desk and repeated the same thing again in case she hadn't heard.

'You lost your mate that is *dear*. *Oh* well, I can't help you with that, I'm afraid, you'll have to see a counsellor for that!' said Hilda, and leant back in her chair.

Joseph heard Erin snigger. He looked at her to see her smirking and felt himself getting annoyed. 'NO, I'm looking to translate what's in here!' he said loudly, pointing to the box, and for a split second he forgot about his surroundings.

'SSHH!' said someone from behind one of the desks to the side of them.

'Oh well, why didn't you say that, my dear? Here, pass it to me, let's take a look at it,' said Hilda, and she placed her large circular glasses on her face.

He placed the box onto the high part of the desk and flicked the clasp open.

'My, what a pretty box that is,' said Hilda, smiling.

Joseph felt his stomach turn when he saw her false teeth staring to fall down in her mouth. Gently he unravelled the last part of the scroll and leant across to show it to her and watched her lean forward from out of the chair and caress the scroll between her fingers.

'Good quality vellum this is made from,' Hilda said.

'What's vellum?' Joseph whispered to her.

'No thank you, my dear, I've eaten already,' replied Hilda.

'What?' said Joseph, screwing his face up at her response, and turned to Erin.

Erin giggled. 'I think he said "what is vellum", *not* "do you want some melon?",' she whispered.

'Oh, it's calf's skin, dear, calf's skin,' said Hilda, and leant back in her chair and took off her glasses, letting them dangle around her neck on the beaded chain. 'I'm sorry, dear, I don't know what it means.'

Joseph huffed with frustration. 'Well, how do I find out?' he said.

'Well, we have books—' said Hilda.

'Great,' Joseph interrupted.

'What's that, my dear?' said Hilda, leaning slightly forward from out of the chair.

'I said, GREAT!' Joseph repeated loudly.

'SSHH!' said the same person again behind them.

Erin snapped her head around and gave the person a filthy look.

Joseph blew out his cheeks, feeling exasperated by the situation.

'Like I said, we have a book, an Old Latin book that might be able to translate it, but it's not here,' said Hilda.

'Well, where is it, then?' said Erin in a demanding tone.

'It's in our vault,' replied Hilda.

'And how do we get to this vault?' Erin asked.

'I'm sorry, dear, it's not for public use. We keep it locked in the vault and only staff can access it. You could contaminate it otherwise!' replied Hilda, scowling.

'Great!' said Joseph sarcastically.

'That's quite alright, my dear,' replied Hilda, and smiled.

Joseph turned around and slapped the front of his forehead, and looked to the ground for it to open up and swallow him.

Erin sighed and unintentionally shifted her eyes to the side of the desk near to her, and she saw Hilda's key-card sat upon it. A cunning streak brewed inside of her and she asked, 'Are there any other Latin books here, Hilda, that we could take a look at?'

'Of course, dear, just down there where that metal spiral staircase is,' said Hilda, pointing to the far corner of the library.

'Maybe Hilda could help you look for some Latin books?'
Erin said, and kicked Joseph in the foot.

'Ouch!' Joseph said, scowling at her.

Erin cocked her head in the direction of Hilda and pulled
a face at him whilst clenching her teeth together at the same
time, which caused Joseph to look confused.

'C'mon, my dear, this way,' Hilda said, struggling out from
behind the desk with a walking stick in her hand.

As they toddled off down the library together, Erin gave
Joseph a cheeky smile and a wave when he glanced back over
his shoulder. Acting inconspicuous she casually leant across
the desk, when out of the corner of her eye she caught sight of
the little nerd who had shushed at them, watching observantly
from behind his book. Irked by him, she gritted her teeth and
screwed up her lips and began to tap the lower part of the desk
with her fingernail, whilst watching him pop his head up and
down like a gopher.

Not the confrontational type, but certainly the type to
speak her mind, she casually strolled over to him. He popped
his head up once more, and Erin saw the panic in his eyes as
she approached and quickly ducked back down again. Erin
slowly lowered his book down onto the table with her finger to
reveal his pimpled face. Seductively she leant her body across
the table towards him and gave a coquettish grin, and watched
him smile through a set of metal braces.

'Hi there,' she said.

'Hi,' the nerdy kid replied, slowly straightening up.

'Here's the thing. I've been watching you, watching me

from over there, and if I catch you one more time looking in my direction, I'm going to gouge those pretty little eyes out – do you understand me?' Erin said, and scratched her nail across the pages of his book and smiled devilishly.

His face sank. Erin gave him a wink as she rose up and watched him cower back behind the book again. Just as she went to turn to walk away, she looked up and caught sight of Joseph at the bottom of the spiral staircase with Hilda following closely behind him.

'Damn it,' she muttered.

In a hurry, she marched back to the desk and when nobody was looking she casually leant across and grabbed the pass. The second she leapt off, she saw Joseph and Hilda only a few feet away. Nervously she smiled at them as she quickly tucked the pass in the back of her jeans pocket.

'So did you find what you were looking for?' she asked calmly, running her fingers through her hair.

'No dear, your boyfriend is hopeless,' replied Hilda, and trundled off shaking her head.

'*What?*' Joseph silently mouthed, holding his arms up.

Erin chuckled. 'Come along, *BOYFRIEND*, let's go and have a look around, shall we?' Erin said grinning, and inter-locked her arm into his.

Just as they turned to head off, a sharp tapping noise echoed around the room and gradually became louder and louder by the second. Everyone who had their head buried in their books and laptops immediately looked up at one another to see where it was coming from. The light began to fade in the room. Joseph and Erin stopped and looked at each with concern. Slowly their glance drifted upwards and they saw lines of crows silhouetted against the windows outside and they all began to hammer away at the glass like woodpeckers.

Before anyone could panic or get up to leave, suddenly out of nowhere, the large window at the far end of the library completely shattered and shards of glass were sent flying through the air. Everyone hit the floor petrified as a swarm of angry crows piled through the broken window. One by one, every window shattered and more and more crows flooded into the room like a dam had burst. Everyone was covered in the razor-sharp glass which was sprawled everywhere, while the crows angrily squawked and began to attack.

On the floor, covered in glass, Joseph heard nothing but a white noise. He rolled over on the broken glass and looked up with horror to see the crows circling above him, and glanced across to Erin who was propped up on her elbows, staring at a cut hand. Before he could reach out to her, chaos broke out. Tables and chairs were knocked over and bookcases on the balconies were sent crashing to the ground as everyone screamed and ran for their lives, trampling past them both on the floor.

Joseph stumbled to his feet, rushed over to Erin and quickly helped her up, when the security guard whom he saw earlier barged past and ran straight into the centre of the chaos. Instantly he was struck by a table and was sent flying to the other side of the room.

They both turned back around to see where the table had

come from, and stared horrified at the Crowman at the far end of the room. The Crowman gave a thunderous squawk and pounded the floor towards them like a charging bull. Joseph yanked Erin by the hand before she could scream and they darted up the corridor. The Crowman instantly dispersed into hundreds of crows and flew past them above their heads and re-emerged at the end of the corridor. They stopped dead in their tracks. Joseph looked to his left and saw another corridor leading behind the staircase. 'Quick, this way,' he said, pulling Erin. Down the short corridor they ran and through an opening that lead into an unlit, small square dead space with a door. Desperately he pushed against it with his shoulder before resorting to kicking it as hard as he could.

Erin turned her head. To the side of the door was a very small black box with a tiny red light. She reached into her back pocket and pulled out the key-card and said, 'Joseph, JOSEPH, *here*, try this!'

Joseph looked at it, puzzled. 'Where did you get that from?'

'Never mind that, hurry and see if it works,' she said.

The box beeped the moment he placed the key-card upon it. Without hesitation, he flung the door open and ran through. The door slammed shut. They backed away nervously, passing offices: some lay empty and others had members of staff cowering behind their desks, when the door suddenly shook. They both spun around and ran up the corridor past the remaining offices where they reached another security door and quickly swiped through.

As they moved away they found themselves walking out

onto a white metal balcony that led onto a huge square-shaped atrium made of brick, which rose high into the air like an high-rise building and was brightly lit from the glass skylight above.

Joseph peered over the balcony and looked around. 'Now where?' he said.

'Quick, down here,' Erin replied, shifting down a white metal spiral staircase.

Joseph paused for a second and he grabbed the handrail. He saw blood smeared down it. When he reached the bottom, Erin was about to run off towards a door when he shouted, 'Hold on, Erin, your hand's bleeding!'

'It's fine,' she said.

'I'll be the judge of that,' Joseph replied, holding her hand to examine the wound.

'See, it's only a small cut. C'mon, we haven't got time for this,' Erin said.

'Just give me a second,' Joseph said, and quickly slipped off one strap of his rucksack and his coat and tugged hard at the sleeve of his top and tore it off completely. Carefully he wrapped it around and tied it in a knot on the back of her hand. 'There, hopefully that will stop the bleeding,' he said, looking up to see her smiling.

Joseph watched her move slowly towards him with her eyes closed and her lips delicately pressed together ready to kiss. Casually he tilted his head to the side and leant forward. He went to close his eyes but stopped when he saw an intriguing rock sculpture over her shoulder in the middle of the atrium floor. It aroused his attention as he thought he had seen it before. His eyebrows shifted together. He hastily pulled away from Erin and promptly walked over, leaving her hanging with her eyes closed and lips pouting.

After a second or so, Erin opened her eyes and shifted them back and forth. 'Joseph?' she said. She swirled around and stopped, flapped hers arms and sarcastically said, 'Cheers, thanks a bunch! What are you doing anyway?' and motioned over to him.

Joseph had his eyes fixed on the rock and replied in a low tone, 'I've seen something similar to this as a kid, when I was fishing with my father . . . *except* it didn't have that hole in it.' And he touched the outer edge.

'C'mon Joseph we ain't got time to marvel over stupid rocks – we need to find the vault!' Erin said.

'Hold on a second, I want to read what it says,' Joseph replied, crouching down.

'*Fine*, I'll find the bloody thing myself then!' she fumed and stormed off.

Joseph rubbed the dust off the gold plaque that was positioned at the bottom of the rock and began to read it out loud to himself.

'This small replica of The Orsín Stone was made by
Dyron Bass and was gifted to the National Library.

"CIRCULUS VITAE SAXEUS" written in Latin, translated into English means: The Stone Circle of Life.

The Orsín Stone, meaning the "God Stone", is a large standing stone situated on a mount at Cregennan Lake. The actual stone stands a staggering 10ft tall and 4ft wide. The Orsín Stone has a hole that is 1ft in diameter all the way through it and is positioned approximately 5ft up from the ground. The runes on The Orsín Stone have been translated into English in the passage below:

Have mercy, O God, through the circle of life,

Show mercy, O God, through darkness be light,

Thou holdest the key to our soul, I pledge my love to thee,

Grant us safe passage to Ettonina – I place my faith in thee.

It is believed that years ago and still to this day, people came to worship the sacred Orsín for religious beliefs that it would bring them health, good fortune, youth and beauty. Many also believed that if the passage was repeated correctly three times, with your hand placed through the hole, you would see your future and pass through into the otherworld.'

Deep in thought, Joseph stared hard at the plaque. 'This must have been what my father was on about when he took me fishing,' he said quietly to himself. Under his breath he began to repeat the words from the passage. As he rose up and went to place his hand through the hole out of curiosity, Erin's voice boomed, making him jump as it echoed all around. He looked over his shoulder to see her waving while she held open a door.

'Joseph, c'mon, quick, I think I've found something!' she said

He took a final glance at the stone and began to back away and followed Erin through the door, down an unlit corridor where a light was coming from the end. 'Where are we going?'

Joseph whispered to her.

'Just follow me,' Erin whispered back.

They reached a T-junction, where a faint emergency light shone above. Joseph swung his head left and right down two extremely long corridors where the lighting continued, and the doors on either side had lit boxes fitted to the wall of every door.

'This is it,' said Erin.

'What is?' Joseph said with a look of confusion.

'The vault,' she replied.

'How do you know?' Joseph asked.

'Because each one of the doors has a sign on the side of it – *look!*' she said, pointing to the nearest door.

'Common Brittonic books,' Joseph read out. 'Okay, well there's a lot of doors so we'll have to split up, you go left and I'll go right,' he said, and motioned to the first door, then quickly zigzagged up the corridor.

Erin did the same in the opposite direction. When she reached the third door on her left she stopped to stare at the sign on the wall which read: *Ancient Latin and Runes Records.* 'PSSTT, JOSEPH, I might've found it,' she whispered up the corridor.

Joseph quickly jogged back up the corridor and saw her yanking at the door. 'Problem,' he said.

'The door's locked and it looks like this *stupid* card doesn't work in these boxes,' Erin replied and swung around to try another door.

'What do you think that other box was back up there?' said

Joseph, thumbing behind himself.

'What other box?' Erin said.

'Didn't you see it? Quick, follow me,' Joseph replied, and darted back towards the centre of the corridor. He turned left down a dead end. 'That box,' he said pointing to a large grey box on the right-hand side of the wall.

Erin stepped closer. 'It looks like it could be a power unit of some sort,' she said.

'Do you reckon it's powering all of these units on the walls?' said Joseph.

'It could be, but I don't know what that one could be beside it,' she said.

'Here, pass me the card,' Joseph said, and moved to hold it up against the red light. She grabbed him.

'Wait a minute, we don't even know what it for, let alone what it—'

But before she could finish her sentence, Joseph impulsively held the key-card up to it, and a single beep sounded and the red light turned to a solid green. The door panel opened next to it.

'– does,' Erin said, finishing her last word.

'Think we know now,' replied Joseph with a grin, and pulled the door panel wide open to reveal security cards in their own individual slots, all labelled with numbers above each one. 'Looks like these are for all them boxes, but what number was it?' he said turning to her.

'Hold on, I'll go check,' replied Erin and darted off. 'Key five!' she yelled.

Joseph whipped out the card and quickly ran back to the door. 'What the hell's that noise?' he asked, looking puzzled and noticing a strange hissing sound coming from it.

They both stared above the door to see a small amount of white gas disperse and then watched the light above the door turn from red to white.

'Try it now,' Erin said.

Joseph slotted the card into the hole on the box. It clicked, beeped once, and then red light instantly turned to green. He pulled hard on the door as it created a vacuum and threw it wide open and stood back. They both squinted from the blinding light that radiated from the large white room that looked more clinical than a vault.

'Jackpot!' Joseph said, and felt Erin throw her arms around him and kiss him on the cheek. They stepped inside, flabbergasted to see each individual book held in glass cases on a ninety-degree angle raised upon shelves and a huge white cube in the middle.

'Whoa, somebody get me a strait-jacket – that's one white room!' Erin said, blinking repeatedly. 'Now all we got do is find the right book.'

Joseph moved to the left of the cube and looked amazed by its flawless finish. Carefully he ran his fingers along the top of the smooth white marble, from one side to the other, and wondered why there was a small black circle embedded into the centre of it. He carried along with his fingers across the top and stepped around the back, when he accidentally pressed a clear embedded button which was a switch. A hologram suddenly appeared above the cube. It was a computer-generated face that resembled a woman. Alarmed by it, Joseph cautiously began to back away.

'This is going to be like finding a black cat in a coal cellar,' Erin said, bobbing her head up and down the shelves.

'Uh, Erin, you'd better take a look at this,' said Joseph nervously.

Erin's eyes grew large when she swung around. '*WOW*, what the hell is that!?' she said.

'SALVE ET GRATA, HELLO AND WELCOME,' said the hologram.

'It can talk!' Erin said.

'YES,' replied the hologram.

Joseph stood shell-shocked. 'Who, who are you?' he said stuttering.

'I AM AVA,' replied the hologram.

'AVA, that's a girl's name,' Erin said screwing her face up.

'ARTIFICIAL VIRTUAL ASSISTANT,' replied the hologram.

Intrigued, Joseph narrowed his eyes. 'So what is it you do exactly?' he said.

'I STORE INFORMATION CONTAINED WITHIN THIS VAULT INTO MY VIRTUAL MEMORY BANK, AND CAN SEARCH, SUPPLY OR CROSS REFERENCE ANYTHING THAT YOU ASK RELATING TO THE INFORMATION I HOLD,' said the hologram.

'*Cooool*,' Joseph said, impressed, 'so say if I wanted to translate something, you can do that, can you?' he asked.

'YES. IF I CONTAIN THAT INFORMATION TO COMPLETE THE TASK,' replied the hologram.

'GREAT! So how do you go about translating something that I have?' asked Joseph.

In a flash, a piece of the white gleaming table top, which appeared seamless, suddenly slid away, and a large black screen lifted up a couple of inches from below and fitted flush into the space provided. Joseph's eyes instantly widened, mesmerized by the inconceivable technology, and he threw a glance to Erin to see her reaction.

'PLEASE SCAN THE OBJECT,' said the hologram.

Joseph quickly whipped off his rucksack and took the scroll from out of the box and carefully unravelled it. He held it face down onto the black screen while a red light scanned across underneath it. He glanced up and saw the computer's face had disappeared, and was replaced with a turning white circle as though it was waiting for the information to be processed.

'INFORMATION UPLOADED AND COMPLETED. WHAT WOULD YOU LIKE TO DO NEXT?' said the hologram.

'I want the Latin section translated into English and read out,' said Joseph in a stern voice.

The hologram began to read the message aloud:

I am neither alive nor dead,

No love to give, no pain to feel, no leaves to shred,

Instead, I stand alone for those to admire,

Hollow and cold to those never warm like fire,

How old am I, it is unknown,

Ancestors worship me like a king to a throne.'

'TRANSLATION COMPLETED. WHAT WOULD YOU LIKE TO DO NEXT?' said the hologram.

'It's another riddle,' Joseph said, turning to Erin.

'AVA, what does it mean?' Erin asked.

'SORRY, I CANNOT DECIPHER THAT INFORMATION. WHAT WOULD YOU LIKE TO DO NEXT?' the hologram said.

'Hold, hold on a minute,' said Joseph as he tried to take it all in.

'I AM SORRY, I DO NOT RECOGNIZE THAT COMMAND, WHAT WOULD YOU LIKE TO DO NEXT?' said the hologram.

'Just shut *up*, would you! Erin, I need something like a pen or something, or anything to make a copy of this message,' he said.

'REQUEST COMPLETED,' said the hologram.

'What are you going on about, you stupid computer!' Joseph said.

Unbeknown to him, a piece of paper appeared from out of a thin slot that was barely visible to the naked eye on the side of the table of where he was standing.

'PLEASE TAKE THE PRINTOUT,' said the hologram.

'What printout?' he said, confused, and shrugged at Erin. He turned to look across the table top and eventually looked down and saw the piece of paper to his right hanging out of the side and snatched it.

'THANK YOU. WHAT WOULD YOU LIKE TO DO

NEXT?' the hologram said.

'Excellent, c'mon, let's get out of here' said Joseph, and threw everything back inside his rucksack. He quickly folded the piece of paper in half and tucked it inside his trouser pocket.

Back up the corridor they both scarpered and turned right. Almost at the door, Erin suddenly stopped and yelled, 'Joseph, wait, we forgot the key-card!' and spun back around and scrambled back up the corridor to the security box. 'Got it!' she said and quickly ran back and handed it to him.

They poked their heads up and peered through the wire mesh windows.

'I don't see the creature, do you?' whispered Erin.

'No, but we need to stay close to each other – right?' Joseph said.

Erin nodded. 'Right' she said.

The lock beeped. Joseph edged the door open slowly. They crept out into the atrium, heading towards the staircase, when they jumped with fright at the sound of the door slamming behind them. Joseph ushered Erin up the steps first and took a step but then stopped. Curiously he turned his head to stare at the sculpture, when suddenly he heard the glass shatter above.

'JOSEPH!' Erin screamed at the top of staircase.

For the split second that he had chance to look up, shards of glass came raining down the atrium from the skylight in amongst a swarm of crows. Up the stairs he sprinted as fast as he could and dived onto the balcony just as the glass struck, ricocheted off the staircase and crashed to the floor. He felt

Erin tugging him by his arm as he stumbled to his feet and glanced back and saw a blur of crows looping back up the atrium.

Erin quickly ran over and swiped the door. 'C'MON!' she yelled.

Frantically they sprinted back past the offices again, which were now all empty, and reached the door where they had first entered.

'Are you okay? Are you hurt?' Erin said, checking him.

'I'm fine, I'm fine,' Joseph replied, trying to catch his breath.

'What were you doing, anyway? I thought you were right behind me going up the stairs?' asked Erin.

'It doesn't matter, c'mon, we need to get the hell out of here, when I open this door, make sure you stick close to me,' Joseph said and grabbed her trembling hand.

He took the key-card from her and swiped the door. His heart was racing as he inched it back and stared through with one eye. He felt Erin squeeze his hand tightly. Nervously he pulled the door back further and crept out into the dark area and peered through the opening. He leant to his left and saw to the side of the staircase a dead body that had been pecked to death on the floor. He swallowed with disgust and quickly turned away and looked down a staircase in front of him.

'Okay, see those steps there, that's where were going, but whatever you do, don't look to your left,' he said.

'Why not?' whispered Erin.

'Because you might not like what you see, okay?' he said,

and firmly pulled her by the hand and shifted quickly towards the top of the steps. He heard Erin gasp for a split second, but he continued down the steps anyway and crept quietly into a low-lit exhibition room filled with armoury.

'Oh my God, what's that awful smell?' Erin said, covering her mouth and nose.

'Not sure,' Joseph replied, grimacing as they slowly crept between the glass cabinets, when suddenly he tripped and fell to the ground.

'Joseph, are you alright?' Erin whispered.

Joseph, face-down, glanced back and saw another dead body and quickly scrambled to his feet. He took a few steps back and swallowed and looked at Erin and saw her bottom lip quivering. 'It's okay, just don't scream,' he said, holding his hands up to her.

Close to tears Erin took a step back and muttered, 'Jo–Jo–Joseph, it's behind you!'

A lump formed in Joseph's throat. He edged around ever so slowly and his eyes flashed open with fright at the sight of the Crowman's burning eyes lurking in the shadows. Its beak chattered together. Then it stepped out and erected itself to its full height. Filled with fear, Joseph became rooted to the floor when he heard Erin scream and then the creature bellowed out a deathly squawk and started to charge towards him. Everything moved in slow motion as he spun around and started to run and yelled at Erin to run as well. Suddenly he felt himself struck from behind and was catapulted through the air and landed on the steps covered in glass.

Dazed, he shook his head and rolled onto his side and looked up and saw the creature heading towards Erin who was on the ground. 'Erin!' he yelled, and quickly clambered to his feet and rushed back down the stairs to her. Joseph ducked as the creature swung its claw and smashed through another cabinet. Joseph yanked Erin to her feet. Frantically they ran up the stairs and glanced back and saw the creature had stopped, as it couldn't climb the steps and began to squawk thunderously. They stopped in the corridor and looked left and right.

'Which way?' asked Erin.

'This way!' replied Joseph.

Down the hallway they ran towards the revolving door, while hundreds of crows followed in pursuit. 'Quick, get in, GET IN!' Joseph said, and shoved her through the door. He glanced back and his eyes grew wide as the crows flew like an Exocet missile towards him. At the last second he leapt inside the door, spun around and fell out on the other side and tumbled down the steps.

'Joseph, are you alright?' Erin said, running over to him.

Joseph groaned on the floor. 'I'm okay, just help me up,' he said.

'C'mon, let's get out of here,' he said, and hobbled down the other steps.

Down the large flight of steps they ran until they reached the car at the bottom and quickly dived inside. Joseph looked back at the building to see all the windows breaking and crows emerging from the building.

'C'mon, Erin, they're coming, they're coming!' he yelled to her.

Erin slammed the car into reverse and crazily drove backwards all the way down the road, mounted the pavement and slammed into the garage door of the green house.

'C'mon, c'mon, c'mon!' said Joseph.

'I'm trying, I'M TRYING!' Erin replied, crunching the gears.

The wheels spun against the fine layer of snow as the car screeched off. Joseph held on for dear life as they tore away, while the rear bumper scraped along the ground until it eventually fell off and was left behind in the middle of the road. Out of nowhere came flashing blue lights and a car was heading towards them at speed.

'Oh no, it's the police!' Joseph said, panicking.

'Hold on tight,' replied Erin. She gritted her teeth and pressed her foot all the way down to the floor.

Joseph scrunched his eyes shut and at the last second they shot past the police car, causing both wing mirrors on the cars to collide and smash clean off. The sound startled Joseph to immediately open his eyes and he turned around to look through the back window. 'They've stopped in the road and they're turning around!' he exclaimed.

'Don't worry, I've got this,' Erin said, and kept her eyes fixed on the road ahead as they zoomed off.

Chapter 22

WHAT DO YOU CALL?

'Are you alright, Joseph?' Erin shouted through the open passenger door.

'Just give me a minute,' groaned Joseph.

Erin frowned, watching him lean over the fence being sick. She quickly reached over to the back seat and grabbed his rucksack and started to rummage through. Not finding what she wanted, she began to search the car high and low.

'Tissues, tissues, tissues, doesn't this car have any tissues?' she said out loud to herself.

She opened the cluttered glove box and lifted up a map amongst other things and finally found a pack lying at the bottom. The car door flew open and out she leapt and hurried over across the snowy layby and handed them to him.

'Thanks,' Joseph said, and wiped his mouth.

'That's okay, how are you feeling anyway?' asked Erin, folding her arms.

He sat back against the fence, exhausted, and replied,

'Better for being sick, that's for sure.'

Erin plonked herself beside him and said, 'Well, I don't think I'll be kissing you in a hurry, Mr Van Puke,' and gave him a friendly nudge with her shoulder.

'It's your bloody crazy driving that makes me sick,' Joseph said, smirking.

'Really . . . and there's me thinking you weren't cut out for travelling,' Erin replied with a wry smile.

'Nah, it's definitely your driving,' Joseph chuckled.

'Well, better than being caught by the police, hey?' Erin said.

'You can say that again,' replied Joseph. All of a sudden his mood changed and became serious as he stared at the ground.

'Hey, you okay?' said Erin.

Joseph nodded to her and lowered his eyes. 'I just hope all of this is not in vain, you know, for the sake of everyone that's died. I don't know what I would do if if I lost my—' he said.

'Hey, listen,' Erin interrupted and began to rub his back, 'you're not going to lose anyone – okay? Sometimes things are out of our hands in life, but how you choose to live your life, *that* can never be taken away from you. You made me realize that.'

'What do you mean?' Joseph asked, looking perplexed.

'Well, because up until I met you, I realized I was drifting along. All I ever did was go to school and work for my parents to help run the family business. *Sure*, my mum wants me to go to university, which I might still do – who knows? – whereas Dad wants me to take over the family business and turn it around. But after everything that has happened, it's made me realize how fragile life can be. I don't want to just slave behind a bar for the rest of my life because it's convenient. The world has too much to offer, you just have to get off your lazy ass and go get it, like you did, the moment you decided to go and find out about that photograph, and from that moment on – we met, so everything happens for a reason, Joseph,' she said.

Joseph pondered for a moment over what she had said and didn't notice she had stood up.

'So what's the plan now, Indiana?' Erin said, rubbing the backs of her arms.

'Hmm . . .' Joseph said, snapping out of his trance to look up at her.

'I said, what's the plan now, Indiana? We can't sit around here all day in the freezing cold,' said Erin.

'Who's Indiana?' Joseph replied as he stood up and started to walk back to the car with her.

'You know, the guy who goes hunting for lost treasure and stuff in the films?' said Erin.

Joseph shook his head and shrugged his shoulders. 'Nope, no idea,' he said.

Erin rolled her eyes. 'Never mind,' she said, opening the car door and climbing back inside. 'Seriously, though, what are we going to do? We can't keep driving around in this car for ever, sooner or later we're going to get caught.'

'I know, I know, you're right, we just need to figure out this riddle,' Joseph said, pulling it out from his pocket.

'So do you have any idea what it could mean?' she asked,

leaning over.

Joseph screwed his lips up and shook his head. 'Nah, not in the slightest,' he replied, scratching his head, and he sighed.

'Well, your grandfather certainly doesn't make it easy for you, that's for sure. Looks like we could be banging our heads against the wall with this one,' Erin said, and tapped her head against the window and then leant against it.

'What did you just say?' Joseph said, turning to her with a surprised look upon his face.

'I said your grandfather doesn't make it—' Erin said.

'No, no the other bit,' Joseph said, cutting her off.

'What, we could be banging our heads against a wall,' she said, partially screwing her face up.

All of a sudden a light bulb lit up inside Joseph's head and his eyes grew large, staring at the paper in his hand. 'That's it!' he exclaimed.

'What is?' Erin asked.

'It's a wall!' he said enthusiastically, turning to her again.

'What's a wall? You're not making any sense, Joseph!' she said.

'The riddle, it's a wall, well, I mean it's not exactly a wall, it's a stone wall,' he said.

'*Great,* so now we're looking for a stone wall, which the whole planet's built with,' she said sarcastically.

'Sorry, I'm not making myself clear. Remember the statue thing back at the library I was looking at?' said Joseph.

'Oh yeah, the large rock thing, you mean,' Erin said and pretended to get excited.

'Yeah, that's the one! And—' Joseph exclaimed.

'And we were about to passionately kiss, but instead you bogged off to look at it and left me hanging like an idiot, yeah, how could I forget!' she said, glaring hard at him.

'Oh yeah, sorry about that,' Joseph said, abashed, rubbing the back of his neck, 'but you remember the statue, right?'

'Yes, I remember the sculpture,' Erin said, and gave a huff and rolled her eyes.

'Well, when I was about eight, my father took me fishing to a place called Cregennan Lakes where I saw a standing stone for the first time, which was identical to that in the atrium, except this was much larger. But when I asked him about it, he said it was something to do with people worshipping them, but also mentioned that there was another one much bigger than the one I saw on a different lake to where we were fishing,' Joseph said enthusiastically.

'Right, so you saw a standing stone that looked like Stonehenge – big deal, what's your point exactly?' replied Erin.

'Ah, so you do know about these standing stone things?' Joseph said and raised his eyebrows.

'Not much,' Erin said and shrugged, 'only that I once went on a school trip to see Stonehenge, but apart from that—'

'Well, I haven't been to Stonehenge, but the point that I'm trying to make is, the sculpture that was in the atrium is the one that my father must have been referring to,' said Joseph.

'And how do you know?' Erin asked.

'Because I read it on the plaque and it said that the real one stood at Cregennan Lakes, plus if you read the riddle all the clues point to it – here,' Joseph said, handing it to her.

Erin read it again. 'I suppose it does kind of make sense,' she said.

'But there is just one problem?' said Joseph.

'What's that?' Erin said, turning to him.

'I don't know how to get to it,' said Joseph.

'Oh,' replied Erin.

Joseph rested his head against the window. 'Without my dad being here to take us there, we're stuffed,' he said, and blew out his cheeks.

Erin clicked her fingers and pushed his legs out of the way. 'Here!' she said, pulling a map from the glove box and placing it down in his lap.

'O-*kay*,' Joseph said, surprised, and fought to open the concertina pages. He held it up, pretending he knew what he was looking for.

After a few minutes, Erin started to tap her fingernail against the door and said, 'Would you like me to take a look at it?'

'Nah, it's okay, I've got this,' he replied.

Joseph could see out of the corner of his eye she was restless, and he was growing frustrated as well, but he couldn't swallow his pride and he continued to search for the location. Unexpectedly she leant her head against his shoulder and peered over.

'Here, there it is!' Erin said.

Joseph huffed. 'I knew that,' he replied, feeling slightly jealous.

'Sure you did,' Erin said, grinning.

'So what are we waiting for? Let's go find us a stone!' Joseph said excitedly and sat and waited impatiently for the car to move. He heard Erin cough and turned to look at her. 'What?'

'Seat belt please,' replied Erin, reaching for hers.

'Oh, yeah,' said Joseph, and quickly buckled himself in.

'And one more thing,' said Erin as she started the car.

'Which is?' he said.

'Don't be sick on me now, will you?' replied Erin and giggled.

Joseph leant across and pretended to be sick all over her and then laughed.

'Eww, gross!' Erin said, pulling a disgusted face with a hint of a smirk.

'Hey, want to hear a joke?' asked Joseph.

'Sure,' said Erin.

'How do you make a tissue dance?' said Joseph.

'Don't know,' Erin replied and shrugged.

'You put a little boogie in it!' replied Joseph, and laughed hysterically at his own joke.

Erin tutted and shifted her eyebrows inwards and shook her head.

'I know, I didn't get it either at first when my mate—' said Joseph, still laughing.

'No, I get it, I just think it's a terrible joke, that's all,' replied Erin.

'Well, I bet you can't do any better?' said Joseph, baiting her.

'Of course I can, I work in a pub full of banter *and* jokes remember. Okay, so a pirate walks into a bar with a ship's steering wheel hanging from his crotch, and the bartender says, what the hell is that? Pirate replies, dunno but it's drivin' me nuts!' Erin said, grinning.

Joseph stared at her with a blank look upon his face.

'Get it – the steering wheel is driving his you-know-whats,' she said, and wrinkled her brow.

'Oh yeah,' Joseph replied, and gave a sheepish smile.

Erin raised her eyebrows and said, 'Oh, this is so going to be a long drive,' and pulled the car slowly away.

Chapter 23

A ROAD LESS TRAVELLED
BRINGS GREAT REWARD

Large man-made stone walls ran parallel to Joseph and Erin as they drove along a very narrow, winding road, which barely fitted the car, and seemed to go on for ever. Behind the walls was an abundance of beautiful countryside covered in snow that had started to melt, and patches of bright green grass began to flourish. The road slipped off into the distance and met majestic mountains that sat boldly like pyramids.

Joseph continued his barrage of awful jokes, when Erin interrupted him and said, 'Hey, I got another one for you.'

'Go for it,' Joseph said, eager to hear.

'Roses are red, violets are blue, if I had a brick, I would throw it at you!' Erin said, laughing uncontrollably and almost letting go of the steering wheel.

'That's not even a joke, that's just blatantly mean,' Joseph said, and crossed his arms in a huff and frowned.

'Ah, c'mon, I'm only playing with you,' Erin said with a cheeky smile and threw a glance at him. The moment she turned back to the road, they passed a road sign and Erin quickly slammed on the brakes.

Joseph's seat belt locked as he was flung forward and the car skidded across the tarmac and ground to a halt. 'Hey, what's the big idea?' he said, turning to her.

'Sorry, but there was a sign back there,' she said and slowly began to reverse the car.

As the sign came into view, Joseph's eyes lit up to see it pointing left which read: *Cregennan Lakes, three quarters of a mile.*

'We've found it!' Joseph said, turning to her with a beaming smile, and leant over and gave her an affectionate hug. 'Thank you,' he whispered over her shoulder.

'For what?' Erin asked.

'For everything! I couldn't have done it without you,' he said, and slowly edged back into his seat and stared deep into her eyes. A bundle of butterflies roamed his stomach as soon as she placed her hand inside his. His eyes slowly drifted down to her beautiful, radiant lips that smiled with a glow. His heart fluttered. He wanted to kiss her but his nerves were getting the better of him.

Before he knew it, she gently grabbed him by his top and pulled him forwards. Euphoria flooded him the moment he pressed up against her soft lips and nervously wrapped his arm around her body. His neck hairs stood on end as they engaged in passionate kissing. Then slowly he edged away, flushed and crimson-faced, to catch his breath, which felt like it had been stolen by an angel. With her eyes still closed for a second longer, he gazed at her pretty face. Then she opened them and gave him a soothing smile. 'Can I tell you something, and promise you won't laugh?' Joseph said in a soft voice.

'I would never do that, unless of course it's one of your terrible jokes,' Erin replied, and gently stroked his face.

'You're the first girl I have ever kissed,' he said nervously. Strangely she buried her head into his chest and wrapped her arms around him tightly. Joseph felt concerned that he might have said something wrong that had upset her, and slowly placed his arms around her and gently stroked the back of her hair. 'I'm sorry, I didn't mean to upset you,' he said softly.

'You haven't,' sniffled Erin. 'Your words meant a lot to me,' she whispered softly.

Out of nowhere a horn blasted, which scared the living daylights out of the both of them and they jumped with fright. They sprang up and glanced around to see a noisy tractor rolling up behind them with a farmer waving his hand in an angry manner.

Erin quickly pulled the car away and turned left and drove a couple of yards down the road and stopped again. She turned to Joseph and at the same time they both burst out laughing. Her laugh slowly wound down and a coy smile appeared. She leant across and gave him another kiss before pulling off again.

Joseph gazed out of the window at the tranquil surroundings. Suddenly they approached a dividing man-made wall with a steel gate. As soon as she stopped the car, Joseph quickly hopped out and opened the gate to let Erin pass through, then quickly closed it behind him. He leapt back inside with a cheesy grin upon his face.

'What are you smiling about?' Erin said, narrowing her eyes and smiling.

'This is it! This is where my father brought me fishing! If you look over there you'll just be able to make out the small lake at the bottom,' he said excitedly, and pointed down the valley.

'Looks pretty big from here,' Erin replied.

'Well, there's a bigger lake than that around here, supposedly, and if you look over there, that's the standing stone I saw as a kid with my father,' Joseph said, pointing through the windscreen.

They continued along the twisting road, passing over a brow and descending down the other side and entered through an open gate. They drove around a very sharp bend to the left, where a row of tall trees appeared on their right, but only for a few yards, when the most spectacular and breath-taking lake suddenly appeared from out of nowhere. The car rolled to a halt. Complete silence fell between them and their mouths fell open in awe. Their eyes became transfixed on the lake's exquisite beauty, even on this gloomy day.

'Oh my God, I think I've died and gone to heaven,' Erin said.

Joseph's eyes were popping out of his head. 'Me too,' he replied.

'Who would have ever thought this was here. It's magnificent!' Erin said, turning to him.

'C'mon, we'd better hurry up and find this standing stone

before it gets too dark,' Joseph said, looking up at the sky.

As soon as Erin had pulled the car into a nearby car park and switched the engine off, Joseph swiftly leant over to grab his rucksack from the back seat, when he saw the hilt of the dagger poking out of the top. He withdrew it and held it up and saw a nervous look in Erin's eyes. 'We need to be on guard if that devil creature returns,' he said, and placed it back inside of the box.

The freezing cold air drifted across the lake and caused goose pimples to spread across Joseph's body the second he stepped out from the car. 'Whoa, that's cold,' he said to himself, rubbing his hands together, before walking around to the other side to meet Erin, who had her arms folded tightly to her chest.

'Here,' he said, raising her hood up over her head.

'Thanks,' Erin replied, smiling and interlocking his arm with hers.

They strolled out of the car park and stopped on the road, a stone's throw away from the water's edge. Joseph peered through his narrowed eyes across the countryside that was shielded by the low-hanging cloud slowly shifting from the southwest of the lake.

'Well, this is going to be like finding a needle in a haystack,' he said, shivering, and placed his hood up.

'What's that over there?' Erin asked.

'Where?' Joseph replied.

Erin pointed left of the lake. 'That,' she said.

'Oh that, it's a boathouse. There was another one of those

on the smaller lake where I fished with my dad,' Joseph said. 'Wait a minute, what's that behind it?' He stared right of the boathouse, but the brief break in the clouds caused him to lose sight as they quickly blended together again.

'What was it?' asked Erin.

'Not sure, but I think we should go check it out, what do you reckon?' he asked.

'As they say, leave no stone unturned,' she said, and raised one eyebrow to him with a smirk.

'Ha ha, very funny, that one I do get. C'mon, last one over there is a rotten egg,' Joseph said and started to run up the road.

'Hey, not fair,' Erin said, chasing after him.

Up the road they ran. It gradually inclined and then became steep. Joseph reached a large white gate which was locked. He stopped and gasped for breath. He looked back down the road and saw Erin walking up just a few yards away and yelled, 'C'mon, slowcoach,' before turning his attention to the boathouse, which he could now see the back of.

Erin finally reached the gate and leant against it, panting. 'Cheat,' she said.

'What, me?' Joseph tittered.

'Yes, you, if you hadn't had such a head start, you know I would have won,' she said, and screwed her face up at him.

'Yeah, yeah,' Joseph smirked. He stared at a man-made stone wall that ran from the boathouse and up the hillside and cast his eyes along it. A little way up he could see a large wooden stile. 'C'mon,' he said, climbing the gate.

'Where are we going?' Erin asked.

'Over to that wall over there,' Joseph said, nodding his head sideways from his position on top of the gate before dropping down the other side.

In no time at all they crossed the partially frozen marshland and reached the stile. Joseph let Erin climb first and he followed quickly behind. No sooner had he stepped one foot onto the grass than he turned to her, baffled, wondering why she looked in a trance-like state.

'What's wrong?' he asked.

'Look!' she said in a hushed voice.

Joseph turned his head and his mouth fell open. The clouds had cleared and shifted across the lake and there on a small mound, in all its glory, was a remarkable standing stone. 'Oh my God, Erin, we've found it, we've found it!' he yelled. 'C'mon! Bursting with excitement, he darted across the marshland like a dog off the leash and momentarily forgot all about Erin.

'WAIT UP!' Erin yelled, running after him.

Joseph reached the stone fairly quickly from his crazy sprint and stood in front of it, blown away by its impressive size. He eyed it up and down and then began to circle around, running his fingertips against all the runes carved upon it, when he completed a full circle and stood back, marvelling. He didn't hear Erin coming from behind him, muttering to herself, until she was standing beside him with an angry look upon her face.

'Why didn't you wait for me? I was calling you!' Erin said.

'Sorry, I got carried away. But get a load of this, check this out,' Joseph said, walking over to the hole and placing his arm through it. 'Look at the size of this hole that goes all the way through it – it's *huge!*'

'It looks like a big rock to me,' said Erin sarcastically and crossed her arms.

'Ah, c'mon, don't be like that, I apologized, didn't I?' Joseph said, turning to face her and pretending to frown by pushing out his bottom lip.

'Anyhow, now that we've found it – what do we do next?' Erin asked, strolling over.

'Well, I guess now we look for clues,' he replied.

'That's all well and good, but it would help if we knew what we were looking for. What else did it say on the scroll?' she said. 'At the end?'

'Something to do with, *what do you see,*' he replied, touching the stone.

'Well, that's a great help,' Erin said, raising her eyebrows as she started to walk around it.

After a long time searching the stone and the surrounding area, Joseph rose to his feet, tired and fed up. His face was pale and drawn, his hands were aching and stiff. The cold drew up through his feet and made him irritable, and most of all he felt famished, which added further to his moodiness. He strolled miserably back around to the other side of the stone where Erin was stood. She also had a peeved look about her and Joseph asked, 'Find anything?'

'Nope, nothing, you?' replied Erin.

'Nothing,' Joseph said, shaking his head and tightening his

lips together. 'I just don't get it, we've been searching for ages and there's nothing here!'

'We're obviously missing something,' said Erin.

'Like what? I mean look at it out here, there's nothing for miles around, apart from us and this stupid stone,' he said, flapping his arms with frustration and huffed.

'Aren't they weird, the markings all over it, though?' Erin said, touching the stone.

'Back at the library it said on the plaque that the words translate into some sort of passage, which you would then have to say out loud three times and place your hand into the hole,' Joseph said.

'What happens then?' Erin asked, turning to him.

'Then supposedly you magically fly off into some sort of afterlife,' he said and sprinkled his fingers up into the air. 'Why do you ask?'

'Hmm, no reason,' Erin said, and bent down slightly to look through the hole.

'Look, I don't know about you but I'm cold and starving and maybe we should head back to the car in case that creature comes,' Joseph said reluctantly.

'Hold on a minute, you should take a look at this,' Erin said, waving her hand to him.

'What, what is it?' he asked.

'See for yourself,' Erin replied and stepped aside.

Joseph bent down and looked through with narrow eyes. 'It's an *island!*' he said in disbelief, and straightened up and shifted to the side of the stone to gaze at the lake. 'How is it we never saw that before?'

'Probably the mist was hiding it,' said Erin.

Joseph stared long and hard at it for a moment and became lost in his thoughts. All of a sudden, he spun around and began to walk speedily up the narrow footpath.

'Wait, wait a second, Joseph, where are we going?' Erin said.

'To see what's on that island,' he replied.

'And how do you propose we're going to get there, fly?' she said sarcastically. 'It's in the middle of the lake'

'Follow me and you'll see,' Joseph said and walked quickly down the marshland.

In no time at all, Joseph reached the stone wall at the bottom next to the boathouse, and hidden amongst the bushes he saw another stile. Slipping and sliding, he quickly climbed over and came back down the other side and turned to see Erin walk through a broken side gate with a grin. He huffed and promptly walked over to the old wooden door and pressed down on the latch and slowly opened it. An almighty gust of cold wind whipped out from the boathouse and blew against him. Cautiously he stepped in and said, 'That's how we get there!'

Erin followed him in and stood on the brittle concrete ledge. She stared at the rickety old rowing boat bobbing up and down on the water and said as she spun back around, '*OOOOH no*, there's no way I'm getting in that thing!' and headed back to the door.

'Wait, hold on a second,' Joseph said, blocking her path

and placing his hands up, 'what's the problem?'

'What do you mean, what's the problem, *that's* the problem!' she said, pointing to the boat.

Joseph grinned nervously. 'What, it floats, don't it?' he said, staring at it, a little doubtful himself.

'You can't be serious, Joseph, that thing will sink before you know it,' said Erin.

'No, it won't, watch!' Joseph carefully climbed down inside and stood in the middle, rocking the boat back and forth with his feet. 'See, it floats,' he said.

'Huh,' Erin muttered, raising her eyebrows. As she went to turn away and head for the door again, Joseph said to her, 'Where are you going?'

'I'm sorry, Joseph, but there's no way I'm getting into that death trap. We've cheated death once too many times and now you want to go and take that old, leaky thing for a row – you can count me out,' said Erin and crossed her arms.

'Fine, I'll go on my own, I don't need you anyway,' Joseph replied curtly.

'Fine, be like that, don't come calling me when it begins to sink. I'm going back to the car,' she said, and headed for the door.

'*Fine*,' he replied bitterly.

'FINE!' Erin replied, and slammed the boathouse door behind her. She stamped across the little footbridge and up the hillside, muttering to herself, 'The bloody nerve of him, after everything I have done, I hope it bloody sinks for all I care.' Suddenly she lost her footing and fell down onto the wet ground in a heap. 'GGRRRRRRRR!' she screamed out, then stumbled to her feet and continued her trek across the marshland.

Gritting his teeth, Joseph climbed back out and ripped the oars off their wall hooks and threw them down into the boat angrily, along with his rucksack, and he climbed down again. 'Leaky boat, HUH, there's nothing wrong with the damn thing, I'll show her!' he muttered to himself and quickly untied the rope and slung it inside. He gripped one of the oars and pushed against the side of the concrete edge. Slowly the boat crept out onto the cold breath of the water, which gave him a chill. He locked the oars into position and unevenly began to row until eventually he found a rhythm and started to power across the water. 'HAH, see, nothing to it!' he said to himself.

His arms began to burn as he rowed faster and faster, feeling his heart beating hard with each and every stroke. Every so often, he glanced around to see where he was, and saw the island growing quickly in size, but he found himself looking more at ominous dark clouds above.

Without warning, and before he knew it, the boat clanged into the side of the island's embankment. Instantly he was propelled backwards off his seat and landed flat on his back inside the boat. He gazed at the sky, exhausted, and breathing erratic. The boat rocking upon the waters made him feel nauseous. Quickly he sat up and glanced around and saw he was slowly drifting away again from the island.

'No, no, no, no,' he said, panicking as he clambered to

the end of the boat, which caused it to sway aggressively, and he stretched out his arm as far as he could. His fingernails clawed into the embankment until eventually he latched onto a scraggy root jutting out and hauled himself in. He detached the right oar and swung the boat around in line with the island and tied the rope swiftly round a root. He slipped on his rucksack and unsteadily stood up and started to climb up the embankment. After a few times of falling back down, he finally reached the top and crawled along on his hands and knees through the undergrowth and heaved himself up onto his feet with great effort. Tired and out of breath, he wiped his mucky hands on his trousers before pulling back a branch to see if he could see the car park from the island. 'Huh, told her it wouldn't sink,' he said smugly to himself, and turned to face his daunting surroundings.

The island was extremely overcrowded with trees, but larger than he'd expected. The light that filtered through the cluster of branches was very dim and caused it to feel shady and unwelcoming. Not a flake of snow had fallen on the ground but a lot of moisture seemed to cling to the air. He glanced around with uncertainty and, feeling on edge, he decided to pull out the dagger. 'Okay, medallion, where are you? I know you're here somewhere – I know it,' he muttered to himself.

Feeling optimistic, Joseph proceeded forward with caution, swinging the dagger carefully at the branches and nettles to create a path. It sliced through the undergrowth effortlessly. Impressed by the blade's sharpness, he took a daring swing at a bigger branch, but overswung and cut straight through a small tree like a hot knife to butter. 'Holy cow, that's incredible!' he said, gawping at the blade. With his back turned, he suddenly heard the tree creak from behind and glanced over his shoulder in shock. 'Uh-oh,' he said as the tree began to fall in his direction and he quickly dived out of the way. The moment the tree hit the ground he looked back to see that it had missed him by a matter of inches. 'Whoa, that was close,' he said.

Gradually he rose to his feet just as a strange murmur appeared from behind him. In a flash he swung around and pointed the dagger outwards. 'Who's there?' he said in a timid voice. He felt his stomach tighten and his shoulders became tense. His eyes darted from side to side while the dagger shook in his hand from the firm grip he held around it. Warily he began to step back, when out of nowhere the blade began to glow a faint red. 'What the hell?' he said, startled, and instantly dropped the dagger to the ground and quickly backed away.

Freaked out, he stared at it for a second or so, thinking his eyes were deceiving him, before he cautiously approached and crouched down and carefully poked it with his finger, expecting something to happen. When nothing did, he reached for it nervously and rose to his feet with it held away from him. 'See, all in your head, Joey,' he said out loud to himself, when the blade unexpectedly gave off a shimmer. His eyes became dazzled momentarily. Then apprehensively he held it pointing outwards and circled it slowly. The moment the blade started to glow once again he gasped and stopped. For a second, he held his breath before easing it out and now he began to make his way in the direction it had pointed.

As Joseph wandered through the woods, little by little the blade grew stronger in hue. He ducked under some branches and emerged on the other side into a small clearing and to his surprise saw a huge tree upon its side. The trunk was heavily covered with ivy and nettles and looked like it had been there for quite some time. Gingerly he followed it along for a short while and stopped at an opening amongst the bushes. He stared at the blade, which still held a strong glow and then peered through the gap where there was a rocky, cratered area.

'Looks like it's this way,' he said to himself, and with some effort he climbed down the rocks that were covered in moss and made his way in. Almost immediately he gasped at the incredible, ghastly sight of a ten-foot-tall wall of mud and sprawling roots at the tree's base. It had been ripped from out the ground and stood upright. 'Oh my God, that's disgusting,' he said, grimacing and quickly turned away.

The second Joseph raised his head, he jumped out of his skin with absolute fright. Petrified, he stumbled backwards, tripped and fell to the ground and clambered back. 'Get away from *me*, stay back, stay *back!*' he yelled, cowering with the dagger pointed at a spirit floating just metres away from him.

Draped in an off-white robe that appeared loosely fitted to its transparent frame, and with long flowing hair that was of a similar shade, the spirit had a sway of elegance which Joseph observed. Though indeed it was clear to him that the spirit resembled a woman in every shape and form, he found it difficult to define the natural features of her face as she emitted a bright white light. But in his fearful, paralysed state, as he lay on the ground staring, something else caused him alarm and that was the dagger. The blade reacted as if it was drawing energy from her and was burning so fiercely, he was convinced it might catch fire at any second, but he was too afraid to let it go.

'What do you want from me?' he said in a shaky voice, but the spirit remained silent and just floated gently back and forth, staring at him.

Joseph felt his legs turn to jelly as he tried to get to his feet. He continued holding the dagger pointed away from him and stuttered, 'Who-who are you? Are you the spirit my grandfather spoke of?' But once again she didn't respond and strangely pointed her floating arm. Joseph kept his eyes firmly fixed on her and turned his head suspiciously to his right. Then he flashed his eyes over in the direction of a rock face, which was completely covered in vines and moss. He flashed his eyes back to her. 'You want me to go over there?' he said dubiously. The spirit nodded in affirmation.

Cautiously he began to step sideways, refusing to take his eyes off her, when he reached the wall and for a split second turned his head to look it up and down and gave it a slight prod, and then swung back to see the spirit had miraculously disappeared. Hunched over, Joseph sighed with relief and held his hand to his chest and felt his heart pounding. He looked at the vines, feeling confused, and wondered what the spirit was trying to tell him, when the blade burning fiery red in his hand caught his attention.

Without a second thought, he started to slice away at the thick vines and in no time at all, he had hacked away the whole lot and stood back nonplussed to see an opening, barricaded over by wooden planks. Eager to see what was on the other side, Joseph clawed at the planks with his fingers, before resorting to kicking them forcefully. After quite a few aggressive kicks, one of the planks broke in half and quickly he knelt down and prised it back with his hands. He stared through into the darkness and then one by one removed all of them until a doorway became clear to see.

Joseph stood at the foot of the opening, slightly on edge, and stared at tenebrous steps that spiralled downwards. Swiftly he whipped off his rucksack and pulled out his torch. With the blazing dagger held out, he took a deep breath and proceeded cautiously down the brittle stone steps. Down and down, deeper and deeper he went, singeing all the nasty cobwebs along the way that were weaved across the stone walls.

Finally he reached the bottom to the smell of stagnant water, though he could see none, and he entered into a narrow passage that was no bigger than an arm's width apart. On tenterhooks, he crept along, shining the light into the pitch black and wondered how far it went and where it was likely to lead him to. After a few more paces, the passage came to a dead end. Faced with a stone wall, he searched around with the light and saw a curved hole at the bottom. He knelt down and shone the light into an ebony tunnel that was crawling with insects. 'Please, Lord, don't let there be anything nasty inside there,' he prayed before squeezing inside.

Out the other side, Joseph leapt to his feet, shaking all of the bugs off him and stepped forward and suddenly felt the floor move. 'What the—?' he exclaimed, shining the torch down to see a stone slab had shifted downwards a few inches beneath his foot. All of a sudden he heard a strange cranking sound and then – *CLANG*. He spun around, shocked to see steel bars had dropped down the tunnel. 'No, no, no, *NO!*' he said, tugging at the bars and striking them several times or so with the blade, which did nothing but spark against it.

Panic-stricken, he shone the light in every direction in what appeared to be a circular stone room. Joseph quickly searched for a way out when he came across a wooden lever set in the middle of the wall. Impulsively, he went to reach for it, but stopped suddenly when he spied a message written above it on a piece of wood and read it out loud:

'*Push the lever up, death it will bring,*
Push the lever down, fate be the same thing,
Which way to pull me, up or down,
If a clown stands on his head, which way does it frown?'

Joseph couldn't think straight. His mind was filled with confusion at being trapped inside the room. 'What does that mean: *death it will bring?*' he said worryingly to himself and looked around the room. As the light slowly crept upwards against the wall and moved above his head, he gasped with horror and stumbled backwards and fell to the floor. His eyes were filled with fear, staring at a razor-sharp, metal, spiked contraption that was circular framed and the same size of the room, which hung like a chandelier only ten feet or so away, pointing down towards him. Joseph started to hyperventilate. He slid up the wall and circled back towards the tunnel, while staring up the whole time. He shook the bars desperately. 'Someone, please help me, I'm trapped, HELLLLPPPP!' he yelled through the bars at the top of his voice.

He slumped against the cold floor with despair and stared at the riddle which the light was shining against. He wrapped his arms around his legs which he had brought up to his chest and rested his forehead upon his knees and closed his eyes. Thoughts of being trapped for ever, or worse still, being killed by the spikes, terrified him, but most of all not being able to see his family and friends again, or Erin, for that matter, was harder to accept. But as he weaved his way through his clouded mind, a memory of when he was a small boy playing with a new toy at Christmas time at home seamlessly floated up from nowhere and caused him to reminisce.

'*Dad, Dad, it's not working,*' he remembered saying to his father.

'*What's not working, son?*' his father said, approaching.

'*My fire engine, it's not working,*' Joseph said.

'*Let's have a little look, shall we? Here, there you go, son,*' his father said, turning the batteries around the other way. '*You know, Joey, sometimes the answer is always there in front of you, you just have to look a little bit harder to find it.*'

Joseph gradually opened his eyes. He rose to his feet and looked up with worry, then trod cautiously across the room. He stared long and hard at the riddle and read it over and over again until his thoughts were burnt out. Once more he looked up to see the tips on the spikes shine from the light. He swallowed, and turned to face the lever with trepidation. 'God help me,' he said, reaching for it with his sweaty hand and took a couple of deep breaths.

'Okay, Joey, here goes nothing – on three. One, two . . . three!' he shouted and simultaneously scrunched his eyes shut and pushed the lever up. An extremely loud sound of metal and stone grating echoed all around the room for a few seconds and then immediately stopped. He gingerly opened his eyelids and realized that he was still alive and quickly flashed the light over to the tunnel to see the bars had lifted.

Joseph leant over onto his knees and sighed with great relief.

As he straightened up and was about to make a sharp exit, he noticed that part of the wall was missing in front of him. Curiously he stepped closer and shone the light inside. His eyes lit up with disbelief to see a dark silver trinket box on four tiny legs resting upon a book. His heart began to race as he reached in carefully. He cast his torchlight over the book, which read: *Cyril Van Pearce: Diary*. 'Oh my God, it's Grand-dad's diary!' he said with elation.

His hand started to tremble with excitement as he unwound the string that held it closed and opened the front page to find an envelope tucked inside. Without hesitation he tore it open, sat back against the filthy wall and began to read the letter.

Chapter 24

FAREWELL

Dear Joseph,

First and foremost if you are reading this letter, I pray that you are safe and well. Secondly, huge congratulations are in order for successfully finding the Dragon's Head Medallion! I want to say how proud a grandfather I am that you have completed the task and the medallion has not fallen into the wrong hands, and I can rest in peace knowing my work on earth is finally done.

I feel that after all you have gone through, a full and clear explanation is probably required of me as to how I came to possess the Dragon's Head Medallion, so please forgive me if I am repeating anything that you might already know. But to set the record straight, I accidentally discovered the piece of metal whilst out fishing with your father on this very lake. Your father caught the largest captivating rainbow trout that either one of us had ever seen before, but as we were removing the hook I noticed something was stuck in its mouth. I quickly got my fishing pliers, whilst your father struggled to keep a hold of the fish in his hands, and carefully pulled it out.

There it was, this beautiful, hypnotizing piece of metal which you see before you, and most intriguing because I truly did not know what it was. Your father laughed and told me it was a piece of broken scrap metal and said to chuck it back in the lake – but I begged to differ. I knew there was something mystical about it, but just didn't know what. As a great believer in fate, I immediately contacted a dear friend of mine, the retired Professor Roy Timbleglas, and paid him a visit at the National Library where he now worked.

After a couple of weeks of running some extensive, in-depth tests and studies, he categorically confirmed it was not made of any of Earth's materials whatsoever! This, as you can imagine, came as a startling surprise to me, along with a flood of questions, like where did it come from? How did it get here? Does it belong to aliens? The questions were endless. Needless to say, over the months that followed no answers presented themselves, but something peculiar did happen and that was that a lot of crows started to appear in and around our home and seemed to follow me wherever I went. But that wasn't the only strange thing that happened.

I have never told anyone this story, so you are the first to know, but one day whilst I was out fishing alone in the boat at Cregennan Lakes I caught a little fighter of a fish and started to reel it in, when out of the blue, a crow landed on the end of the boat and began to squawk annoyingly. At my wits' end with these blessed things, I stood up and tried to shoo it away whilst fighting to keep a hold of the fish, but without warning the line snapped and I fell backwards, banged my head on the side and was sent flying overboard.

As I was sinking I opened my eyes to see a tiny white light which appeared from the darkest depths of the water. It drew closer and closer and suddenly stopped in front of me. With my blurred vision I stared at what seemed to be a white spirit in the form of a lady, floating. It really was a surreal moment as I thought I was dead. But intrigued as I was, and with the assumption that if I was dead she couldn't harm me, I decided to extend my arm out to her – and she did the same.

From the moment our fingertips touched, Joseph, life as I knew it would never be the same, and what happened next was unimaginable. Flashing images appeared before my very eyes of the most bizarre and random things: a green moon, a waterfall, a black creature, a glowing pool, a beautiful woman in a cloak, death, the dagger, the piece of metal and the lake. I quickly pulled away, at which it all stopped, and suddenly I began to choke on water so I swam back to the top as fast as I could and clutched the side of the boat for my dear life. I looked down to search for the light again but it had completely vanished. Once I climbed back inside the boat, I started to shiver as though I had been electrocuted, and the flashbacks started again like I was having a seizure.

Disturbed by what happened to me and by what I had seen, when I finally got home I locked the piece of metal away in the garage and left it there until I could figure out what to do with it. As the months rolled on, I continued with life as normal (apart from the odd nightmare here and there, and the blessed crows), and completely forgot all about it. Until one day — as we were travelling home from visiting your parents, and you, Mary and I were laughing about something, and a crow flew unexpectedly directly into the windscreen of my car and cracked it. Thankfully I still had full control, but your grandmother was white as a ghost and terribly shaken up by the incident.

After that frightful moment, a few weeks later the unthinkable occurred. Your father was killed in the line of duty, which as you know ripped our family apart, and most certainly left me a broken man. From that moment on, I firmly believed that the piece of metal was cursed and was to blame for Michael's death, so I decided to take it back to the lake where I found it and toss the regrettable thing back.

As I stood near the water and went to throw it in, suddenly the white spirit lady rose from the lake. She floated across and stopped in front of me at the water's edge. At first I was nervous after what happened to me last time, and then I thought of Michael and got extremely cross and started to shout at her. Just as I was about to throw it once again, she reached out for me to touch her hand. Reluctantly (but curiosity always being my downfall) I reached out once more, but this time not only did I have a flashback and catch a glimpse of her life and how she came to enter into our world and die, but I also had a flash-forward in which you were involved.

As you know, the spirit's name is Quindella, and for what reason she entered into our world I am unsure, but she entered through a water portal and was followed by the creature called the Crowman. She fought at the edge of the lake with the Crowman, who wanted the Dragon's Head Medallion (but the creature didn't know that Quindella only had one half of it), and struck her dagger into the water. Defenceless, she tried to run but the creature grabbed her and soared high into the air over the lake. Quindella managed to wriggle free, but from the height that she fell and the speed in which she hit the water, she was knocked unconscious and ultimately she drowned.

Unable to recover the medallion from the water, over the years the Crowman killed no end of people that went near the lake. But soon it became wise and grew watchful and instead chose its victims carefully, looking for any it thought might have found it. Then hundreds of years later I came along and accidentally discovered it and so my fate was sealed: I now became the target unknowingly. From that moment on I was doomed and destined to die at the hands of the Crowman. How and when, it did not matter, only that it was going to happen.

But that wasn't all I saw. Before I discovered the medallion, I saw the Draigar Dagger being discovered by a fisherman and saw it trading hands, being sold to the British Museum and then locked away in an underground chamber. I also saw the Crowman hunting after you for the medallion, it killing your mother and Mary and our world in destruction and chaos. After knowing what I saw, I came to realize that it would be simply foolish of me just to hand you over the medallion. Furthermore I thought that if these events had not happened *yet, we stood a chance of changing the future, and the only way to ensure our family's safety was to hide the medallion and guide you to it.*

I, on the other hand, could not change my future. But I believe my sacrifice will hopefully spare our family's lives and allow you to fulfil the prophecy that the spirit foresees, and you will become the chosen guardian of it – that I am sure of. You will forever remain in my heart, Joseph. Make sure you live your life without regret and to the full and I hope to see you again someday – but not too soon.

Let God be by thy side as thou peregrinate the darkness.
Love
Granddad X
P. S. Find the spirit, Joseph, she will help and know what to do.

~

Joseph felt crushed by a cocktail of emotions: anger, sorrow, resentment and despair all seemed to collide inside him at once. He closed his eyes momentarily and clenched his lips and teeth tightly together from the overbearing pain, while tears rolled down his face and fell onto the letter and soaked through it. After a few minutes of weeping he regained his composure, folded the letter away and gave it a kiss and placed it down to his side. He dried his eyes quickly and picked up the dainty trinket box and delicately touched the curved lid that had raised foliage all over it. Finally the moment had come, he thought. After all the problems he had faced and the countless times he had cheated death, he was ready to see why the medallion was so important that he had to risk his life for it. Butterflies grew in his stomach as he slowly began to lift the lid. Strangely it started to coruscate and glittering light filled every inch of the room, but it soon stopped when it was fully opened.

Awestruck, Joseph could not believe his eyes as he stared inside the purple-velvet-lined box. His trembling hand carefully reached in and lifted out the Dragon's Head Medallion and he held it up between his fingers and thumb. It shimmered wondrously against the light, causing his neck hairs to stand on end and his eyes to grow the size of golf balls. Hypnotized, he gazed in amazement at the deep red, flawless detailing carved into it of half a dragon's head, raised, surrounded by star cogs, rivets and then a twisting rope on the outer edge.

'Whoa, you are something special . . . I can see why Granddad would hide you now,' he said under his breath. He swivelled his hand to see peculiar markings etched upon the back of it and was intrigued to know what they meant. Quickly he slipped it into his trouser pocket and stuffed the letter and the diary into his rucksack. He then picked up the dagger, which by now had ceased glowing, and with the torch in his hands he rose to his feet with greater confidence than he had ever felt before.

A look of revenge flickered in his eyes. 'Time to find that murdering crow,' he said to himself, gritting his teeth, and then he walked over to the hole in the wall and crawled out.

Chapter 25

THE SPIRIT OF THE LAKE

Back in the car, Erin anxiously rubbed her hands together to keep warm. The anger she felt towards Joseph had long since passed and now with every minute that ticked by she grew more and more concerned for his safety. Dreadful thoughts began to eat away at her and slowly but surely she was getting herself worked up. *What if he's injured, how am I supposed to get to him?* What if that evil creature has found him and has hurt him? she thought. The condensation on the car windows blocked her view to the island, so she quickly wiped it away and stared with desperation for him to get back in the boat.

'C'mon, Joseph, where are you?' she said, fretting.

She held off as long as she could from starting the car, but her fingers began to ache and became stiff. Reluctantly she placed the key inside the ignition. As she was about to turn the key over, out of nowhere a crow landed on a stone wall to her left. She gasped and felt her heart skip a beat. Her eyes grew wide as she sat terrified by the evil crow and froze like a statue, holding her breath. The crow squawked repeatedly, then ratcheted its head and stared around with its burning eyes.

Riddled with fear, Erin cowered down in her seat. She began to worry herself sick how she could warn Joseph of the imminent danger. Slowly she extended her neck up and nervously peered over the dashboard to see the crow still perched there and quickly ducked back down again.

'What do I do?' she repeated over and over again to herself. After a few intense minutes had passed, Erin once again raised her head and saw to her relief that the crow had disappeared. She clambered up in her seat and wiped the windscreen crazily and stared through the smeared window. To her great surprise, she saw Joseph over by the island, standing up in the boat, waving his arms in the air. Panic-stricken, she threw open the car door and frantically ran over to the edge of the lake and shouted to him at the top of her voice.

~

'ERINNN!' Joseph yelled out, excited to see her, as he continued to wave. Suddenly he stopped and slowly lowered his arm and stared with concern at her distressing behaviour. Unable to hear, he immediately shifted his head upwards and stared at the sky and felt a sense of danger approaching. Without hesitation he slashed the rope with the dagger and rushed over and picked up the oars and pushed off quickly against the embankment. The oars pounded the icy water.

Faster and faster they whipped in and out of the lake as he rowed, whilst frequently he looked to the sky with trepidation. He felt himself grow tired quickly and his arms began to burn with agony. For a split second he thought about stopping to take a breather, but then came the dreaded sound – the sound of crows. He motioned his head from side to side searching for them, but they sneakily hid amongst the clouds out of sight. Fearing he was a sitting duck, he leant down to grab the dagger and looked at the boat with utter shock and disbelief.

'Oh no, the boat is bloody *sinking!*' he said to himself, alarmed. 'It must have got damaged when I hit the island. He stared at the water slowly beginning to fill at the other end where there was a crack in the wood. Panicking, he quickly grabbed his rucksack and chucked it behind him and placed the dagger down on his lap. He gritted his teeth and began to row harder than ever.

~

Meanwhile, Erin paced back and forth on tenterhooks with her hands held to her head, watching him row vulnerably across the lake. 'Oh my God, oh my God, oh my God!' she said to herself, panicking, and then looked across the lake. 'The boathouse!'

Up the road she ran as fast as she could towards the white gate. Breathless, she finally reached the gate and started to climb over but stopped in her tracks as the sky all of a sudden became filled with crows. Erin froze in a state of shock as the swarm soared high up into the clouds and returned back down as the Crowman. Horrified, she watched helplessly as it swooped down at great speed towards the lake from the west, heading directly behind Joseph.

'JOSEPH!!' she screamed. But it was too late. The Crowman swooped down and snatched Joseph right out of the boat and soared high into the air.

Joseph squealed out like a pig in pain from its overpowering grip on his arms. Desperately he fought to break free, but its hold on him was too strong and up and up he rose, higher and higher. He glanced down and watched as the lake looked frightfully further and further away. Suddenly the Crowman changed direction and U-turned in the sky. As they continued their ascent, Joseph swung the dagger wildly numerous times at the creature's legs, but failed each and every time. He continued to wriggle like a maggot, trying everything possible to break loose, when suddenly he felt his left arm release from the Crowman's grip. With his one arm still held by the creature, he dangled dangerously and took one last look at the lake, before he took an almighty swing upwards and cut the Crowman's foot completely off.

The Crowman bellowed out the most horrific squawk, which echoed all around. Blood splattered against Joseph's face, and for a split second he felt his body become light. Then suddenly he felt his stomach shift and his eyes flashed wide open from the initial shock as he began to freefall. He watched the Crowman shift quickly further and further away in the sky. As he hurtled down towards the lake at tremendous speed, the air felt extremely cold as it whipped past him. He knew he was about to die, so he closed his eyes and immediately images of his family and happy moments he shared with them flashed before him. Joseph held his arms out as if he was embracing death, then suddenly he smashed straight into the water like a torpedo.

~

Erin watched him hit the water and screamed out hysterically at the top of her lungs 'NOOO!' which seemed to last for ever. She felt her heart had completely stopped along with everything else. No longer could she feel the cold wind blow or the chill in the air, or see a cloud move or a blade of grass. Every one of her senses had ceased; she became numb. The only thing that she could now feel was something inside of her had died right there and then along with Joseph. She held her hand to her mouth in shock. Her eyes instantly welled with tears, her legs became weak and gave way under her and she collapsed to her knees.

~

Joseph's body sank deeper and deeper into the murky depths of the water and eventually came to rest at the bottom of the lake's bed. The medallion slipped from out of his pocket and was now lying next to him. He lay motionless, his life slipping away, when out of nowhere a small white light appeared from the darkness of the waters. It quickly grew larger and larger in size and suddenly stopped and hovered over him.

The spirit slowly swayed back and forth, staring at Joseph's young peaceful face resting there. Then she delicately stroked the dagger he still held in his hand with her floating fingers. She turned to the medallion and began to whirl her finger above it, which created a tiny whirlpool. The moment she stopped, the medallion drifted down into the palm of his hand. The spirit placed her hand down on top of the medallion and his hand. All of a sudden their hands burst into a small red-hot flame and tiny bubbles rose to the surface. The spirit began to speak in an ethereal manner, in a language that could never be understood by any mortal. But even for Joseph in his unconscious state, the interpretation was clear, and she said this to him:

'A chosen fate, a chosen hand,
Reign of fire across the land,
Protect all creatures from those who dare,
Protect all mortals by those who care,
Lead with strength, love with thy heart,
For thou art chosen, O Draconemerus,
Desolation follows in the wind,
To save thy world thou must go to the stone.
Take the Medali-Draco to the one they call the Gatekeeper.
Go, O Dragon God, thy destiny awaits, guard it with thy life.'

The spirit released her hand, causing the flame to die out

instantly. The spirit started to move her floating arms over him, and slowly but surely Joseph's body began to rise from the lake's bed. Up and up it went until it reached the top and lifted him straight out of the water. The spirit followed closely behind his limp body as it floated along just above the surface, and gently laid it to rest on the frozen ground not far from the boathouse. The spirit stared at him for a brief moment and then disappeared back into the dark water.

~

While Joseph lay blue-faced and motionless, images flashed before him of random events of the spirit's life, parts of the otherworld, destruction and chaos of his world and death. Then suddenly his eyes flashed open and he immediately began to choke and cough up water from his mouth. Quickly he turned onto his side and threw up, and then gasped for air like a new-born baby drawing breath for the first time. He felt weak and was shaking uncontrollably, and also heard a whining sound as though water was swishing around in his brain. With great effort he rolled himself onto his hands and knees and once again threw up violently. After what felt like the last of what was in his stomach, he took a couple of deep breaths before he stumbled to his feet.

Joseph wobbled about, disorientated, and shook his head to get rid of the annoying sound. But amidst the noise he heard another weird sound like a faint voice. He looked up through his blurry vision and saw two Erins running towards him in the distance. Slowly his sight realigned and he saw her waving at him. He went to wave in acknowledgement but hesitated, feeling a tremendous burning sensation in his hand. As he was about to open his palm to look, Erin interrupted with the wailing sound of her voice, which had all of a sudden became crystal clear.

'JOSEPH, IT'S BEHIND YOU, IT'S BEHIND YOU!!' Erin screamed to him.

Joseph's eyes widened and his heart felt as though it had skipped a beat. Nervously he turned around and the moment he did, within a split second the Crowman landed on top of him and he was slammed to the ground.

Erin screamed and picked up a rock from the floor and charged towards the creature. She was less than a few steps away and was about to strike it, when she suddenly stopped dead in her tracks. A gasp came from her and the rock fell from out of her hand. Erin held her hands to her mouth and stared in shock. The Crowman suddenly turned into a man, now lying on top of Joseph with the dagger pointing straight out of his back.

Joseph wrestled to get free and pushed the man off him and quickly let go of the blood-smeared dagger and leapt to his feet. He stepped back, panic-stricken.

The tall, pale, thin man, whose profile was uncannily very similar to that of a crow with his peculiar long nose, wore black trousers that were torn at the knees, long straight jet-black hair trailing his shoulders, and deep-set eyes, which were as dark as his hair. He lay clutching his bare chest where the blade had been driven through. He began to choke from his own blood and cough it up from his mouth, and in a strained, deep voice spurted out, 'Thank you, you have saved me . . .'

Joseph felt confused and angry by his comment and shouted, 'Who are you? And why did you kill my grandfather?'

'My name is Cornelius Crow, and I am sorry, I did not mean to hurt anyone, I was cursed by—' he said, but was unable to finish his sentence as he took his final breath and passed away.

Erin stood beside Joseph, staring at the man, and then suddenly turned and threw her arms around him. 'I thought you'd drowned!' she said in a soft, broken voice over his shoulder while tears rolled down her face.

'I guess not,' Joseph replied, placing his arms around her. He raised up his right hand to see the medallion in his palm and quickly slid it into his pocket. Just then, he felt her pull away and give him a huge kiss on the lips, before she rested her forehead against his. The moment he closed his eyes, white powerful flashes like bolts of lightning struck him and he quickly let go of her and stumbled backwards, giddy and off balance.

'Joseph, what is it? What's wrong?' Erin said, reaching to grab hold of him.

Joseph shook his head. He tried to focus on her but she became blurred, along with her voice that suddenly sounded slurred. The flashes continued and everything around him started to spin. 'Not sure. I feel strange,' he replied, holding his head.

'It's probably the shock from the freezing water, but you're really warm, considering,' said Erin, holding his arm.

'I feel warm,' Joseph replied, taking some deep breaths.

'C'mon, we'd better get you back to the car,' said Erin.

'Hold on, there's something I have to do first,' he replied, taking his coat off.

'Like what?' Erin said, shifting her eyebrows inwards.

Joseph stood and took a long hard look at the man and felt slight remorse inside. He held his breath, grabbed the dagger and cringed as he pulled it out from him. He draped his coat over the man, sighed, and then wiped the bright red blood from the blade into the ground. He turned and made his way down towards the water, leaving Erin by the body.

'Now where are you going?' asked Erin, who looked baffled by his unusual behaviour.

'I'll be back soon, just give a minute,' he replied.

Joseph crouched down at the water's edge and nervously opened his palm, which felt like it was on fire. He stared at the burn mark of what he thought to be a dragon's head. The burn freaked him out so he tore off his other sleeve and quickly wrapped it around his hand. Then he dipped it into the cold water, but when he glanced up he saw the boat moored on the embankment. He jogged over and felt relieved to see his rucksack still inside the boat. Quickly he unzipped it and slipped the dagger inside and slung it over his shoulders and made his way back up the hill towards Erin, who was looking rather miffed.

'So, what is it that you have to do then?' she said in a demanding tone.

'I need to go back to the standing stone,' replied Joseph.

'What *for?* Didn't you get what you needed from the island?' asked Erin.

Joseph sighed and bowed his head. 'Yeah I did, but—' he said.

'So why can't we just go home then? Please, Joseph, I want to go home,' replied Erin, and reached for his hand.

Joseph raised his head and saw her eyes were beginning to glisten. At that moment he felt lost for words. He didn't know how to explain to her what he had seen and what he had to do. All he could say was, 'We will. I just need to do this one last thing,' and stroked her hair behind her ear and then touched the side of her face with his hand and smiled through tight lips.

Erin nodded. She closed her eyes briefly and placed her hand on top of his but then asked, 'What's wrong with your hand?'

Joseph sheepishly pulled away. 'Oh, nothing, it's just – it's just a scratch. I did it over at the island,' he replied. 'C'mon.' And he took her by the hand and walked her across the marshland.

As they drew closer, all Joseph could think about was what she had said in the church; the words repeated over and over again in his head like a broken record. '*Sometimes you gotta leave something behind, sometimes you gotta leave something behind, sometimes you gotta leave something behind to get where you're going in life . . .'*

He wanted nothing more than to take her with him, but if the otherworld was anything like they had experienced, or far worse, then the risk was far too great; because if anything ever happened to her he could never forgive himself. Deep down, he knew that the *something* he had to leave behind was her and also his family. A decision he did not want to make, but he felt there was no way of telling her. He thought she wouldn't understand; he didn't have the courage to explain either. Instead he held her hand a little tighter to comfort his guilt and continued to traipse through the wet snow. They reached the stone quicker than he anticipated and felt everything was moving way too fast, so he stood and stared at it for a moment and thought about his life, his family and her.

'So what now?' Erin said, turning to him.

Joseph rubbed his thumb over the medallion in his pocket and sighed. He turned to her and cradled her pretty face in his hands and stared into her beautiful eyes one last time and said in a soft voice, 'Promise me something, Erin.'

'Like what?' Erin replied.

'Promise you'll live your life with no regrets,' Joseph said, and gave her a long, meaningful kiss on the lips and then proceeded over to the stone. He looked down at the medallion in his palm and then stared long and hard at all of the runes, which made no sense to him at first. But then suddenly they all magically began to shift and move about until they became crystal clear for him to read.

Joseph glanced over his shoulder at her. He couldn't find

the words to say goodbye; in his heart he believed he was going to see her again soon. So instead he half smiled and then turned away quickly before his emotions got the better of him. He held the medallion in his right hand and placed it into the stone's hole and began to recite the words.

'Joseph, what are you doing now?' Erin asked.

He heard the nervousness in her voice, which bordered on panic, but chose not to reply and remained calm and focused on his spoken words and continued to repeat them. When he reached the final recitation of the passage he closed his eyes and said softly for the third time,

'Have mercy, O God, through the circle of life,
Show mercy, O God, through darkness be light,
Thou holdest the key to our soul, I pledge my love to thee,
Grant us safe passage into Ettonina,
I place my faith in thee.'

All of a sudden the ground started to shake around them. Erin took a small step back and cried out: 'Joseph!' Her eyes darted all around and caught a glimpse of the sky and realized the clouds had strangely stopped moving. It was as if time had physically ceased. Then out of nowhere an enormous white flash appeared before Erin's eyes and blinded her momentarily, followed by a loud boom. She stumbled back, dazed, and turned away to cover her face with her hands. When the ground stopped shaking, she slowly opened her eyes to flashing stars. She rubbed them until they cleared and turned around – and saw that Joseph was missing.

'Joseph?' she called out anxiously while she looked around

for him. 'Where are you?' She felt a hard lump form in her throat and called out to him once again as she walked around the stone, thinking he was hiding, until she reached right back around again to where she was first standing and realized he wasn't there.

An onset of panic began to overwhelm Erin. She whirled around and called out at the top of voice: 'JOSEPH, WHERE ARE YOU?' Her bottom lip quivered and her eyes started to well up. Frantically she searched all around the stone and then repeatedly began to thump it with the side of her fist until it hurt her hand.

Erin collapsed in a heap, distraught, and started to cry. Her tears streamed down her face in torrents as she leant her sorrowful head against the stone. She felt truly heartbroken by his sudden disappearance, and had an awful gut feeling she wasn't likely to ever see him again. She held one hand up against the cold stone with despair and said in a choked voice, 'Joseph, can you hear me? Please, please come back to me, I need you . . . I . . . I love you . . .'

Chapter 26

WHERE AM I?

Joseph pressed his back hard up against the tree. His breathing was out of control. The desperate run he had just made through the forest had completely exhausted him. He was too scared to look around to see if the monsters on horses were still chasing him. Nervous sweat trickled down the side of face, and his stomach was tied in knots. The corner of his lip throbbed. He ran his tongue over the swollen part and winced from the stinging pain. The bitter taste was distinctive, but not something he was accustomed to dealing with. Gently he touched the area with his fingertips. A shocked look came over him to see them tipped with blood. Suddenly the sound of horses' hooves galloping and pounding the ground echoed through the shadowy forest. It had him petrified and on tenterhooks.

Then unexpectedly a gust of wind blew past him and caused his neck hairs to stand on end. He followed with his eyes as the wind swept across and funnelled through an opening between the trees. It was as if it ushered him to go through. So he sucked in a deep breath as though he was about to jump into water, and made a sprint for it.

Joseph looked back constantly over his shoulder as he ran down a narrow gravel path, and paid little attention to what was ahead. When he glanced around at the last second he noticed he had passed all the trees and there was nothing but grey sky in front of him. A look of sheer panic flashed in his eyes when he saw a cliff edge. He tried to stop himself from running, but he was moving way too fast, and he slipped and fell to the ground, slid along the gravel and went over the edge.

Hanging onto a tree root for dear life, Joseph dangled dangerously down the side of the cliff. His feet scraped desperately against the side to climb back up, when out of the blue he heard the dreaded sound of a horse. The horse snorted as it clip-clopped along the gravel path, drawing nearer and nearer to the cliff's edge. Joseph's heart was in his mouth. He glanced down at the almighty drop below with a ferocious river at the bottom and rocks protruding out from the water like sharp tines.

His fingers were beginning to slip on the root. Joseph looked up, and to his horror he saw a black horse with a demonic monster straddled upon it. The horse's jet-black, bulging eyes stared down at him, while steam rolled from its nostrils. Joseph gasped. His eyes flared with fear as he stared death right in the face. The moment the monster leant down and extended its arm out to grab him, Joseph let go of the root and instantly plummeted.

~

The shock from the fall caused Joseph to shriek and gradually open his eyes. It was a dream but yet so vivid. He found himself face down on the damp ground, staring with blurry eyes at something in the palm of his hand. His mouth was extremely dry and he felt groggy. Ever so slowly he pushed himself up on his weak, trembling arms and gently eased his head up off the ground. But under the immense strain he collapsed back down with exhaustion. All of his energy had been zapped out of him. He lay, vulnerable, huffing and puffing. But after a little while, a warm sensation travelled through his body like his energy was slowly returning along with his vision. With a great effort he rolled one leg up under his chest, and with an almighty push heaved himself over and landed in a slumped position against his rucksack.

Heady and out of breath, Joseph gazed around, confused by his surroundings which had a queer tinge of green. He wondered where the hell he was and how had he got there, as he couldn't remember. Slowly he raised his weak arm up and held aloft the peculiar object between his fingers and thumb.

'What is that?' he muttered under his breath. His narrowed eyes continued to stare at it, when the night's sky suddenly drew his attention. Something was illuminated behind the object. He barely shifted his head an inch to the side when he saw to his astonishment a pale green moon. Intrigued, he slowly lowered his arm and gazed, but the longer he stared the more effulgent it seemed to become.

Then out of nowhere, like a bolt of lightning, Joseph was struck with white flashes before his eyes. His body went into a fit and he started to shake uncontrollably. His eyes rolled into the back of his head. His memory came flooding back to him in one hit. Then suddenly it stopped and he began to pant heavily and immediately thought of someone and said, 'Erin!'

Joseph heaved himself up onto his feet and faced the unwelcoming forest with unease. A chill swept through him and sent goose pimples spreading across his bare arms. He looked at the medallion before slipping it into his pocket and called out for Erin. He frowned when she didn't answer back and soon realized he was on his own. Sadness fell upon him, but before he had time to wallow in his own self-pity, a rustling sound came from the undergrowth nearby.

Startled, he swung around and narrowed his eyes. He crept forward nervously. 'Hello?' he said in a shaky voice. The bushes shook again. Then suddenly there was a vicious growl. A lump formed in Joseph's throat and his hands began to shake. He edged away, when unexpectedly he backed into something hard. He gasped and froze. 'Please don't hurt me!' he said, trembling. His hand felt for what it was, which appeared cold and rough in texture. Cowardly, he turned his head and saw a small standing stone. He sighed with relief but it was short-lived when the growling appeared again, even closer now.

Joseph looked up to see big yellow eyes shining in the dark. Then to his horror, a big black wolf's head emerged, snarling with white razor-sharp teeth. It appeared much larger than an ordinary wolf, especially with all of its hair standing on end. It gave it a very aggressive stance.

'Nice wolf . . .' Joseph said through quivering lips.

As it padded slowly towards him, Joseph started to edge around the standing stone. Then without warning, the wolf let out a long howl. Joseph jumped with fright, turned and made a fast break for it.

He ran aimlessly through the unearthly forest, striking branch after branch along the way as the wolf chased him down. Over logs he leapt, down a dip he ran, through the trees in and out, but there was no letting up by the wolf; it was right behind him every step of the way. Joseph didn't know how much longer he could keep up the pace, when just as he leapt over some rocks, the wolf snapped at his heels. He thought the ground was on the other side, but it wasn't and he fell straight down a huge drop.

'HOLY—' Joseph yelled on the way down before he hit the sloping ground and tumbled head over heels and skimmed through the trees, landing at the bottom in a prickly bush.

'OW, OW, OW!' he cried out in agony, as he desperately tried to get out of the prickly branches.

Finally he emerged, scratching his arms like a dog that had fleas. He looked around for the wolf and to his relief it was nowhere to be seen. Subconsciously he placed his hand into his pocket and immediately panicked.

'Oh my God, the medallion – it's gone!' he said.

A cold sweat came over him as he frantically searched around, when something shimmering in the sward caught his eye.

'There you are, thank God,' he said to himself, holding his chest, and swiftly moved in to scoop it up. 'Can't afford to lose you, you're my ticket out of this place.'

As Joseph slipped it into the side pocket of his rucksack, he unintentionally looked up and spied an orange, nebulous glow through the thicket in the distance. He stared for a moment, wondering what it was, before looking around the murky woods with uncertainty. He pressed his lips firmly together and then turned his attention to the green moon, which was a quarter formed and sat clear in the night's sky.

'Looks like I'd better find out where I am and who this Gatekeeper is,' he said to himself, and made haste towards the light.

Acknowledgements

I would like to express my sincere gratitude to the people who have helped assist in the edit, proofread, translation, illustration and design of my book: Bella, Leena, Sue, Dr Armand, Julie, Mark and the whole team at Clays.

I would also like to thank those of you who have chosen to pick up my book and read it, and continue to do so and follow Joseph through his saga.

12/8/17

Newport Library and
Information Service

X023776